Arboriah Lux

Kathleen I. Lyons

Lyons Publishing

This is a work of fiction. Names, characters, places, and incidents either the product of the author's imagination or are used fictitiously. Any resemblance to actual persons, living or dead, events, or locales is entirely coincidental.

First Edition April 2023

Book design by Kathleen I. Lyons

ISBN 979-8-9878973-0-0 (paperback)

ISBN 979-8-9878973-1-7 (ebook)

Published by Lyons Publishing

Arboriah Lux

Kathleen I. Lyons

Lyons Publishing

To my parents and my friends that have been supporting me on this crazy journey of mine to achieve my dream. And more importantly, to all the readers who want to delve into the imagination to escape reality, if only for a little while.

Also by

Seraphim Awakening

Seraphim Bloodlines

1

The White Tree with Ruby-Colored Leaves

I'm not sure how I'd arrived at that place, or even where that place was, but before me, in a field of lush green grass, was a magnificent white tree. It towered so high over me I believed if I had tried to crane my head back to glimpse the very top, I would have fallen backwards. The tree was truly beautiful; each branch bore brightly colored red leaves that seemed to shimmer like gemstones. I walked with naked feet around the wide tree, and I stopped when a glimpse of a different bright color caught my eye.

Hanging from one of the tree's many branches was a single, plump apple.

It was enticing to behold, for the supple flesh of the fruit was a golden yellow in color. I reached up, even so far as to stand on the tips of my toes, trying to touch the fruit. It was still a little ways over my head, and when I'd grown tired from my strained reach, I nearly lost my balance as my weight shifted fully back to my feet.

And then, an odd thing occurred.

The branch of this great white tree that bore this seemingly forbidden morsel of color seemed to lower itself, as if it were a parent giving a child a treasured toy. I felt myself drawn to the gesture, not thinking it odd in the slightest, and I reached my hands out to receive it. The golden apple dropped in my hand, and as I looked at the fruit with childlike awe, I felt a pat on my head.

I looked up at the tree once more.

The tree itself had extended its branch, and it gently stroked my head with its bushel of ruby leaves. A slight breeze blew, causing the leaves to rustle ever so slightly.

'Take a bite, child.' A voice whispered in that gentle breeze.

I'm not sure how I understood, but the tree was inviting me to eat the apple.

And what should have been frightening to any normal person, a tree seeming to have conscious thought and will certainly being an off thing to see, caused me no distress. For me, for that tree to have a voice of its own seemed like the most normal thing in the world.

And with that in mind, I looked at the fruit in my palms and drew it closer to my lips. I closed my eyes into the bite, juice as sweet as honey dribbling down my chin as my teeth pierced the flesh with a satisfying *pop*. There was a growing warmth in my chest, and a wave of drowsiness overcame me. I laid down, leaned against the tree's massive roots, and laid my head against its wide trunk. Sleep numbed my body, and I felt the apple fall from my hand, tumbling and thudding across the green grass as my eyelids slowly closed.

When I awoke, there was no magnificent white tree with ruby leaves towering over me; instead, I lay in a field of tall yellow grass with a grayish sky overhead. I sat up to further observe my surroundings, and I found this field bore dull-colored wildflowers, muted compared to the bright colors of that wondrous tree.

However, they were still beautiful to me, even though it felt like something very crucial was missing.

'A dream of such a beautiful tree.' I felt a longing to see it once more.

I stood from where I had been laying, the tall grass brushing against the thin fabric of the skirt of the white dress I was wearing. Surrounding the field were ashen-white trees, their branches bare of any leaves, and where a dazzling white sun was rising—or setting; I couldn't really tell which—was a solitary, steady-sloped mountain, black and gray. Mountain was probably being too generous; it was more of a large hill. But, even so, the sun seemed to reflect off the surface of the structure as if it were itself made of black glass.

'Where in the world am I that the sun is bleached white and I can't feel its heat?' Another thought then came to me. 'Wait... *was* there a time when the sun was any other color than white? Or a time the sun would give off warmth?'

In all honesty, I couldn't recall such knowledge. A crisp breeze cutting through the open field brought me out of my thoughts, making me shiver with the chill and pulling me from my thoughts.

'I should look for shelter.' I shivered, hugging my trembling form. 'The trees should block most of this wind.'

My pondering would have to wait until I was safe from the elements and could really sit down and think. I wasn't about to risk sickness. And it was in that moment that I longed to see the noble tree that seemed to be so welcoming and warm. My cheeks flushed with color at the odd, seemingly childish desire, and I shook my head of the thoughts.

'I don't have time for daydreaming. Let's just find shelter and get warm.'

I rubbed my arms as I walked to the edge of the field where the trees led to the black-glass mountain. Fields of tall grass and wildflowers gave way to heavy-trodden forest paths. I paused as I reached the forest's edge, suddenly very weary of the shadows of the trees against one another. I took a deep breath to steel my nerves at the unknown, and I trekked forward.

As it turned out, the white sun had indeed been setting; the light gray skies became darker with a pale rose-colored moon illuminating the night sky. The moon was the only celestial body; there were no glittering constellations of stars to guide me. It would have been a comforting sight, considering the forest was silent as the grave except for the howling winds and the low groans of the trees' naked branches. I continued straight on my path, not bothering to look around. The cool air sapped my strength and burned my lungs as I walked, my bare feet sore and numb to the cold. I stumbled a bit, which prompted me to stop and rest against a tree to catch my breath. I slowly lowered myself into a small cradle of tree roots, and as I rested, I thought back to that odd-yet-beautiful dream, shivering in my reminiscence.

'Why do these pale trees have no leaves?' I wondered. 'Is it winter here... wherever "here" is? Why do I feel like it should be warmer?'

There had been no fallen leaves on my trek through the forest, only twigs and damp soil. I rubbed my feet to warm them, and I noticed minor cuts bleeding on my soles.

'I must have been walking so long in the cold that I couldn't feel my feet getting cut.'

Seeing no possibility of shelter soon, I tore strips of fabric from the hem of my skirt and gingerly wrapped them around the arches and balls of my feet. I inspected my work with a proud smile.

'Time to keep moving.' I thought as I moved to stand from the tree roots.

As I did, there was a new sound that echoed in the pale rose light. I slowly lifted my head, a different chill prickling up my spine.

The shadows of the trees yielded a single pair of glowing red eyes.

Another pair soon joined it.

And then another pair.

And another pair.

My heart pounded in my chest. The red eyes leered at their prey, low growls emanating from their hidden forms.

I faced a decision: stay still or flee. If I stayed, I would certainly meet my end, and if I fled, these unknown creatures would surely catch up with me and kill me.

'Either way, I'm dead.' I realized, slowly gripping the tree with the hand I'd used to stand. 'But if I run, I might find help.'

And with the possibility of help refreshed in my mind, I hastily turned and started running.

The creatures gave chase behind me as I wove through the trees to avoid them. Adrenaline coursed through my veins, dulling my previously aching feet. My lungs burned as I wheezed the chilling wind, fighting to give me a push. The growling behind me gave way to terrible howls and snarls, signaling that the hunt was on. Low-hanging branches whipped at me as I ran, scratching my skin and tearing at my now muddied white dress. I breathed heavily as exhaustion set in. I tripped and fell to the muddy ground with a shriek, and before I could recover, I froze despite my heart pounding against my chest, massive paws pouncing on the ground on either side of me. Jaws full of sharp teeth breathed rotten breath against my skin as the creature snarled.

My breath grew rapid as I panicked.

I let out a horrified scream as I squeezed my eyes shut, waiting for the pain I would no doubt experience before the cool fingers of death would lull me to a never-ending sleep.

There was a warm gust of air and then something warm and smelling sickeningly dry splattered across my face. There were no more growls from the creature that towered over me, no nauseating breath. I trembled as I slowly opened my eyes to find that the creatures that had pursued me—three massive creatures with matted, coarse fur and sharp spines along their backs to the ends of long, whip-like tails—all lay slaughtered, surrounding a lone figure, a silhouette of black. I slowly pushed myself up to look at the one who had saved my life, this mysterious silhouette with pungent blood dripping from his hands. My voice caught in my throat as the figure turned to face me. It was a man dressed all in black, making him able to blend in well with the shadows. He wore a hood over his face, but peeking from under his hood was a pair of glowing red-amber eyes. When he took a step towards me, I flinched and crawled backwards to keep my distance. The man stopped and looked at me.

"I'm not gonna hurt ya." The man's voice was young, though it was far from gentle. As if in an attempt to calm me and solidify his claim, he sighed and then took down his hood, revealing a handsome face framed by messy, black-to-ashen-gray hair. "I wouldn't have saved ya from those hellbeasts if I meant ya harm."

We stared at each other for several long minutes before the area became illuminated with a soft reddish glow.

"You certainly have a poor bedside manner, Esilas."

I turned to see another man dressed in black, though his hood was down. In the pale glow of the red-flamed torch he carried, I saw the face of a young man with white hair tied in a loose ponytail over his shoulder and a pair of soft red eyes, almost the color of rose petals.

"She won't let me approach her to see if she's hurt." The first man, called Esilas, said, frustratingly running a hand through his hair.

The second, kinder man seemed to give an amused sigh.

"Well, did you state that intention?" He approached me slowly and knelt down, though I moved back a bit, still on guard. The man only smiled softly. "You'll have to forgive my comrade, miss." He spoke with a kind voice as he held out his hand. "I'm afraid his manners are still in need of a bit of work."

The man, Esilas, gave a low groan, annoyed.

"You do realize that you're the only one with gentlemanly standards in the entire Watchmen's Guild, don't you, Elderik?"

The man, Elderik, simply smiled.

"Not all fights can be won with brute force." He looked at his comrade for only a moment before looking back at me. "If you'll allow us, miss, we can treat any wounds you sustained from these beasts."

I looked at each of them and then slowly reached to take the kinder man's hand. However, before my fingers could graze his own, Esilas grabbed my wrist, his grip so tight that it triggered my flee response.

"Let me go!" I screamed as I squeezed my eyes shut once more, fighting his grip in panic.

"Esilas, you're scaring her!" Elderik scolded his comrade.

At this, Esilas' hand loosened a bit, but his grip was still firm.

"Elderik, *look*," his breath was shaky as he spoke, sounding as though he had seen a ghost; "her chest."

I peeked open my eyes a bit and looked down at my chest.

What I saw made my eyes pop open in shock.

Just below my collarbone and framed by my fire-red and gold hair was a skin-brown mark that resembled a deep-rooted tree with wide-spreading branches with what appeared to be leaves and flower buds.

I snapped my head up to look at the two men. Elderik's eyes were also wide with shock as the two of them stared at me, and more specifically, at the mark on my chest. The man, Esilas, just stared at me, his light tan skin growing pale. I could feel my cheeks gather heat from the embarrassment of their stares. It was Elderik who spoke first, his voice of utter disbelief.

"A Heart-Mark... it's not possible..." the kind man muttered and then looked at me. "You're... an *Aster-Blood*?"

2

The Meaning of Lux

THE TWO MEN, ESILAS and Elderik, brought me back to their camp. Tending to the fire was another young man clad in black; well, he was more of a boy, maybe around age fifteen. He had short, sandy-blonde hair, and his eyes were the same color as Elderik's.

"What took ya both so long?" He whined, standing from his position by the campfire. "Surely, it don't take en eternity to kill some mangy beasts." He turned, about to continue his childish complaining, but he paused when he saw me, wrapped in Elderik's cloak to keep warm. "Who's she? Some whore escape her brothel?"

My cheeks grew red with the heat of embarrassment.

"Whore?!" I exclaimed, offended at his assumption.

Elderik sighed and turned to me.

"My apologies, my lady," he said, bowing his head. "This is Ephrem, one of the other members of the Watchmen's Guild, particularly of our order, the Keepers of the Watch."

"He also doesn't know when to shut up." Esilas said as he set a place for me to sit by the fire.

The boy, Ephrem, looked at Esilas, offended and trying to make sense of the situation their group seemed to have found themselves in.

"Hell's going on here?! Esilas—!"

"She's an *Aster-Blood.*" Elderik explained as he gently sat me down. "She was attacked by hellbeasts, and our honorable patrol leader saved her."

Ephrem's eyes widened to the point I thought they would have popped out of his skull, and his head snapped towards me.

"An *Aster-Blood*?!" His demeanor was erratic, and it sort of startled me. "I thought yer kind was extinct! Can I see your Heart-Mark?!"

"Ephrem!" Esilas and Elderik both turned to him and scolded their younger comrade, but my blood ran cold at his words.

"Extinct..." I muttered, clutching the cloak tighter around my body.

Elderik looked at me and gently wiped the blood from my face with a rag.

"Unfortunately," he said, softly. "It is true. You are the first *Aster-Blood* that anyone has seen in the past half century."

When he was finished wiping the blood from my face, I watched as he gently unwrapped the bled-through rags on my feet, wincing at their newfound tenderness. The adrenaline from the chase had long-since left my system, but despite my tiredness, my curiosity of the entire situation refused to let me rest. And after I contemplated Elderik's statement, I spoke up with a need to know more about what he had meant.

"I don't understand." I spoke up, just above a whisper. "What... is an *Aster-Blood*?"

Ephrem, in his naivete, looked at me with bewilderment.

"Ya don't even know what you are?! Yer not very bright, are ya—Ow! Esilas!! The hell, man?!"

Esilas had hit his subordinate in the head again, considering that the boy's mouth was certainly without bridle.

"She's been through an ordeal, Ephrem." He warned as he sat beside the fire, a little ways away from his subordinate. "Don't be rude."

Ephrem grimaced, grumbling that he would keep his mouth shut unless spoken to; he, to an extent, respected Esilas, even though it required a bit of abuse to get the message through.

"To answer your question, my lady," Elderik cleared his throat, trying to ease the tension and return to the topic at hand. "*Aster-Blood* refers to purity of spirit, ephemeral like the starlight described in ancient texts. The word *aster-* is a root that means 'star.' Star-blood, therefore *Aster-Blood*."

"They're beings that are the embodiment of the word 'pure'." Esilas further explained, crossing his arms as he leaned against a fallen log. "They were once seen as treasures by those in the Courts."

The tone of his voice didn't escape me when he mentioned "the Courts"; whatever they were, there was hatred in Esilas' voice, as though there was an injustice that couldn't be forgiven.

"But," I spoke up once more, wincing again as Elderik carefully bandaged my feet and treated the scratches on my arms. "What happened to them? From what you said before, you made it seem like I'm possibly the last of my kind, s-so..."

I trailed off, not exactly knowing what to say.

The three of them were silent: it appeared they were having a hard time trying to answer my question.

"You should get some rest." Esilas was the one to break the silence. "Any more talk of this will only impede your recovery."

He laid down, preparing to sleep. I had been about to speak up, needing the answer to my question, when Elderik spoke up.

"But before that," Elderik's words caused Esilas to pause, "could you perhaps tell us your name, my lady? We neglected to ask you."

When he asked for my name, I felt my heart stop for only a moment; it occurred to me I could recall nothing about myself. The only memory I had before waking in the field was the dream of the white tree with red leaves. I looked down at my poorly bandaged feet.

"I... I don't know." I whispered, just loud enough for them to hear. "I remember nothing of myself."

Elderik put his hand on my head.

"Fret not. Until you can remember your name, perhaps we can give you a nickname." He seemed to ask for my approval at his suggestion.

I simply nodded, causing the man's kind smile to return with a light chuckle.

"Alright, but what kinda name would fit an *Aster-Blood*?" Ephrem spoke, propping his chin on his hand.

The three of them were silent again, each of them contemplating what sort of name would really suit me.

And then Esilas spoke a single word.

"Lux." He said, softly. "The word is a root that means 'light.'" He laid down and turned his back to the campfire. "A fitting name for an *Aster-Blood*, no?"

The expression of surprise that crossed Elderik's face as he looked at Esilas didn't escape me. He then gave a tired chuckle and turned to me.

"It does seem to fit you," He said. "Would you accept that name as your own?"

I looked at him; he seemed hopeful. Ephrem seemed to be in agreement with his leader's suggestion as well. And with no other options, I nodded.

"Lux does sound appropriate." I commented.

The name sounded familiar, but I felt as though there was something missing. Elderik chuckled and then gave me a pat on the head.

"Well, now that the matter of your name is settled," he said, smiling "Why don't you get some rest? We'll have more time to talk tomorrow as we return to the barracks."

I nodded, covering my mouth as a yawn escaped me. I leaned back against another tree, staying close to the warmth of the campfire, and I felt myself drifting into a much-appreciated, peaceful slumber.

The next morning, I was being nudged awake by a large snout with fangs protruding from its upper jaw. I opened my eyes, and I could smell rotten breath. My near-death experience was provoked upon my awakening and spurred me to shuffle away from the hellbeast. The creature was different compared to the creatures that had tried to eat me; its coarse gray fur was marked with streaks of what appeared to be charcoal paste, and the creature's body resembled more of that of a large dog. The creature tentatively took a step forward and lowered its head before laying its body at my feet. There wasn't any malice from the creature, but rather a sense of submission. I didn't feel any fear like I had before. I hesitantly reached my hand out, and soon the creature's wet nose nuzzled my palm, and a low noise rose from its throat as if it were a purr. The large animal then moved to lie at my side, laying its head in my lap so that I may further pet it. A soft smile formed on my lips as I continued to run my fingers through its fur.

"It's called an infercanis." I turned with a slight jolt to see Esilas holding a large, fanged rabbit in his hand. He'd gone hunting, it seemed. "But we at the barracks just call them hell-mounts."

I turned back to the animal and continued to pet its head.

"He's gentle." I said.

"You might be the only exception besides us and Elderik's younger sisters." Esilas said as he sat down to skin the kill he'd made. "Make no mistake, though; those beasts are merciless hunters and killers, especially in the wild like their counterparts."

I sat where I could look at Esilas as he worked.

"You said that I might be the only exception," I said, remembering how unforthcoming information had been made before; "is it because I'm an *Aster-Blood*?"

Esilas paused for a moment and then sighed.

"Yes," he said, cutting the skin and putting the animal on a spit; "*Aster-Bloods* attract all manner of life to them. The innocence they carry humbles most creatures." He stopped his work and looked at me; "however, as you saw last night, that innocence also makes you vulnerable."

I fought the sudden urge to shudder at the terrifying experience, still fresh in my mind. I looked at him, about to ask more questions, when I saw he had returned to his work, building a fire to roast his kill. He didn't want to be pestered by further questions. I hummed softly in disappointment as I continued to pet the infercanis at my side. Not long after mine and Esilas' brief conversation, the sound of footsteps was heard. I turned to see Elderik and Ephrem returning to camp, the latter carrying the familiar fang of one of the slaughtered hellbeasts. Elderik was the first to greet me of the two.

"Ah, good morning, Lux." He smiled. "I see Esilas' mount has taken a liking to you."

I returned his smile. Ephrem looked absolutely baffled.

"How come that thing likes everyone but me?!" He complained. I chuckled softly, and I laid my head on top of the creature's, minding not to bother his ear.

"Maybe it doesn't like you because of your damn childish attitude, you newborn." Esilas suggested nonchalantly, which gave rise to another tantrum from Ephrem, while my curiosity was piqued by the term he had used.

"Ya ain't no bright ray of sunshine either, Esilas!"

"Now, now, you two." Elderik chuckled; "let's not have a bout this early in the morning."

He seemed to be the oldest of the three of them, and it showed in how mature he was.

"What does he mean by 'newborn'?" I asked; Elderik had been about to answer when Ephrem spoke up.

"Esilas is making fun of me because I was turned while he and Elderik were born the way they are." Ephrem's answer only confused me more.

"Turned..?" I muttered.

"Ephrem is a first-generation vampire," Elderik explained; "a human was turned by a Noble vampire."

My eyes widened, and I looked at Ephrem.

"Vampire?" The word was another familiar bit of information, but I couldn't place it in my memory.

"Yep." He said, his voice reflecting a sense of resentment of his predicament. "Elderik, here, is a fifth-generation vampire, and Esilas is a dhampir."

"Ephrem, I swear," Esilas' red-amber eyes leered at his younger comrade. "If ya don't keep your damn mouth shut–"

"She needs to know, Esilas," Elderik sighed, a sudden reluctance in his tone. "You know the law."

"Fuck the law." His head snapped to Elderik, answering him quickly. "We take her to the Courts, and she'll disappear... just like *she* did."

He stood up and hastily walked away in his anger. Elderik sighed and rubbed the back of his neck. Because of Esilas' words, a chill prickled up my spine.

"I swear... despite his age, he can be stubborn." He muttered, rubbing his eyes.

"W-What did he mean?" I asked, my heart rate steadily climbing. Even Ephrem seemed hesitant to answer my question as he looked at Elderik.

"Esilas... well, he doesn't have the best experience with higher-rank vampires or the Courts." Elderik said. "He and his sister were separated when they were children because she was an *Aster-Blood.* It's been nearly fifty years since they've seen each other."

"But why?" I asked. "Was she not allowed to see him?"

"Because dhampir are just above humans." Ephrem said in an uncharacteristic seriousness in his tone. "*Aster-Bloods* are presented to the Courts at the Royal Estate in the city, and they never associate with *lower blood*."

"Society in the city of Obsiditourma is ruled by a hierarchical rank system." Elderik took over the explanations from there. "At the bottom, making up the most of the city's population, are humans, first-generation vampires, and half-breeds like dhampir."

"Don't forget about the succubi and incubi." Ephrem said. "They're just called half-demons."

"Half-demons?" I asked.

"Offspring of demons and humans. Demons hold more power than vampires by their birthright." Elderik said. "They make up the entire royal family... but there are several half-demon bastards in the Outskirts."

"So... demons rule the city?" I asked.

"Indeed." Elderik answered before continuing. "Above the city's majority, there are those referred to as Low-Bloods, vampires of second to fifth generations."

"You're a fifth-generation, aren't you?" I asked.

He nodded and smiled at me.

"That's right." He said. "My family lives in the Mid-City with other Low-Bloods and Aristocrats."

"Aristocrats are vampires of six or more generations." Ephrem elaborated. "Low-Bloods can become Aristocrats if they show a specific talent for a craft or study. Medicine, architecture, arts and music, the works."

I looked at Elderik.

"That means that your family's next generation will move up in the hierarchy if they show a talent, right?" I asked.

Elderik chuckled as he turned the rabbit on the spit.

"You catch on quick." He said. "Very good."

I couldn't help but smile brightly at his praise.

"So, based on that, the Courts come next, don't they?" I asked.

Elderik's proud smile became a somber one, and he nodded.

"Indeed." He said. "The Noble families of the Courts are considered inarguably pure-blooded, though if you go back far enough in any of the Noble family's lineage and you'll find human blood, back even farther for the royal family."

"The Nobles are also the only vampires with the ability to turn humans." Ephrem's tone was hateful; he didn't seem to have a liking for them either.

Elderik cleared his throat.

"Besides that ability," Elderik said, "they have other powers that have aged and developed as their families grow with each new generation. At least, that is what is believed. No one really knows for sure. And above the Courts–"

"Are the royal family, the Morgensterns." Ephrem finished. "The highest of the *High-Bloods*. Descendents of the Gods' Tree itself."

Suddenly, it felt as if my heart had skipped a beat.

'The Gods' Tree...'

It seemed familiar, as if it were a part of me, somehow. I hesitantly put my hand to my forehead, straining to grasp at the memory that seemed so far away.

'Why... why can I not remember...?'

"Ah, Esilas." I was brought out of my own thoughts as Elderik addressed the returning comrade. "Have you calmed down now?"

Esilas didn't answer as he sat down. He was silent for a moment, as if deep in thought.

"We can't take her to the Courts." He spoke up finally.

"Esilas–"

"We can't take her to the Courts... because she's not a citizen of Obsiditourma." Esilas elaborated, looking at Elderik. "There wouldn't be any record of her birth or her family."

Elderik's eyes widened with the realization, and then he seemed to be deep in thought. I looked between him and Esilas; the latter seemed hopeful, waiting in anticipation for Elderik's thoughts. The fifth generation vampire, after moments of contemplation, nodded.

“That is true.” Elderik said, looking at Esilas and then turning to look at me. “It is a slight loophole, but it’s still best to advertise her existence.”

“Well, that’s obvious.” Esilas said with a scoff. “I’m not a damn idiot.”

The mood seemed to have lightened a bit as the two discussed the plan for the return to the barracks, and more precisely, how I was going to be smuggled in. And all I could do was listen, because I was too lost in their jargon to really understand what they were talking about.

The plan that Esilas and Elderik came up with was gruesome, to put it mildly; they had decided that it would be best if I was smuggled in as a corpse, a servant girl who’d somehow escaped the city and was killed by hellbeasts. The only downside to the lie would be that patrols would be doubled and every wagon leaving or entering Obsiditourma would be thoroughly inspected, but it was the only plan that seemed practicable. Ephrem was thoroughly displeased, seeing as Esilas had volunteered him to be the one to paint parts of my arms and legs with the grotesque-smelling blood of the dead hellbeasts that he had also been forced to collect.

“We sure that this is absolutely necessary?” Ephrem gagged, trying not to vomit because of the smell. “No one should have to look like this...”

"We have no other means of smuggling her into the barracks." Elderik said as Esilas packed his bedroll and his pack onto the back of his hellmount.

"And afterwards, she has to look the part of one of the new recruits when we actually head for the city." Esilas added.

I'd been about to say something when Ephrem smeared some blood down the side of my face. I involuntarily shuddered, and he stopped.

"S-Sorry, my lady." Ephrem said.

The youngest of the three comrades seemed to trust me a bit more, and he understood the gravity of the situation; he agreed with Esilas that I should be kept hidden from the Courts. And oddly enough, Ephrem seemed to treat me as a sibling.

"It's alright, Ephrem." I said as some of the blood was soaked in my dress and hair. "It won't last long... hopefully."

Elderik looked at me.

"We'll make sure you have proper clothes and a bath when we get you smuggled in." He promised.

I nodded and took a deep breath as Ephrem's job was finished; it was hard to breathe because of the ripe-smelling blood without gagging on bile, but I could manage.

"Are we ready?" Esilas asked, turning to us. He looked at me. "You look like you just crawled out of your own grave."

He was trying to hide a smirk.

I narrowed my eyes at him; he was making fun of me.

"Your humor in this situation is not appreciated, Esilas."

My comment made the dhampir show his smirk in full, and Elderik walked over to help me into the saddle on Esilas' infercanis. I sat side-saddle on the back of the massive creature, and Elderik covered me with his cloak.

"This will help cover your scent during the rest of our journey." He said, covering my head.

I laid down to let the cloak further cover me, and we set out for the barracks of the Keepers of the Watch. As we rode to the barracks, I felt myself dozing off every once in a while because of the soft rocking of the hellmount's back and things being quiet, though Ephrem was humming an odd tune to himself, which was getting on Esilas' nerves.

"I really wish he'd stop with that damn song. It's so morbid." He groaned under his breath, which brought me out of my light sleep.

I'd been about to move a little when I heard Elderik address Esilas.

"I've been trying to figure it out," Elderik spoke up; "why did you give the girl *that* name?"

"You're asking this now?" Esilas asked, sounding amused. "You had plenty of time to ask about it last night while the girl was asleep."

"She's probably asleep now, considering the fact that she's not moved in a while." Elderik said. "So, why did you give her your sister's name? Was it because she was an *Aster-Blood* as well?"

I kept myself quiet, resisting the urge to grip the mount's fur at the revelation.

"No," Esilas mumbled in a somber tone; "that's not it." I felt him gently pet his mount on the neck. "It's just... there's an odd sense of hope that this girl gives off... just like *she* did..."

I could feel Esilas' pain, a desire that appeared it was always out of his reach, and a tear gently rolled down my cheek. There was something in me that felt as though something horrible had happened to his sister. I heard Elderik breathe a sigh, drawing me from my thoughts.

"Your human is showing, my friend." He pointed out, his voice gentle. "You know that you can't get attached to her."

"I know." He sighed, sounding defeated. "A bastard has no right to be attached to anyone..."

"That's not what I mean, Esilas, and you know that." Elderik said, his voice somber with an audible frown.

Esilas said nothing else, only continuing forward. So many questions stirred in my mind.

'If he and his sister were close as children, then why didn't his sister try to contact him? Was she forbidden from doing so? Or did something or someone else stop her from contacting him?'

I winced a little, my head aching from all my inquiring thoughts.

"And where have you three been?" A haughty voice sneered as our small party came to a stop. I bit my lip to keep quiet.

"On patrol, like we were ordered to." Esilas answered with little enthusiasm; it appeared he was used to this sort of treatment.

"Impure vampire blood like you should have been feasted on by hellbeasts." The snob-sounding man—obviously a superior—didn't hold back any disdain for Esilas. "The Gods' Tree knows you belong with the animals, *dhampir.*"

"Now, now, captain," Elderik soothed, trying to diffuse the situation before it escalated. "You know Esilas is a valuable asset to the Watchmen's Guild and the Watch-Keepers."

"Valuable because of who his father is." The captain said, distastefully. "If it weren't for that man, then I would have made the boy a permanent stable hand. He should count himself lucky that he even gets to leave the barracks instead of scraping hellmount shit all day."

I could feel how Esilas was feeling, the loathing in his heart; it didn't seem directed towards the captain as it was to whoever "that man" was. I wished so much that I could reach out and hold Esilas' hand, to comfort him as well as to soothe my nervousness.

"And just what the hell is that on your mount, half-breed?"

I heard armored footsteps approaching the infercanis, and I fought to keep my heartbeat calm.

"I wouldn't look, sir." Ephrem said, preventing the man from touching the cloak covering me. "We found a citizen being mauled by a pack of hellbeasts. A servant girl."

Ephrem lied so nonchalantly; I was impressed, actually.

"We thought it best to return the girl's body to her family so that they can give her a proper burial." Elderik elaborated.

"Bringing a corpse back to the barracks?" The captain sighed with a posh sort of disgust. "You three truly are lower rank. Just get rid of it before the stench attracts other hellbeasts." I heard him gag and cover his mouth. "How vile."

"Will do, sir." Elderik said.

A few far-off shouts and we were allowed through the gate of the barracks.

'I'll have to commend Ephrem and Elderik for their quick thinking of their lie.' I thought to myself, amused.

A few turns later, I could tell we had entered a building, and I heard other hellmounts nearby.

"I'll make sure no one is near our room." I heard Ephrem as he dismounted.

I had been about to move as well when I felt a hand on my back.

"Stay still." Esilas whispered.

The infercanis lowered himself to lie down, and Esilas picked me up, still wrapped in the black cloak, and carried me close to his chest. I thought back to the interaction with the captain; Esilas was treated so poorly simply because he was a dhampir, while his sister was an *Aster-Blood*, treated as a treasure. Despite this, Esilas didn't resent her at all; he missed her so terribly. I wondered what it would be like for someone to miss me like that or I them. As I contemplated those feelings while hidden by the darkness of that wrapped cloak, I felt warm tears stream down my face, mixing with the dried hellbeast blood.

3

A Nightmare in the Mirror

Esilas held me close the entire way to the comrades' shared room, and there was a lot of stopping and starting along the way. In all honesty, I'd been so absorbed in my thoughts that I hadn't even noticed when Esilas had stopped and set me down until he pulled the cloak from my head.

"Hey, what's wrong?" I jumped when I felt his hand touch my cheek, having brought me out of my deep thoughts. "Look at me."

His voice was softer than it had been when we first met. I looked at him, and then, upon remembering my thoughts, I hastily wiped my tears.

"I-I'm sorry." I whimpered, my voice cracking from the emotions I had felt. "I'm okay, I promise."

He gently took my hands away from my eyes, making me look at him. His red-amber eyes stared into mine, tense but very calm. The emotion I associated such traits with was concern.

"Hey." He whispered. "Tell me what's wrong."

His voice was tender and soothing. He *was* concerned.

He took a rag, gently wiping the blood and tears from my cheeks. I was silent for a few moments, contemplating my answer, and I heard Esilas sigh.

"Or don't. It doesn't really matter." He mumbled in defeat. "You'd probably like to talk to Elderik more than me–"

"The captain…" I spoke, looking down as I felt tears form again; "… what he said to you was so cruel… you suffer so much disdain here, just because of the blood you bare…" I shook my head. "It's not right… no one should be judged on how they were born…"

I stopped when I felt Esilas' hand flinch as I spoke, but it was offset by a dry chuckle.

"You truly are pure." He lowered his hand to my cheek and gently brought my eyes to meet his, his red-amber hues piercing into mine with a melancholic longing. I could feel my heart pounding in my chest at the odd sense of familiarity.

"Esilas?" I whispered. "Who… is Lux?"

I had said the words before I even knew they had come from my mouth. His eyes widened slightly, filling even more with that shaken and somber emotion, and his touch wavered a little as his form visibly flinched. I'd hoped he wouldn't be angry with my inquiry. He was silent for a while, and I feared he would slip back into that darkness that he carried with him.

"I-I'm sorry. I shouldn't–"

“Luxia.” Esilas breathed, and his sudden answer made me stare, it being my turn for widened eyes. “Her name was... *is* Luxia... and she’s... my twin sister...”

I watched him as he walked over to a washbasin to clean the rag he’d been using. He was withdrawn once more into his solitude as if it were a sanctuary from his painful memories. I’d been about to apologize when there was a series of three quick knocks at the door. Esilas looked at the door with a sigh.

“You can come in, Elderik.” I tilted my head, looking at the door.

My curiosity turned into bewilderment when the door opened to reveal that it was Elderik. I looked between the two of them, wondering if it was some sort of secret knock.

“Even before we brought Lux here, you always knock on doors, especially when there isn’t a need to.”

Esilas had a slight smirk on his face, and I found myself slightly even more shocked by his statement.

‘Elderik is the only one who knocks on doors in this place and *that’s* how he knew he was at the door?!’ I thought to myself.

I looked at Esilas, and I could tell that his expression wasn’t just one of amusement.

“Sorry, it will always be a habit of mine.” Elderik chuckled and then looked at me. He had a set of dark clothing with him. “Here. These should be about your size, maybe bigger.”

I took the clothes and nodded.

“Thank you for this.” I said. “I’m sorry to have put you through the trouble.”

“It’s no trouble at all.” He said. “Get cleaned up and changed. We’ll make sure no one enters the room.”

“But be quick about it.” Esilas said as he filled the wash-basin before joining Elderik at the door. “It’ll look suspicious if we’re seen standing outside our own room.”

I nodded silently as the two men left me alone to bathe and change clothes.

The water was cooler than I would have liked, admittedly, but as long as it got the dried blood off my skin and out of my hair, I decided I would not complain. I quickly yet thoroughly washed what was left of the dress, figuring that I could use it to hide my chest. As I finished bathing and dressed myself, still shivering a bit from the damp fabric binding my chest, I glimpsed myself in the mirror. My damp, red and gold hair was wavy, almost looking like liquid fire, and my eyes were a bluish-green, with a depth of sea-colored gemstones. The Heart-Mark on my chest was still what captured my eyes most of all. I traced my fingers over the intricate lines, almost as if it had been a designed tattoo.

‘It sort of reminds me of that tree from my dream.’

I recalled a name Ephrem had spoken when he and Elderik were explaining the hierarchy of Obsiditourma.

‘The Gods’ Tree.’

At my recollection, I felt a slight pain in the back of my mind, and I glimpsed a figure phasing in and out of focus in the mirror. It was the figure of a young woman with light tan skin, long black hair that faded into ashen-gray and a familiar pair of amber-red eyes. There was a mark on her chest—a Heart-Mark—that resembled an elongated, eight-pointed star.

'Wait, could this be—'

Before I could even finish my thought, a shadow appeared behind her—the only feature visible of the silhouette was a pair of glowing eyes—with a dagger raised above her head. My eyes widened, and I took a step back, covering my eyes as I heard a dying scream and a sickening splatter echo in my ears. After a moment of silence, an unfamiliar voice echoed in my head, a sinister voice that dripped with hatred.

'Death to all the High-Bloods.'

A knock startled me, and I turned to the door.

"Lux, are you decent?" It was Elderik.

I turned back to the mirror; the vision of the woman had vanished, my panicked form the only thing visible in the reflection.

"Lux, we can't stand out here forever." That voice belonged to Esilas.

"J-Just a minute!" I stuttered loudly as I hurried in putting on the clothes. I leaned against the wall as I pulled on the boots.

'That woman...' I thought back, my hands still shaking; 'w-was that Luxia?'

I braided and tied my hair up and off my neck, covering it with a spare piece of black cloth before the door opened. Esilas had been the one to open it, and Elderik had been about to say something to reprimand, but stopped. The two of them stared at me, and I could feel heat rush to my cheeks.

"W-What?" I stuttered. "Why are you two looking at me like that?"

I was worried that I'd put the clothes on wrong in my haste.

"D-Did I put these on wrong?"

"N-No, you put them on right. It's not that." Elderik said, rubbing the back of his neck as he looked at me. "I-It's just that–"

"We almost didn't recognize you." Esilas finished, slightly flustered. He walked over to me and looked at me.

He tightened the strings on my shirt and then gently pulled my bangs over my eyes.

"There we go." He said. "You look closer to a first-generation vampire now." He smirked a little. "A proper disguise, though there will be many people taking second looks at such a pretty boy."

Elderik looked at him with wide eyes.

"Esilas!" He hit him on the shoulder.

I blinked at his smirk, and then I realized he was making fun of me again. I narrowed my eyes and shoved him away.

"Don't make jokes at my expense, Esilas!" I said before crossing my arms, feeling self-conscious about how I looked. Elderik chuckled at my reaction.

"Well, you've got spirit." He said. "Luckily, we're heading into the city tomorrow to restock our supplies and to report to the Watchmen's Guild."

"Elderik is heading to his family's clinic for our medical supplies." Esilas said. "He'll be able to smuggle you through the Mid-Gate."

I looked at him, slightly surprised.

"Wait, are you not coming with us?" I asked him, feeling slightly disappointed.

"Not to the clinic." He elaborated. "I have business in the Outskirts."

Ephrem soon came in with a plate of dark rye bread and some cheese.

"I was able to smuggle some food out of the kitchen." He said, and then his eyes turned to me. "Wow, is that you, Lux?!"

"Ephrem!" Esilas' head snapped to him, hissing. "Keep your damn voice down!"

"Sorry." Ephrem whispered, and then he walked over to place the plate on an old trunk. "It's not much, but it should help if you're hungry." He was talking more to me than he was to his two comrades.

"Well, aren't you smitten?" Esilas said bluntly as he went to leave the room.

"Wait, Esilas, where are you going?" I asked.

"Out." He said curtly, before closing the door behind him. His expression had been a lonely one, maybe a bit of jealousy as well.

'Understandable. His sister received a lot of attention because she was an *Aster-Blood* as well... it's only natural for this to seem all too uncomfortably familiar...'

I shuddered involuntarily at the terrified chill that prickled through me.

I had heard her scream.

Luxia's scream.

'What happened to her?'

I felt Elderik put his hand on my shoulder.

"Don't worry about Esilas." He said, offering a smile of reassurance. "He goes off by himself, particularly when he feels overwhelmed."

I'd been about to say something when he gently led over to a rather shabby-looking desk.

"Now, let's redress those wounds, shall we?"

The room the three comrades shared was more the size of a storage room. There was a single set of bunk beds on one end and a hammock on the other, and at a small window was the shabby desk where Elderik redressed the wounds on my feet.

"They're already nearly healed." The vampire said, sounding surprised.

"Is that... normal for an *Aster-Blood* like me?" I asked.

"I'm not sure, in all honesty." Elderik said. "My parents might know a little more, or even Eshrik."

"Who's he?" I looked at him.

Elderik looked up at me as he finished bandaging my feet, smiling softly.

"He's my elder brother." He said. "He's a medical scholar in Mid-City, closer to the Royal Estate, actually."

"The guy's a proper genius." Ephrem said, swinging in the hammock. "Quite the chipper fellow, too. A bit too excitable, really."

"He's worked his way through the academy and is aiming towards running the Archives." Elderik spoke with such pride about his brother.

"He's been working on a drug for the blood hunger that dhampir and first-generation vampires experience." Ephrem said.

This immediately caught my attention.

"Blood hunger?" I looked from Elderik to Ephrem.

"Yeah, because of the physical changes we first-generations go through, we can't control our hunger." Ephrem explained. "Dhampir have it a lot rougher because their human blood and the vampire virus they're born with are sometimes at odds."

"It's why the older generations garner so much respect." Elderik added.

"And it's why we're treated like trash." Ephrem grumbled with the same resentment as before. "I envy Esilas and his ability to not give a shit about it."

I frowned a little; that wasn't what I had picked up from anything Esilas had said.

"How long have you two known Esilas?" I asked them.

Ephrem chuckled.

"Elderik's been his bunkmate since before I was dumped here." Ephrem said.

Elderik chuckled a bit, though it sounded tired.

"I'm one of the few that Esilas actually lets himself be close to." He said. "Besides myself, there's my family, and then Ash."

I blinked at the name.

"Ash?" I tilted my head to the side.

"It's the name of his hellmount." Ephrem elaborated with a chuckle.

"Esilas has never really trusted anyone else or let himself get close to anyone." Elderik said. "He was only ever close with his twin sister–"

"Luxia." I said.

Elderik looked at me with wide eyes, but he gave a sad smile.

"So, Esilas finally said her name." He said, sitting on the bottom bunk. "That's a relief."

"I don't understand." I said. "What do you mean?"

"Well, from what I understand, Esilas and Luxia–"

Before Elderik could explain further, the door opened to reveal Esilas, his clothes slightly torn and what skin he was showing was covered with slight scratches and new-forming bruises. He closed the door behind him.

"Giving her a damned history lesson, are we?" He walked in, slightly limping, and Elderik stood up to catch him as he stumbled.

"She asked how long the two of us had known you." He said. "One thing led to another."

Esilas muttered something unintelligible as Elderik helped him lie down in his bunk. The moment the dhampir fell onto his bed, he was asleep. In stark contrast to how distant he'd been since we met, Esilas looked so calm as he slept.

"E-Elderik... why is he hurt?" I frighteneddly whispered, going to kneel at his bedside. Elderik sighed a little.

"The barracks aren't exactly different from the wilds of the Pale Woods." He said as he cleaned Esilas' scratches.

"The higher rank Watch-Keepers like to beat up Esilas." Ephrem said. "It's not just because he's a dhampir, either."

I looked at him.

"What do you—"

"It's because of *who* brought him here." Elderik answered. "His own father."

My eyes widened at what he'd said, and I looked at Elderik as he gently pet Esilas' sleeping head, a gesture a parent would give to soothe a child. I understood Esilas more with the information I'd learned in such a short time. He felt as though he was alone, even with Elderik, his family and Ephrem supporting him. He longed to see his sister, to know what had become of her. He resented everyone, though he never showed it. I hummed softly and then moved to lie down next to the sleeping dhampir.

"Whoa, whoa, whoa!" Ephrem whispered frantically, freaking out so much that he fell from his hammock with a *thud*. "Lux, what are you—?"

"If I can help to ease this loneliness that is so consuming him," I said calmly as I gently put Esilas' arm over me; "then I'll do whatever I can to that effect, even if it's just a little."

Elderik hushed Ephrem from saying anything else, and I felt him put his hand on my head with a soft chuckle.

"Your empathy knows no bounds, Lux." He whispered, his hand gently petting my head. "I leave him in your capable hands."

The lamps were extinguished, and as soon as the light of the pink moon slowly rose to illuminate the room, I fell asleep, carefully snuggled close to the dhampir that was so broken inside.

I was brought to the surface of consciousness by the brushing of hesitant fingertips against my cheek. I hummed softly as my eyes gently fluttered open, and I was met with the uncharacteristically gentle, red-amber eyes of the man I'd slept beside.

Remembering my decision to do so made my cheeks flush with heat.

"E-Esilas, I'm sorry.." I stuttered in a whisper as I moved to give him room. "I-I just–"

"It's fine." He whispered back, his voice a hoarse whisper as he gently wrapped his arm around my waist to bring me closer to his chest. "It's warmer... and safer for you, as well."

I could feel my muscles become tense a bit with hesitation before relaxing, but the situation only made my cheeks darken all the more.

"S-Safer for me?" I repeated, feeling comfortable in his warmth. "How?"

"If the other Watch-Keepers find out that you're an *Aster-Blood*, they'll be obligated to bring you to the Courts, no doubt expecting a handsome reward." He explained, his arm tightening slightly. "And if they find out you're a woman, they'll either use you themselves or bleed you dry." I could hear the shudder in his voice. "You'd either disappear into the Courts... or they'll break you here..."

There was a fear in his voice, a reminder of his sister and how he'd lost her. His silent, despairing heart made mine break, and without thinking, I gently wrapped my arms around his neck and softly ran my fingers through his hair. I felt him flinch at the contact.

"I won't disappear." I whispered reassuringly, as my fingers combed through his slightly knotted hair.

Esilas relaxed for a moment before he tensed up once more, pushed me away a bit, and pressed himself against the wall. I sat up and looked at him.

"Esilas?" I reached out to touch him, but his hand grabbed my wrist, stopping me and keeping me at bay.

"D-Don't..." He strained, his voice laced with pain. "It'll pass in a moment... I-I'll be fine..." He was seething, his breath passing through his fangs in a hiss. "Damn hunger."

My eyes widened, and I recalled what Ephrem had said about dhampir having a more difficult time dealing with than other vampires did.

"Do you have any medicine for it?" I asked, wanting to help.

Esilas shook his head as he was about to grab his throat. I took a deep breath, deciding.

"Take my blood." I said.

Esilas' head snapped up to me, his wide eyes glowing a little more red than usual.

"What..." he said, his eyes filling with a mix of fear and fury. "What the hell did you just say? Do you even know what it means to offer your blood, woman? *Your* blood especially..."

His eyes pulsed a brighter shade of red, and his grip on my wrist tightened. I winced a bit at the bruises that were no doubt forming, but I didn't back down.

I *couldn't* back down.

"If it means that your hunger will be sated, and your pain relieved," I whispered, gently putting my hand on his that gripped my wrist so tightly; "then I want to be of as much help as I am able."

He was baffled, and his eyes reflected that much. His grip loosened slightly, but he pulled me closer to him.

"A-Are you... not frightened?" His voice was soft, full of uncertainty.

I nodded a bit, but I had a smile on my lips despite that fear.

"I am," I said; "but you shouldn't be in pain because of something that is beyond your control."

Esilas stared at me as if searching for any crack in my resolve, and when he couldn't find any, he let out a shaky breath of defeat.

"You're determined..." He muttered, sliding his grip to my hand, interlacing his fingers with mine. "Your consideration and kindness... will get you killed..."

He brought my wrist to his mouth, his hot breath sending chill bumps to prickle along my skin. He swiped his tongue over his dry lips before his fangs pierced my wrist. The sound of the *pop* made my heartbeat quicken, but the pain was only there for a moment, like that of a pin-prick, though there was a dull ache that penetrated my bones. Esilas took very little, only enough to be considered a drink from a waterskin. He slowly pulled away, letting out a breath as if he'd come up from underwater, and he gently licked the bite he'd made. Afterwards, he turned on his back, looking up at the underside of the top bunk.

"Esilas?" I whispered. "Do you feel better?"

He didn't answer; he sighed and laid his forearm over his eyes. After several moments, I had been about to speak again when the dhampir beside me spoke.

"You're a fool..." he answered back softly after a long pause. "You can't go worrying about everyone else except for yourself." He took a deep breath and sat up. "We need to dress your wound. Last thing we need is Ephrem stirring from his sleep and his hunger acting up as well."

He reached behind him to a small table and grabbed a piece of cloth to wrap my wrist. We didn't speak at all as he gently wrapped the cloth around my wrist and my hand. The silence wasn't uncomfortable; it was a sort of mutual understanding, and this was his way of thanking me for helping him during such a vulnerable time.

Early the next morning, Esilas and Ephrem smuggled me into the covered supply wagon as Elderik cleverly distracted the callous barracks captain. Esilas had been rather attentive since the night before, but he wasn't very good at hiding his change in behavior. Well, from Elderik at least; Ephrem just thought he'd slept well because he was hugging a pretty girl. This remark, admittedly, made heat flush to my cheeks and earned the first-generation vampire a punch in the gut from Esilas. Ephrem was left at the barracks, which he was still pouting about when we left. I hugged my knees close to my chest as the supply wagon traveled from the muddy roads to cobblestone. The gentle rhythm had almost lulled me to sleep.

"So," I heard Elderik speak to Esilas, which stirred me from my light sleep; "are you going to tell me about your sudden change in behavior?"

I kept quiet as Esilas answered.

"What makes you think my behavior has changed?"

"You hate these visits to the city and the Watchmen's Guild," Elderik said; "and not to mention how attentive you've been to Lux all morning." When his comrade didn't answer, he sighed. "If you won't tell me, I'll ask the girl when we drop you off—"

"My hunger returned last night." Esilas cut him off. "It was stronger than the last time around."

There was a long pause before Elderik spoke again.

"You didn't... please, tell me you didn't—"

"She offered." Esilas answered quickly. "She wouldn't let me refuse." He let out a chuckle. "She's stubborn."

Elderik sighed, sounding relieved.

"I'm sorry." He said. "That might have been my fault."

"I don't really see it as your fault." Esilas said. "Somehow, I doubt her nature would let her not help anyone."

"Even so," Elderik said, his tone sounding concerned; "I never imagined that you'd have an attack. It's been three years since you started on the medicine."

"We both know that the effects of Eshrik's medicine would lose their efficiency after some time." Esilas' voice sounded melancholic. "I can only imagine how *her* condition is faring..."

Elderik was silent for a bit again before he spoke.

"There's something else you're not telling me." He said. When Esilas didn't elaborate, Elderik sighed. "If you're worried about her hating you, you know that there's not a reason for her to."

Esilas said nothing else; I didn't see his face, but I could tell that he was deep in thought just by how silent he was. The wagon came to a slow stop, bringing me out of my thoughts of their conversation. There was a shuffling outside the wagon, the sound of armored footsteps, and I held my breath once more.

"Elderik and Esilas!" A rather cheerful voice greeted them. "It's nice to see you both again!"

The man's voice was cheerful, like a child's; his friendliness sort of caught me off guard. It appeared that they knew each other well, exchanging pleasantries as the gateman went over the paperwork for them to enter the city. After he confirmed Esilas' and Elderik's papers, the guard gave a shrill whistle, and I heard a cranking metallic sound as something heavy was being lifted. The wagon started forward once more, and after we were some ways away, I heard Esilas speak up.

"That man is perhaps the oddest first-generation vampire I've ever met in my life." He said with a sigh.

"I think it's quite refreshing." Elderik chuckled. I heard a shuffle, and the canvas flap was pulled aside.

I looked to see Elderik smiling at me.

"Want to join us up here?" I blinked.

“A-Am I allowed to?” I asked with a stutter.

“Yep, you can come on up here,” he said as Esilas helped me to climb over the seat to sit in between them; “this is your first time seeing the city, after all.”

I looked around, and my eyes widened at the incredible depth of the city.

“Welcome to the city of Obsiditourma, Lux.”

4

The Mid-City Gate

THE ENORMOUS MOUNTAIN OF black glass I had seen from the field was, in reality, a steady-sloped city, a monolithic beacon. The outskirts of Obsiditourma were a mosaic of different shades of dark gray and ashen-white brick, and at the top of the city was a large black castle, the Royal Estate. There were shops ranging from low-wage seamstresses and tailors to baking and blacksmithing. Their trades were simple, but I could tell that these professions were all that they had. The people in the city's outskirts were poverty-stricken, their clothes ragged and patched in some places while they were poorly stitched in others. It was a melting pot of species, and I could tell who was human from who had become a first-generation vampire by the features they bore. There were some traits that I didn't recognize; some people had normal colored hair but had eyes of a pale pinkish-gold hue.

"They're the half-demons we spoke of before." Elderik answered my question before I could even open my mouth to ask it. "You looked confused by their eye color, so I thought I'd elaborate."

I looked at him; had I really been that easy to read? Soon we reached a clearing, a town square where market stalls were set up around a large water-fountain. Stall keepers were shouting advertisements about the goods they sold, but I could tell that food was scarce.

"I don't understand." I said, looking at Elderik. "With a city as big as this, there should be farms that can provide food of all kinds."

Elderik had a sad look on his face.

"There *are* farms just outside the walls of the city," Esilas said, "but they've not produced anything substantial."

"Food has been scarce for a while." Elderik further explained. "Even when Esilas and Luxia were children, the farms outside the wall had hardly grown anything. It appeared the soil simply swallowed up any effort to grow produce. Even the Pale Woods haven't budded with new leaves."

"How long has this been going on?" I asked, bewildered by this. "Has no one attempted to help these people?"

"No one really knows how long this has been the way of things." He said. "Most believe that it started around three years ago, and others believe it was longer before that. And if you talk to those particular others, they'll tell you that these hard times started when the Morgensterns first came into power."

I was deep in thought then.

'Three years...'

There seemed to be a pattern emerging, but I couldn't understand how it all tied together.

'Three years since Esilas had his last attack... What is the significance of three years? And why has no one attempted to help?'

My pondering thoughts were interrupted as Elderik slowed the wagon to a stop, and Esilas stood from the wagon's seat and jumped down.

"I'll pick you up after we resupply at the clinic." Elderik said.

"You mean *after* you've caught up with your family and had a nice home-cooked meal?"

Esilas may not have been smiling, but I could tell that there was a joking tone in his voice.

"You know that you're invited as well." Elderik said. "They'd love to see you again."

"Maybe next time." Esilas said.

"That's what you said last time."

Esilas said nothing else further as he turned to me, looking at my bandaged wrist before he looked up at me.

"Be careful." He said, his voice low with concern. "Elderik's family is the only exception. No one else can know."

I could tell by the urgency of his voice that he was serious, afraid of history repeating itself. I nodded and pulled my sleeve down over my wrist. Esilas looked at Elderik, nodding with a silent understanding, before turning and walking into the crowd of market-shoppers. I suddenly felt a bit of anxiety as he seemed to disappear like a shadow, and then I felt Elderik put his hand on my head.

"He'll be fine, Lux." He reassured me as I looked at him. "He's just got a lot on his mind."

He took the reins and gave them a flick to urge the two hellmounts forward.

After a bit of driving, Elderik finally broke the silence and spoke up about his conversation with Esilas.

"You must have questions about what you heard." He didn't bother asking me if I'd heard anything; he already knew that I had. I nodded and put my hand over the makeshift bandage. "We have time and privacy, so you can ask whatever you want."

"Is... Esilas mad at me?" I asked. "Because I offered my blood to help with his hunger?"

"I don't think he's as mad at you as he is at himself." Elderik answered. "Truth be told, Esilas has never been cared for by anyone before, let alone have anyone actually offer their blood to him."

I could understand a bit of that truth; the other Watch-Keepers at the barracks treated him so poorly, so it was doubtful that they'd ever help him if he needed it. Then again, it wasn't really like Esilas was the type to ask for help from what I could tell. I looked at my wrist.

"Dhampir need blood to survive, too, don't they? Just like vampires? I don't understand–"

"That's not exactly true." Elderik said, suddenly. "While we are creatures that feed on blood, we've developed to where we don't need it all the time to stay sustained. Generations as old as fourth and fifth can survive on very little blood, and Aristocrats see more blood as a luxury than a necessity."

"So, the older a generation you are, the less you rely on feedings?" I asked. "That means you can eat regular food, too, right?"

"Indeed." He confirmed. "Dhampir and first-generations experience hunger in the form of attacks because of the anomaly in their blood, though first-generation vampires are more likely to grow accustomed and coexist with their hunger than dhampir are."

"Ephrem said that their human blood and vampire blood are at odds with each other."

"Well, that's only half true." Elderik said. "When first generations are turned, their bodies experience a lot of changes because of the virus that they are given. It mutates their system, and that's why they experience their hunger in such a way. Dhampir differ in that regard because they are born with that virus and it fights to mutate their human genes, and that volatile clash makes hunger worse for them."

"You mentioned before that it had been three years since Esilas' last attack." I said. "Was that because of the medicine your brother made?"

"Yes." Elderik said. "It's meant to help dhampir and first-generations keep a firmer hold on their hunger so they don't accidentally attack someone."

I thought back on their conversation; if this was the case with Esilas, then how was Luxia's condition? Was she suffering the same way as her twin? Or had she been able to find something that helped her? I wondered more and more about this odd series of events.

"I'm curious about something," he said as he turned to me; "how much did he take from you when he bit you?"

At his question, I paused for a moment to think, humming softly.

"I think... it was enough to be considered a single drink from a waterskin, maybe?"

There was a slight jerk, and when I looked at Elderik, he was staring with wide eyes.

"That's it?! A drink from a waterskin?! That small of an amount?!" He nearly screamed. He remembered where we were, and he cleared his throat before continuing onwards. "After three years, it should have been much more than 'a single drink from a waterskin.'"

"He didn't seem like he needed any more than that." I wondered if he had stopped before his hunger had been sated.

"When we get to the clinic, I want to take your blood to run a test." Elderik said, bringing me out of my thoughts. "Will you let us?"

"Y-Yeah, I guess..." I said, stuttering a little; "but what are you hoping to find?"

"According to legend, every *Aster-Blood* is said to have a unique ability." He explained.

"Like the Aristocrats?" I asked.

Elderik nodded and smiled at me.

"That's right." He said with a smile. "Those powers are different, though. They were given to them by the progenitor of the Morgenstern family, Lucien Morgenstern. His powers were given to him by the Gods' Tree, and in order to keep the balance, the Tree also gifted certain members of humanity with pure spirits when times would get hard, creating the first *Aster-Bloods*."

"I'm not sure I understand–"

"Your Heart-Mark is a deep-rooted tree with new growth leaves and budding flowers on its branches." Elderik said. "And based on what's happened, that is not a coincidence."

I had been about to ask what he was implying when he slowed the cart; we were nearing another gate.

"Elderik—?"

"Don't say a word." He whispered to me, his tone urgent as guards approached.

These guards were clad in black armor, the crest of a crescent moon conjoined with an elongated four-pointed star embossed on their chest plates.

"State your business, Watch-Keeper." The guard spoke with an unpleasant tone, and I could see piercing red eyes through the guard's visor.

A chill ran down my spine at the sight, but I stayed still, watching the interaction between the two men.

"I, Elderik Dargrin Passor, am here to visit the Passor Family Clinic to resupply the barracks and report to the Watchmen's Guild." Elderik spoke so formally that I almost didn't recognize him as the same person who'd taken such parental care of Esilas the night before.

I watched as Elderik gave the guard some papers to show that he had passage to enter. The guard turned his gaze from the papers he'd been given to me, and I froze in place as his eyes narrowed.

"And who is this shrimp?" I flinched at his harsh tone.

"This is one of our new recruits." Elderik answered, lying so cleverly.

The guard's eyes analyzed me, seeming to pierce my soul. He then scoffed.

"Those are some pretty soft features." He said menacingly. "Looks more like a girl than a boy."

He had been about to reach for my arm when a hand clapped onto his shoulder plate, giving both the guard and me a scare. I turned my attention, following the hand to another guard; he wasn't wearing a helmet, showing his eyes to be a dark red, a familiar shade I'd seen mixed with another, and his hair was silvery-gray and slicked back.

"Now, you wouldn't be trying to scare the youngster," his voice was kind, and yet it was almost menacing towards the guard. "Would you, soldier?"

The guard turned on his heel in a near blur of motion and stood at attention.

"N-No, captain, sir!" He shouted. "I wasn't doing anything of the sort, sir!"

It was sort of amusing to see a person who'd been so stern to suddenly become so panicked in stature. I bit my lip to hold back a snicker, but when the captain's eyes turned to me, my amusement quickly turned to that same panic.

"Step down, boy." He commanded, though his voice sounded more gentle than before.

I looked at Elderik and he nodded once, though with much hesitance. I took a deep breath and then stood up. I stepped down and looked up at the captain; he stood a head taller than me. I clenched my hands at my sides as I stood straight.

"How old are you, boy?" He asked. It was a question that I had been unprepared for, and I didn't know if I should answer because Elderik had told me not to speak.

"Sir, he's–"

"Nineteen, sir." I said, lowering the pitch of my voice as I looked up at the man. "I was abandoned by my maker at the barracks."

I would have to apologize to Elderik for not following his instruction. The captain looked at me, as if trying to find any falsehood in my eyes, and for a moment I thought he would call me out on my lie. He moved his hand, and I tensed, fearing he would take off my head covering, but he gave me a pat on the head. The gesture was almost... fatherly.

"A first-generation, huh?" He said. "That explains why your scent still smells human. Make sure you tell Elderik if you have an attack."

I looked at him and nodded. He then helped me back up into the wagon.

"Help Elderik keep an eye on that boy at the barracks..." He whispered. I looked at him, blinking at his request.

"He's already helped Esilas a great deal." Elderik said as he put his hand on my head. His tone towards the man was polite, but there was a coolness to it, almost protective.

The captain seemed to tense a bit at his tone, and he nodded before giving one of the hellmounts—coincidentally, Ash—a slap on the rear to urge the wagon forward through the gate.

"Good," he said, though only I could hear him. "He needs someone."

I turned to look at him as the wagon moved, and when I saw the look on his face, I remembered where I'd seen that shade of red.

Those familiar somber eyes.

"Elderik... isn't that–"

"That," he said; "was the vampire who fathered Esilas and Luxia... as well as the one who split them up."

There was a protectiveness in his tone as Elderik spoke; he thought of Esilas as family. Elderik told me a bit about Esilas' father and how he had split him and his sister up, how Esilas held a burning hatred for the man. He didn't tell me much after that, believing that Esilas should be the one to divulge further information. The conversation had since diverged from the topic and focused more on the scenery.

The wagon climbed a steady incline, and on either side of the smooth brick road were sleek gray buildings on either side. At the top of the hill, when the roads leveled out, we were met with elegant carriages drawn by dark-colored horses with curved horns on their snouts and two pairs of dark orange eyes.

"They're called Hellsteeds." Elderik chuckled at my shield-like wonderment. "It's said that Lucien Morgenstern used the gifts he received from the Gods' Tree to bring the dead horses of his people back to life and they mutated into such elegant beasts."

"They're beautiful." I said, before looking at him. "Will you tell me more about the Gods' Tree?"

"I'm not that much of an expert on that subject." He admitted with a chuckle. "If you want to know more, you'll have to ask my father."

I hummed a little and then asked a different question.

"How did you come to be a Watch-Keeper if your family owns a clinic?" I asked. Elderik looked at me as we stopped at an intersection.

"Well, Low-Bloods like me are given the same handsome education as Aristocrats," he explained; "but after a certain year, we're given the choice to either volunteer or follow in the family practice."

"So you volunteered to become a member of the Keepers of the Watch?" I asked.

"That's right." He nodded. "And my brother, Eshrik, is pursuing medical research."

"Isn't it difficult for you?" I asked. "You only get to see your family once a month."

"It can be difficult at times, yes," he admitted; "but every second son has the option to volunteer, whether it be as a Watch-Keeper or as part of the Ebony Guard, in order to keep reserves up. It's always been like this."

He slowed the wagon to a stop outside a pale-charcoal, two-story building with a sign outside that had an image of a bird in flight. The lettering underneath read "Passor Clinic."

"The old homestead." Elderik chuckled and hopped down from the driver's seat.

As he helped me down as well, the door of the clinic opened to reveal two children—a pair of young girls with silvery-white hair and pale rose eyes.

"Elderik is home!" One girl, who had her hair in pigtail braids, exclaimed.

The fifth-generation vampire turned and smiled brightly as the two girls came running to embrace him. He knelt down and picked them up.

"You two have gotten so big!" He held them close. "You must have grown half a foot since the last time I visited."

I couldn't help but smile at the sight, concluding that the two girls were Elderik's younger sisters.

"Big Brother, who is she?" The second of the girls, her hair cut short with a small bow barrette to hold her bangs back.

Elderik turned to look at me, smiling. He said nothing, but he turned to his sisters and then whispered something in their ears. The two of them looked at me with wide eyes.

"We've gotta tell Mama!" The two girls said simultaneously.

Elderik chuckled at the girls' enthusiasm and let them down.

"Be gentle, girls." He playfully warned as the girls took me by the hands and pulled me up the stairs towards the clinic.

"W-Wait, Elderik!" I looked back at him.

"You'll be fine, Lux." He chuckled. "I'll be inside shortly. I'm taking the wagon to the back courtyard."

I blinked as he practically left me with his sisters.

"Come on!" The girl with pigtails said. "I'm Tana!"

"And I'm Twiny!" The short-haired girl said. "Tana and I are identical twins!"

I chuckled nervously.

"I-I can tell." I stuttered as the two girls brought me through the clinic and up a set of stairs to a small dining room.

"Mama!" Tana called out.

"Elderik brought a guest home!"

"Yeah, a *special* guest!" Twiny giggled.

"A special guest, you say?" There was a voice from the kitchen that answered, and into the dining room walked a beautiful woman with a silvery-blonde in a long braid down her back.

She wore a white button-up blouse with a green silk bow around the collar, a glittering gold brooch pinned to its knot, and up to her waist was a blue-black skirt and a white work apron with pockets. I knew she must have been Elderik's mother, because her eyes were the same rose-petal red as his. Her smile was kind, with a hint of playfulness.

"Elderik brought a girl home, huh? Wonder where he found you." She mused as walked over to me. "Might I, dear?"

I blinked a little, a small blush of embarrassment on my cheeks. I nodded shyly, and she gently reached around to untie my head covering, letting my hair fall. She gave an amused chuckle as she smiled at me.

"A *human* girl, too. How interesting."

"She's a human?!" Tana exclaimed.

"Shhh, Tana." The woman said. "Your brother brought her disguised, and there must be a reason for him to do so. We shouldn't breathe word of this. Promise, girls?"

The two girls looked at each other, and then Twiny looked at me.

"Are you Brother's lover?" My cheeks immediately burned bright red at the girl's innocent question.

"She's much more precious than that." I heard Elderik's voice and turned to look at him. "I'm sorry for all the sneaking around, Mother. This was the only safe place that Esilas and I could think of."

The woman looked at him and then at her daughters.

"Girls, could you tend to the infercani?" She said, and as the girls were about to protest, she simply shook her head. "No protesting or complaining, girls. Run along."

The girls pouted but complied with their mother's request. She then turned towards her second eldest.

"Now, Elderik," she said, "are you going to be an adult and tell me why you've gone through the trouble of disguising her as a boy and smuggling her into the city?"

Elderik sighed and rubbed the back of his neck and then looked at me before looking back at his mother.

"Mother," he said, taking a deep breath, "she's an *Aster-Blood.* Esilas insisted she would be safer here than at the barracks."

The woman didn't seem surprised; she looked from her son to me, eyeing me. She then took a deep breath of her own, letting it out slowly through her nostrils, before she turned back to Elderik.

"I better put on some tea." She stated simply. "I believe that an explanation is in order."

She turned on her heel and entered the kitchen once more. I looked at Elderik, and all he could do was offer a reassuring smile.

5

The Passor Clinic

THE WOMAN, WHO INTRODUCED herself as Dahliah, sat across from Elderik and me at the dining table, listening intently as we told her everything, from how I'd met Esilas and his comrades to the present. She calmly took a sip from her teacup, absorbing the tale. After a few moments of contemplation, she finally spoke.

"I figured she wasn't an ordinary human," she said, before turning to me. "Not with features like yours, dear."

She leaned in a little closer, her soft pink eyes analyzing me.

"And I bet Esilas was the one who gave you the name Lux." She said with a knowing smile. "Am I right?"

I looked at her, a bit confused.

"Wait, what do you mean? How did you know Esilas gave me that name?" I asked, still warming my hands around the teacup she had given me.

"My, those boys must have told you very little." Dahliah said with an amusing smile on her lips. "Traits like yours are uncommon, even among humans. Extremely rare."

She didn't answer my question about how she figured out that Esilas had given me my name.

"The older a generation of vampire you are, the whiter your hair and the redder your eyes become. It's a result of the vampirism mutation." Dahliah continued to elaborate.

"First-generation vampires carry traits of those who turn them, their human features fading after the change is made." Elderik added. "Like their hair color or their skin color."

"So," I started, recalling Ephrem's appearance; "Ephrem's hair color is from the one who gave him the mutation when he was turned?"

Dahliah smiled and chuckled softly.

"Indeed." She said, looking at me with a kind smile. "You're very intuitive." She then set her teacup aside. "If I might ask, dear, could I see your Heart-Mark?"

I blushed a little and looked at Elderik. He nodded, confirming that it was alright to show her. I let out a deep breath and started to slowly untie the strings of my shirt. I gently pulled my shirt collar apart to show her the mark. Dahliah stood and came closer to inspect. She hummed in thought and then went to sit back down. I gently closed the collar of my shirt, not bothering to retie the stings. I felt safe with her being there and knowing my secret.

"Rather curious." She said, looking at Elderik. "Your father would be intrigued by this. It's not like anything I've seen."

"What do you mean?" I asked, leaning forward on the table a bit.

Dahliah looked at me.

"Well, Heart-Marks were said to be the remnants of times long past." She explained. "For example, Luxia's Heart-Mark was a depiction of a glowing star. The stars had disappeared from our skies long ago."

"Legend says that they died with every *Aster-Blood* that was slaughtered during the Trials." Elderik added.

I looked at him.

"The Trials?' I asked, suddenly feeling a heavy feeling in my stomach.

"It was a rather ghastly affair." Dahliah hugging her arms a little, her hands on her elbows as she spoke. "It was a period around when Lucien Morgenstern came into power. The humans, fearful that those with Heart-Marks would join the demons, killed them in cold blood."

"Very few survived, and they went into hiding." Elderik said, sadly.

"But," I looked at him, "I thought the *Aster-Bloods* were created by the Tree to keep the balance."

Elderik sighed and then looked at his mother.

"Humans fear what they don't understand." She explained, sitting back in her chair. "Back then, humans were corrupt with religious zealotry, believing that everything unnatural came from evil. They butchered anyone who contradicted those beliefs, whether they were anyone with a Heart-Mark or they were the ones who tried to protect them."

"That's why *Aster-Bloods* are so protected now, right?" I asked. "And that's why Esilas doesn't want anyone else to know that I'm an *Aster-Blood.*"

"And no one else will." Dahliah said, her soft voice hardening with determination. "I lost Luxia to that damned law, and I'll be damned to the gates of the Abyss before I break that boy's heart again."

I admired her strength of will; it was comforting in a way. She thought of Luxia and Esilas as part of the family, her own children. And that was a relieving thought; it meant that Esilas wasn't as alone as he believed himself to be.

"Mother, there's something else." Elderik said, straightening a bit. "Esilas had an attack last night... and Lux's blood quelled that hunger just after a bit of a drink of it."

Dahliah's eyes widened by a fraction.

"Now, *that* is certainly intriguing." She hummed in thought. "Eshrik would be interested in learning this."

"Could it have anything to do with her Heart-Mark?" He asked. "What it symbolizes..."

"It could very well be. Your father is more of an expert on this subject than I am, even if it's by a small margin." She tapped her chin. "But the question is... why now? Eshrik's medicine he's been producing nothing but positive results."

She then looked at me.

"The most puzzling mystery is your sudden appearance, dear. You remember nothing before you met them in the Pale Woods?"

I looked down at my teacup.

"No, ma'am." I breathed, feeling embarrassed. "All I remember before waking up in that field is my dream."

"A dream?" Elderik questioned, straightening a little in his seat. "You never mentioned this."

"I'm sorry." I apologized, looking at him. "I didn't really think it was relevant."

"What kind of dream was it?" Dahliah asked, leaning in a little. "Could you tell us what you remember?"

I looked at her, and upon recalling the dream, a soft smile grew on my lips.

"A great white tree," I said, feeling light at the memory. "A white tree with ruby red leaves that shone like gemstones. There was a single golden apple on its branch. The tree placed it in my hands, and it whispered for me to take a bite. When I did, I fell asleep under the tree and then awoke in that field." I looked down fondly, running my fingers over my lips. "The apple... it tasted sweet, like honey..."

When I looked back up at Dahliah and Elderik, they were staring at me in silence.

"W-What is it?" I asked with a stutter, growing nervous because of how quiet they had become.

"What you described is called the Gods' Tree."

I turned in my seat as a male voice spoke up behind me. Standing in the doorway to the kitchen was another man, older than Elderik, with a snow-white stubble and his hair pulled back in a ponytail at the base of his neck. He wore a pair of glasses, and through the thin glass were a pair of reddish-pink eyes.

"The Gods' Tree that was planted by the Dark Gods and gave power to the Morgenstern family and the *Aster-Bloods* to maintain the balance of nature." I blinked in confusion as the man came to the head of the table. He knelt beside me, as if to get a closer look. "So, you are the *Aster-Blood* of the Gods' Tree. Hair red like fire and eyes like ocean-colored jewels. Certainly a double-edged sword for you, child."

Elderik chuckled at my confusion, and I looked at him.

"Lux, this is my father, Dargrin Bastien Passor." He introduced. I nodded my head to the elder vampire.

"I-It's nice to meet you, sir." I said.

The man hummed with a soft smile.

"Lux, huh?" He said. "Meaning 'light.'"

"E-Esilas gave me the name." I said, blushing a little. He hummed in thought.

"It is a fitting name, but I think I have a better one for the child of the Gods' Tree."

He leaned down and then whispered a name in my ear. When I heard it, my eyes widened at the familiarity. It resonated deep within me, and I felt my heart skip a beat.

"That's it, isn't it?" He looked at me. "Your true name."

A small smile pulled at my lips, and I nodded. He chuckled as he gave me a gentle pat on the head.

"What is her true name?" Elderik asked, looking between the two of us in anticipation. Dargrin chuckled heartily at his son's eagerness, a twinkle in his eye.

"I think she should tell you when the time is right." I looked at Dargrin with a questioning look, but he simply smiled and put his finger to his lips.

"You're such a tease, dear." Dahliah smiled at him.

She then stood from her chair and looked at me.

"Well, Miss Lux, why don't we take those blood samples?" I nodded and smiled.

I stood from my chair and followed her down to the clinic so that she could take my blood.

Dahliah wore a face mask as she drew my blood for the tests Elderik wanted to run. I recalled how Elderik had told me that more recent generations born could control their hunger.

"He did a rather excellent job with such little training." Dahliah said, having eyed the makeshift bandage on my wrist. "Elderik must have been teaching him at the barracks."

"How long have you known Esilas?" I asked, looking at her.

She looked at me as she bandaged my arm where she had taken the blood. There was a sad smile that had reached her eyes.

"I knew their mother." She answered. "I helped her deliver Esilas and Luxia. I had met her and her sister back when the Passor Clinic could volunteer in the Outskirts." She was melancholic in her nostalgia. "When she died, I begged that we be able to take them in… but their father was obligated by law to present Luxia to the Courts."

"Because she was an *Aster-Blood…*" I whispered.

Dahliah nodded as carefully laying the tubes of blood in a stand and then taking off her facemask.

"Indeed… and then Esilas was taken to the barracks…" She continued. "I thanked the Tree that Elderik was there for him. Hell, he practically raised him."

I smiled softly and then looked at her.

"If Elderik is a fifth-generation, then that makes you a fourth, right?" I asked. "Elderik told me how the rank system works."

She looked at me and smiled; it was more of a smile of amusement.

"Actually," she said, taking off her apron, "I was born a seventh. Elderik's father is a fourth, and that is why he is technically considered a born fifth-generation."

She washed her hands in a basin as I stared at her.

"A seventh." I repeated. "Then that makes you an Aristocrat. How did you meet Dargrin?"

She turned to me as she dried her hands on a towel.

"His father let me apprentice here in my youth." She explained. "My family wasn't at all thrilled about my passion to learn medicine. They wanted to raise the family rank by marrying me off to a Noble in the Courts."

"That's horrible." I frowned.

"It was," Dahliah's somber smile was loving, "but I had Dargrin and his family. They accepted me as one of their own. And in the end, I gave up my status to marry Dargrin, who loved me for me and cared nothing about my status."

"Was... was it hard for you?" I asked hesitantly. "To leave your family behind, I mean."

Dahliah chuckled a little and shook her head.

"There was no love lost between my family and me." She said, "They completely disowned me, but I gained so much more from them doing so. A loving husband, and four beautiful children that I couldn't be more proud of."

I wished more and more that Esilas could have had a family like the Passors. I looked down at my bandaged wrist.

"I wish Esilas and Luxia could have both stayed here and lived happily with such a warm family," I said as my voice cracked and tears formed, "but Esilas pushes everyone away from him. He forces himself to be alone...",

I felt Dahliah's hand gently take mine, her cool skin soothing to the touch. I looked up at her, and she gently brushed my tears away with her fingers.

"Precious starlight," she soothed with a motherly tone; "Esilas is not alone, no matter how much he tries to be. He has

Elderik and our family." She gently tapped me on the nose with a smile. "And he has you."

I smiled with slightly warm cheeks at her encouragement, and I felt my heart become somewhat lighter at her words.

I gently pet Ash's fur as I stood out in the courtyard at the back of the clinic; Elderik and his family were devising a plan to help me stay masqueraded as a normal human who worked in the clinic as an aide. The cover story was more my idea, and though Dahliah insisted I didn't need to do anything, I told her I wanted to pay their family back for the kindness and generosity they had shown me in allowing me to stay with them. Even though it was my idea, I thought about Esilas and what his thoughts would be on the situation, suddenly feeling apprehensive. I worried about Esilas and how he was treated by the Watch-Keepers at the barracks. I was worried that his hunger would resurface and that he wouldn't have a way to ease that pain he would feel if he didn't feed. Ash gently leaned into my touch, purring softly; he seemed to sense how scattered my thoughts were. I smiled softly at the large, gray-white creature and scratched behind his ear.

"Ash really seems to like you." I squealed in surprise and turned on my heel to see Esilas leaning against the uncoupled supply wagon.

"Esilas?!" I whispered urgently. "But I thought you had business in the Outskirts!"

"Admittedly," Esilas sighed as he pushed himself off the wagon, "I trailed back and caught up with the wagon just before you reached the Mid-Gate."

He walked over and stood next to me, gently petting Ash on his side.

"But, what you said before–"

"I was concerned." He blurted, not letting me finish my sentence. He didn't even look at me. "The Mid-Gate soldiers are not as friendly as the ones at the City-Gate, not so easily distracted by pleasantries."

"You..." I started, questioningly, "were worried that I might have been found out?"

"... Yes." Esilas said, after a pause. "But I guess *that man* had a good enough job overlooking the fact that you can't sound like a male, let alone look like one."

My cheeks flushed red with embarrassment.

"H-Hey, I didn't expect to be put on the spot like that!" I said defensively. "Don't make fun of me when this disguise was yours and Elderik's idea!"

Esilas turned to me, a slight smirk on his lips.

"You think I'm making fun of you?" He asked.

I opened my mouth to say something, but my words were caught in my throat with hesitation; I couldn't very well tell what Esilas was thinking at that moment. Esilas chuckled at my befuddled silence.

"You really think as much as you worry." He said, his comment making me snap my mouth closed and narrow my eyes at him.

"You're sometimes impossible to read." I stated. "I feel more things from you compared to others I've met."

"And you're too open." Esilas said, his smirk fading a little but still ever present. "You worry about everyone but yourself."

"You're indifferent to whatever you suffer!" I was growing frustrated. "You take it all upon yourself without ever complaining when you have every right to! All the pain and hardships that you take on yourself! And what you fail to realize is that you have people supporting you! Elderik and his family care for you so deeply!"

I'd been about to continue when Esilas grabbed my wrist and jerked me towards him. At the sight of his red-amber eyes glowing in the fading light of the sunset, my words caught in my throat.

"Ya done analyzing me?" He said, his voice as low as a growl; his smile was long gone now, and his lips were pressed into a thin line. "Your empathy is going to get you killed. You wear your bleeding heart on your sleeve for all to see. Do you realize how often I feel as though I can't leave you alone because of how carelessly compassionate you are to others?!"

It was the first time I'd ever seen him convey such heavy emotions; his eyes were a swirl of frustration and concern, befuddlement and protectiveness. He then sighed heavily and dropped his forehead on my shoulders, shocking me further.

"E-Esilas?" I stuttered in a whisper.

"I'm protective of you, and that's what I find so frustrating about you." He muttered, his form slightly trembling. "Why do I feel this way? Because you're an *Aster-Blood* like she was? No, that's not it..."

I didn't know how to answer his questions, or even if he wanted me to answer it. I could feel every ounce of his frustration and protectiveness. He took a deep breath, a shaky exhale leaving his mouth as he lifted his head to look at me.

"Because you offered me your blood so selflessly? Why...?" He muttered. We both stared at each other in complete silence.

"Oh, for the Gods' Tree's sake, just kiss the girl already!" Esilas and I jumped apart, our heads snapping towards the door to see Elderik and his family—even a giggling Tana and Twiny—standing at the backdoor. "You two are practically dancing around each other."

Elderik continued teasingly. Esilas' eyes narrowed at his comrade as he straightened his posture.

"I'm not some lovesick puppy." He said, returning to his distanced nature.

"Oh, I beg to differ, boy." Dahliah said. "I know that look you were sporting particularly well."

Dargrin and the twins chuckled as Esilas simply looked to the side.

"So, have you two adopted her as well?" Esilas said, changing the subject.

Elderik chuckled at his younger comrade's attempt to dodge the previous topic further.

"Mother is going to talk to some friends she still has in the Aristocracy." He said. "It'll probably be best for Lux to lie low for a while."

Esilas nodded and then put his hand on my head, gently shaking it.

"You heard him, Lux." He said, nonchalantly teasing me again. "Keep out of trouble."

I pouted and swatted his hand away.

"I do *not* get into any trouble." I said. "And I already figured that I would have to lie low."

I heard Dargrin chuckle as I narrowed my eyes at Esilas.

"This will also give you more of a reason to come and visit." The elder Passor said. "Sad that it takes a girl for you to come and visit family."

"We better see you come around here more, Esilas." Dahliah added.

Esilas stared at the Passor family with wide eyes as Tana and Twiny came running to tackle his legs, and they begged him to come and visit. I couldn't help but giggle at the endearment they showed him. There was warmth there in the courtyard of the Passor Clinic as the pink moon rose over the city.

Esilas and Elderik left the clinic after a filling dinner with Dahliah and her family just before night completely fell. Dahliah led me up to what had once been Elderik's bedroom. She had even given me some spare clothes to sleep in, and after I dressed out of my disguise, I settled into bed. Sleep, however, didn't come to me easily; my thoughts were absorbed by the day's events. From meeting Esilas' father to the emotional altercation with the aforementioned dhampir, I felt slightly overwhelmed. I was more focused on Esilas' outburst that he had returned shortly after my own; his heart was so full of complex emotions, and when he looked at me, his eyes were filled with such longing. I sighed a little, ignoring the warmth in my cheeks, and gently turned onto my side towards the window. I closed my eyes once more to fall asleep, and the silence of the room was broken by the sound of singing.

"*There once was a spider*
Who fell in love with a butterfly,
Her wings as blue as starlight."

The sound was haunting, an addictive melody.

"*The spider entangled the butterfly*
In precious melody and serenade.
And the butterfly was enthralled,
Forgetting to fly."

The lyrics faded into a soft hum, and when I opened my eyes, I found myself in a dark room, a single lantern illuminating a worktable. Sitting at the table was the silhouette of a man, sharpening a knife with every line of that sick melody. I felt an uneasiness in my stomach as my heart beat so rapidly in my chest. I recognized that knife; it was the same one I had seen in my vision at the barracks.

"Yes..." the figure spoke, holding up the knife; *"an intricate web, and with the pull of a single delicate thread, everything will come crashing and tumbling down."*

He tilted the knife, and in the reflection of its blade, I saw a pair of pale, pinkish-gold eyes with pupils like slits.

"One by one, every tragedy will destroy her perfect life."

The man suddenly brought the knife down, stabbing his worktable, and as the blade penetrated the wood of the table with a hard *thud*, I opened my eyes and shot up in my bed. Sweat clung to my skin as I fought to control my breathing.

"What... was that?" I whispered to myself in the dark. "Another vision?"

I closed my eyes, remembering those pale pinkish-gold eyes with slit-like pupils. I ran a hand through my hair, taking deep breaths through my nose. I could feel the horror Luxia had felt, but Luxia hadn't been in the vision. As my mind raced with erratic thoughts of anxiety, a soft whisper echoed in the air; the voice wasn't sinister as the tone of the figure had been, but a soft and motherly tone.

'*You are not alone.*'

And at the sound of that whisper, I felt a sense of relief ease my shaking form. I laid back in bed once more than the adrenaline of the nightmarish vision waned enough to bring me to the verge of sleep.

'I'll do it.' I decided then. 'I'll find Luxia... for Esilas... for Elderik and his family...'

I felt an odd sense of safety then, a safety I remembered from my dream of the Gods' Tree; I felt as though the Tree was watching over me, shielding me with his full branches of gemstone-like ruby leaves from any further nightmares. And in that safety, I fell into a peaceful sleep.

6

The Brother, Eshrik

Two weeks had passed since my arrival at Passor Clinic, and Dahliah's friends in the Aristocracy had helped tremendously in acquiring the documents that I needed to legally stay in the Mid-City and be employed by Dargrin and Dahliah as a medical aide. I needed a proper name—a *female* name—for the documents, and so I chose one that honored Esilas' sister and Dahliah, who had welcomed me so warmly into her home: Luxahliah. During those two weeks while we waited for the documents to be officiated by a notary solicitor, Dargrin taught me about the medicinal plants they used to make medicine and what ailments they treated. It was fascinating to learn, and I picked up the material rather quickly. And by the end of my first month at the clinic, I'd garnered a reputation for my skill and compassion, according to Dahliah and Dargrin. I'd just finished with a routine check-up for a young Aristocrat boy with fair skin and rosy-white hair, named René Carkwright.

"Thank you so much for your care, miss." He smiled shyly at me as he held his mother's hand.

I returned his smile and curtsied.

“It was my pleasure.” I looked at him, gently folding my hands in front of me and bowing respectfully.

The boy’s mother smiled softly at me, showing a sense of awe.

“It’s remarkable.” Lady Carkwright admired. “René hates these routine check-ups, but after one visit, he’s absolutely come out of his shell. I dare say he’s smitten.”

The aforementioned boy blushed softly and hid his face in his mother’s skirt.

“I’m glad I could help make him comfortable.” I smiled genuinely. “I do all that I can so that the patients here are met with care.”

“I’m glad that I came here, even if it was to satisfy my curiosity.” The Lady said, which caught me off guard. She smiled softly, amused by my expression as she looked up at the clinic. “When I heard about the human physician that Dahliah had taken on as her apprentice, I admit I was skeptical, but your care and compassion eased my son during his appointment.” She then looked back at me and smiled. “I’ll definitely recommend you and the clinic to anyone I know that may have an ailment.”

I bowed my head, thanking her as she and her son boarded their carriage. As the carriage drove away, René waved from the back window with a bright, little-fanged smile. I smiled and waved back.

“Ah, so you must be Luxahliah.”

I turned my head from the road to see a young vampire male, maybe a year or two older than Elderik, wearing rather expensive scholarly robes and a pair of thin eyeglasses, his straight silvery-white hair cut to just at the top of his shoulders.

"My, Elderik forgot to mention that you were as blinding as the white sun."

I felt a slight heat rise to my cheeks at his words, but I was all the more confused. After a moment, I finally realized who he must be.

"Might you be Eshrik, Elderik's older brother?" I asked him. "The one who developed the medicine for Esilas' hunger?"

"That I am, miss," he said as he pushed up his glasses, "but I don't plan to stop there! No! I plan to eliminate even the possibility of attacks for dhampir and first-generations! No longer will they have to live in fear of the probability that they will attack their loved ones in pursuit of carnal bloodlust! I, Eshrik Evelander Passor, shall be the one to achieve this brilliant feat!"

I felt a bit startled by his rather extravagant declaration, and then I felt a hand on my shoulder.

"I see you're as flamboyant in your fervor for research as ever, Eshrik." I turned to see Dahliah as she playfully scolded her son. "And you've so extravagantly introduced yourself to my protégé."

"Indeed, Mother." Eshrik looked at me, now completely calm and composed. "She's the one whom Brother mentioned in his letter." His eyes slightly narrowed as he analyzed me. "The one with a... *special* trait... about her." His lips curled into an intrigued smile. "Yes... it would seem we have much to discuss..."

I helped Dahliah serve the tea as Eshrik spoke of the contents of the letter he had received from Elderik.

"When Brother wrote to me, telling me he, Esilas, and Ephrem had found an *Aster-Blood* in the Pale Woods," he started as he leaned against the table, "I was understandably skeptical. There hasn't been an *Aster-Blood* born since Luxia. But when he mentioned Father had called her the *Aster-Blood* of the Gods' Tree, my academic curiosity and personal interest was piqued." He looked at me as I sat down with Dahliah on the other side of the dining table. "After all, it is said that it was the fruit of the ancient Tree that gave Lucien Morgenstern the powers that his descendents have inherited today. For an *Aster-Blood* to have the Heart-Mark of that very Tree, I knew I had to meet you in person."

"What all did Elderik tell you about me?" I asked, taking a sip from my teacup.

"He mentioned it was by drinking your blood, Esilas' hunger was curbed." He answered as he took a sip of tea. "I found it rather interesting, especially given the results of your blood test."

"My test results?" I asked, looking at Dahliah.

It had been such a busy two weeks that I had completely forgotten that she had taken my blood for those tests.

“Yes.” She nodded. “While purity in *Aster-Bloods* pertains to their spiritual energy, it doesn’t even describe your blood, Lux. It has healing properties.”

Eshrik set his teacup aside and steepled his fingers in thought.

“Those properties make whoever drinks even a bit of it stronger.” He added, and at his words, my head snapped towards him.

“Wait, is Esilas–?”

“He’s fine.” Eshrik reassured me. “He’s actually more than just fine. His recent growth in speed and hunting instinct has helped him rise through the ranks of the Keepers of the Watch. Even that fool of a barracks captain is singing his praises.”

I felt a sudden heaviness on my shoulders and it wasn’t out of dread; it was a heaviness I associated with responsibility. I knew the impotence of the Gods’ Tree, the balance that the *Aster-Bloods* maintained. I felt that weight on my shoulders, and it was a responsibility that I didn’t feel that I was ready for. I looked at Eshrik.

“What should I do?” I asked. “What do you need from me to help make a more efficient medicine that will help other dhampir and first-generations with their hunger?”

Eshrik looked at me and then reached for his teacup to take one last sip.

"All I need from you are a few tubes of your blood." He answered simply. "I can synthesize a better version of the medicine at my research lab."

His pale-rose eyes shone with an unmistakable determination, and in the end, I agreed.

Eshrik had taken six tubes of my blood with him when he left the clinic, and Dahliah gave me the rest of the day and all of the next to recuperate. I laid in my room, playing over the conversation with Eshrik and Dahliah, and for some reason, I felt very uneasy, and it had nothing to do with the responsibility on my shoulders; while it was near miraculous that the medicine to help with blood hunger had had a breakthrough in its development, there was something that was disrupting my peace of mind.

'Why hasn't there been more of an effort for aid for the dhampir and the first-generations before now? It's almost as if they're *experiments*... as if someone doesn't want there to be any hope for them... someone higher in the system, maybe?'

I recalled my nightmare of the silhouette at his worktable; he'd said that one by one, *her* perfect life would be destroyed by tragedy. I sighed and laid my forearm over my closed eyes.

'But what does Luxia have to do with the medicine for those having to deal with their hunger? And what did that silhouette mean by *death to the High-Bloods*?'

Even recalling the phrase from my first vision sent a chill down my spine, my skin prickling with nausea at the sinister tone. A realization hit me and I opened my eyes. I sat up in my bed.

"The voices from either vision..." I muttered. "They were different..."

The first had sounded monotone underneath that dark cadence, but the second voice was much more sinister, almost as if he was enjoying the melancholic tragedy he had created.

"Two different people, maybe? Or is one of them the true mastermind?"

I put my hand to my head, my vision spinning slightly. I laid back down and my lightheadedness caused me to fall into a deep sleep.

I hadn't been asleep long when the sound of rustling leaves woke me, and when I opened my eyes, I was met with white sunbeams shining through clusters of purple-black leaves. I sat up to find myself in a pristine white courtyard, and at its center was a large water fountain with a statue depicting a man holding a sword up in victory, large feathered wings on his back, and a crown that resembled horns.

'Where is this? I've never seen this place before... and yet–'

My thoughts were interrupted by the sound of giggling, and I turned back to the tree to see a couple sitting not a few feet away from where I'd woken up. One of the two was a familiar face, Luxia, dressed in a beautiful gown that kept her modest while proudly displaying her Heart-Mark. The man beside her had shoulder-length feathery black hair, pale skin, and golden eyes like the color of honey. He wore a white frock with lace cuffs on his long sleeves, tight black trousers and black boots with gold trim. He was tenderly holding Luxia's hand as she read to him from a book of poetry.

"I can listen to your voice all day." He smiled as he gently lifted her hand to his lips and kissed her palm. Luxia giggled softly and returned his smile. The two then touched their foreheads in a tender gesture of affection. *"You're rather flattering in your words today, my prince."*

My eyes widened at her words, and I looked at the man that she was with.

'This... is the prince of the Morgenstern Family?!'

"Can I not be flattering or affectionate toward my darling starlight bride?" The man chuckled with a love-struck smile, running his thumb over her knuckles. *"The future queen of Obsiditourma?"*

"My love, we're not yet married." Luxia smiled, though it seemed oddly somber. *"I want to bring Esilas into the Estate. I want him to share in this life that I've been given here, whether or not he is an Aster-Blood."*

I felt some relief then; Luxia loved her brother and wanted to give him a better life than the one they'd had before they were separated.

"He's not returned any of your letters, Luxia." He said sadly. *"I've had my men search the Outskirts, but there's been no sign of him."*

He gently stroked her cheek. *"But, we will find him, my starlight. I promise."*

'That doesn't sound like Esilas at all.' I thought to myself. 'Esilas has been wanting to find her for years, and he's made it seem like she had fallen off the face of the world..'

"I want him to be here." Luxia said softly as she leaned into the prince's hand. *"I want him to be here for the wedding.. And for the birth of his niece or nephew..."*

Her words sent a cool wave throughout my body, and the shock was enough to send me awake, shooting up from my bed. My hands trembled at what I'd just witnessed.

'Luxia... was she really pregnant?'

I covered my mouth.

'Was that why she was killed? Because of her baby?'

I buried my head in my hands.

'What the hell is going on?'

I looked at the window as the black sky was graying out, signifying the start of a new day.

'What should I do? I can't tell Esilas any of this. It would break his heart.'

I clenched my fists as I laid them in my lap, and I shook my head.

'No, I need to further investigate this... somehow...'

I slowly touched my feet to the cold wood floors and stood up, wanting to wash my face to calm myself. I was still feeling faint, so my pace would be slow. I glimpsed myself in the mirror, where I noticed the leaf buds on the branches of my Heart-Mark had grown into full leaves. I stopped and stared at my reflection with wide eyes. I shakily traced the branches and leaves with my fingertip. I wasn't sure how, or even why, but the Gods' Tree had grown.

7

Mariam, the Mother of Esilas and Luxia

THE DAY AFTER MY recuperation was a slow day for the clinic; there were a few check-ups here and there, but there wasn't anything too severe. I was left to do most of the check-up appointments, Dahliah having taken Tana and Twiny out to get some fresh ingredients for dinner. It had been a full month since I had come to the clinic, and that meant that Elderik was coming to visit, possibly with Esilas in tow. I was waiting in the small office near the lobby for the next patient to come in, and during that spare time, I went and talk to Dargrin. I had spent the previous day in bed, deep in thought about who I could confide in about my visions and the questions I had, and the most logical choice was Dargrin Passor; after all, he knew the most about the Gods' Tree and the powers of the *Aster-Bloods*. So, while the clinic was in a state of malaise, I wandered out back to the greenhouse, where Dargrin grew the medicinal plants and crafted the medicines we used. I took a deep breath as I stood in front of the greenhouse door, and then I knocked.

"Dargrin?" I called softly, putting my hand on the doorknob. "Could I talk to you about something?"

It was silent behind the door, and I curiously cracked the door open to look. I found the greenhouse was void of who I was looking for.

'That's odd. Dargrin usually spends his time here during the workday.'

I strolled into the greenhouse, looking at all the different plants he had growing in the recycled flower boxes. His work table was cluttered with parchment filled with notes and medicinal formulas, and under some stray sheets, I noticed a picture frame. I eased the papers aside and leaned down to inspect the photo. It was a family photograph taken when Elderik and Eshrik were still young children. It looked like a happy photograph, but I noticed something odd about Eshrik; the look in his eyes made it seem like he was an outsider looking in. Dargrin was trying to pull him in closer to the family, but he looked like he was dreading it. It was definitely odd to see Eshrik as an introverted child when he seemed so boisterous when I had first met him. That change in demeanor made me hopeful for Esilas; I hoped that one day, he could smile freely.

However, those dreams aside, Dargrin was not in his greenhouse. I sighed in defeat. I left the greenhouse and closed the door behind me. I hummed in thought and crossed my arms.

'Where could Dargrin be? Did he leave to go shopping with Dahliah and the twins?'

I was brought out of my thoughts by the front bell ringing, signaling that someone had come into the clinic lobby. I composed myself and straightened my apron before heading back to the lobby. However, once I reached the doorway, I froze; standing in the lobby was the familiar figure of a man clad in black armor, his dark red eyes catching me.

The captain from the Mid-Gate.

Esilas' father.

"H-Hello, sir." I welcomed him, trying to smile confidently. "What brings you to the Passor Clinic?"

The man looked me over, his lack of response rather unnerving. He then let out a throaty hum.

"So, you're a woman." He said, his voice giving off an air of confirmation. "You look better in those clothes rather than those black rags you were dressed in when we first met. Dahliah certainly has her way with clothes, as always."

I was confused by this interaction, and my composure completely shattered.

"W-Wait, you knew I was really a girl when we came to the gate that day?!" I asked, panicking as I rambled. "W-What else do you know? Please, don't punish Elderik for the disguise! Does anyone else know about—?"

"Calm down." He gently put his hand on my shoulder. "If I had told anyone what I knew, then my sister and her family would have been in danger the moment I breathed a word."

“Y-Your sister...” I muttered, calming down a little. My eyes then widened when I realized what he was saying. “That means—”

“Dahliah and I are siblings,” he confirmed with a nod. “And that means that Esilas has the blood of an eighth-generation vampire, whether or not classified as a dhampir. I assume Elderik told you who I was, yes?”

“He just confirmed it.” I nodded. “I recognized your eyes.”

The captain simply nodded.

“Dargrin was right.” He chuckled. “You certainly are astute in your observations.”

I was surprised by his words; Dargrin had told him about me, and I wondered why he had told the captain the truth.

‘Just how much does he know...? And how close are he and Dargrin that they spoke about me?’

He took his hand off my shoulder.

“Perhaps we could talk in private? There are some things that I would like to discuss.”

I took the captain upstairs to the dining room and made some tea as he sat down at the table for our conversation.

“Allow me to introduce myself.” He started. “My name is Ailgraym Solani, the firstborn of the Solani family and the captain of the Ebony Guard.”

I passed him his teacup and sat across from him.

“It’s nice to meet you.” I nodded. “I go by Luxahliah now, but everyone still calls me Lux.”

"It's my understanding that Esilas gave you that name." He spoke. "And Dargrin has been very cheeky whenever he spoke about what your true name is. The man refused to tell me anything aside from the minute details." He sighed in frustration, and it reminded me of Dahliah's reaction when Dargrin had teased my name the month before.

"You and Dargrin seem to talk about a lot." I commented.

"Aye." He nodded. "Despite my rather strained relationship with Dahliah, Dargrin and I actually converse quite a bit. We bonded over a singular commonality."

He took a locket from under his breastplate and held it out to me. I gently took it in my fingers and opened it to reveal the faded photograph of a young woman with long black hair, wearing a dark gray and white dress.

"She's beautiful." I commented and looked at him, and from the look of somber reminiscence on his face, I knew that this wasn't an ordinary woman. "Is... she Esilas' and Luxia's mother?"

"Yes... she was..." He said as I handed the locket back to him. He stared fondly at the woman's picture. "Her name was Mariam... and she was the love of my life... my strong-willed hellfire." He smiled sadly. "I had met her not a year after Dahliah had left the family to marry Dargrin... I hadn't been able to understand her choice to do so until I met *her*..." I warmed my hands around my teacup as I invited him to tell the story of himself and Mariam.

"Mariam was a rather spitfire barmaid." Dargrin began. "She was the daughter of a tavern owner in the Outskirts. I was still a patrolman at the Front-Gate, and after every shift, I would go out drinking with my men. I... must admit that I was like the rest of my men; I demanded blood from the barmaids... a-among other things... and treated them worse than one would treat livestock."

He shook his head a little and continued on with his story.

"One particular night, the barmaid my men had chosen to be their next victim proved to be quite stubborn, and after many unwanted gestures, she promptly kicked us out. She lectured us that we soldiers on the outer wall were treated just as anybody was treated in the Outskirts. With no respect and having to work our way up the ladder. She told us all to piss off and slammed the door behind us. The other comrades on my patrol were too drunk to really act on any retaliation; they went to the next tavern. But... I found myself oddly captivated by this strong-willed human woman with hair as black as midnight. It had taken an apology to her and her father and two months' worth of my wages. I thought it was worth it to get to know this woman with a heart like hellfire. For several months, that tavern was my destination after my shift. The relationship had started off rather... strained, because of the horrible first impression my men and I had made... but after half a year, Mariam and I had grown so close. I loved her so much that I wanted to marry her, but I knew my father would never agree to it, so I suggested we elope and we live in the farm villages outside the wall. But... unfortunately, our happiness was not meant to last.

"My father had caught wind of the rumors of me and my affair with Mariam, and just as I had suspected, he refused to let me give up my status as my sister had to marry someone below my station, least of all a human. So... he gave me an ultimatum..."

Captain Ailgraym took a shaky breath.

"I could either break things off with Mariam, or my father would use the family's influence to have her falsely accused of some ridiculous crime and have her be executed. So... in order to protect her, I broke her heart... as cruelly as possible. And I took every curse and every scream that she spat at me. I made her hate me."

I saw how his hands trembled, and with a deep inhale, he continued.

"After that... I lived in utter despair. My father used his influence to promote me to captain in the Ebony Guard at the Mid-Gate—probably to deter me from going to see Mariam again—and I was married to another Aristocrat, all for the sake of maintaining the family name and honor. I was a shell of my former self, and I felt nothing, even for that crass woman that I am forced to call my wife. But five years later, my heart would break even further.

"I received a letter from her, and in horror, I rode my hellsteed towards the tavern-house. I found her there... in her bed, so gaunt and pale... her *deathbed,* and beside her, a pair of dhampir twins... Esilas and Luxia..."

He muttered.

"She had been pregnant when I had broken things off so cruelly with her... and she had carried them to term and gave birth on her own, my sister as her midwife. I crumbled then. I fell to her knees at her bedside and apologized. I never stopped loving her, but I would rather she hate me than be killed for some ridiculous crime that she couldn't have committed... all because I loved her. To my short-lived relief, she told me she had long since forgiven me... but she wanted me to take Esilas and Luxia through the Mid-Gate to Dahliah's clinic. She wanted a better life for them than the one she offered. I told her I would do all that I could for her... no, *our* children... and as I held her in my arms, she died..."

Ailgraym's voice was near its breaking point. But he continued.

"There... was a flower that I wanted to give her, a flower from the gardens in the Mid-City... and when she died, I spread her ashes under those flower bushes. I smuggled Esilas and Luxia to Dahliah... and after she gave me a hefty lecture about my cowardice towards our father and my own feelings, she welcomed me back. But just like with Mariam, that warmth didn't last; Luxia was discovered with a Heart-Mark. I was obligated by law to present her to the Courts... and if I refused, she would have been taken by force, and I, along with Dahliah and her entire family, would have been killed. I then made the same difficult choice that I had been given those five years before: I separated Luxia and Esilas, despite her begging and pleading to stay with her brother and incurring the hatred of my sister and my son, and I presented her to the Courts. However, instead of returning Esilas to the Outskirts to live penniless and hungry on the streets, I brought him to the barracks of the Keepers of the Watch, entrusting him to Elderik."

Ailgraym lowered his head and covered his eyes with his hand.

"I have done all that I can to keep them safe... all of them... and it makes me wonder if I shouldn't have just taken Mariam away from this place, where we could leave peacefully, without this damned rank system."

It was odd to see such a firm presence devolve into a broken man, but I couldn't help that my heart broke for the captain as his heart was laid bare; his tale was filled with tragic forbidden love and the pain that came with having to choose between family and love. I placed my empty teacup to the side, and I reached out to touch his hand. He flinched a little and looked up at me, tears still in his eyes.

"Mr. Ailgraym... you shouldn't blame yourself any longer for what happened to Mariam. I don't think she would have wanted that. You did all that you can for Esilas and Luxia, and your choices have protected them, especially Esilas." I offered my handkerchief with a soft smile. "You've had to bear all this guilt alone, but it takes a substantial amount of courage to relive such harrowing memories."

The captain stared at me with wide eyes, and with a nostalgic smile, he dried his eyes with the handkerchief. Once he'd composed himself, he stood from his seat at the table.

"You truly are pure." He whispered, his voice still raw with emotion. "And if I trust anyone with Esilas' care more than Dahliah or Elderik, it's you. And don't worry; your secret's safe with me... *Aster-Blood* of the Gods' Tree."

I was surprised at his trust in me, and I smiled softly at him.

"Thank you, Captain Ailgraym." I said as I walked him out of the clinic to his hellsteed.

I stood at the bottom of the steps as the captain saddled his mount. He'd been about to ride back to the Mid-Gate when a query came to mind.

"W-Wait, Captain Ailgraym!" I said as I jogged towards him. "I wanted to ask... when was the last time you heard anything about Luxia?"

He looked at me with wide eyes.

"About Luxia?" He echoed. "But why do you ask?"

"I... was just wondering..." I said, hesitant to tell him about my mysterious, and often disturbing, visions of his daughter.

The captain hummed in thought before answering me.

"The last time I had heard anything from her must have been around three years ago," he said. "It was around the time she was looking for Esilas. One of the Royal Estate Guard she had sent was searching the Outskirts, but I told him that Esilas was at the barracks outside the city."

I flinched a little at his answer, but I nodded, patting his hellsteed's side with a smile.

"You should probably get back to the Mid-Gate. Your men could scare children." I joked.

The captain chuckled and nodded to me before he rode off. As I watched him ride back to the gate, my smile faded.

'Three years ago...' a chill running down my spine. 'The last time Esilas had an attack was around the same time before Eshrik had given him medicine.'

I looked down at the street, deep in thought.

'And Ailgraym knew Luxia was looking for him... but then, why couldn't she and the prince find him?'

"Lux!"

My eyes widened at the familiar voice and I turned to see a rather familiar supply wagon being drawn by two Infercani hellmounts. Of the three young men clad in black that were riding in the wagon, the youngest of which practically jumped out, much to the displeasure of the second eldest, and ran to hug my waist.

"Ephrem?" I asked as the young Watch-Keeper looked at me with a bright smile. "You came with Esilas and Elderik this time?"

"He wouldn't stop pestering us until we agreed." I looked up at Esilas as Elderik stopped the wagon just outside the clinic.

"He's been like a puppy waiting for his owner to come back this past month."

Elderik bit back a snicker as he covered his mouth.

"You shouldn't complain after how *you've* been acting for the past month, Esilas."

"Shut up, Elderik." Esilas sighed, trying to hide how flustered he was as he jumped down from the driver's seat.

He'd been about to grab Ephrem by the collar when the young first-generation pulled away and hid behind me. I chuckled softly, welcoming the familiarity of their banter and mannerisms.

"Well, Dahliah and the twins are still out—"

"Looks like we came back just in time." I turned to see Dahliah, the twins, and Dargrin walking towards the clinic.

"We just got ingredients for a welcome home dinner for the three of you, as well as celebrating Lux's first successful month of employment at the clinic." Dahliah smiled brightly at me.

"Wait, this is for me too?" I asked, my cheeks flushing with heat.

"Of course." Dargrin said. "You've been such a help to the patients at the clinic. You deserve to be celebrated."

"Just accept it." Esilas said, putting his hand on my head. "They won't let you refuse their praise."

Elderik chuckled softly and then picked up Tana and Twiny.

"Why don't we all head inside?" He suggested.

"Could you make tea for everyone while we cook dinner, Lux?" Dahliah asked. "And you three can tell us all about what's happened this past month."

I nodded and walked with everyone up to the apartment to prepare for dinner. I'd been worried that any of the family or Esilas would mention Ailgraym's scent being present at the dining table, but to my astonishment, no one said anything.

It was after dinner, however, that someone had finally said something to me about it, and the one who had done so was Dargrin. He asked to speak with me in the greenhouse just as everyone was retiring for the night in order to discuss the matter.

"Captain Ailgraym came to speak with you." He spoke as he sat down at his worktable. "He didn't scare you, did he?"

I shook my head as I stood with my hands clasped in front of me.

"No, sir," I answered, shaking my head. "Honestly, we just talked… and he told me about the story of Esilas' and Luxia's mother."

Dargrin smiled sadly and then took his glasses off to sit on the table.

"Mariam…" He said softly, "I remember her very well. She and Dahliah were close, especially after Esilas and Luxia were born."

I was hesitant to say anything, but I knew that if I didn't tell him what I had wanted to tell him before, then I wouldn't get another chance to do so.

"I... asked Captain Ailgraym about Luxia." I spoke. "He said the last he had heard anything of her was three years ago, that she was looking for Esilas in the Outskirts, by a proxy. But no one ever told her he was taken to the barracks after they had been separated, even though the captain had told the proxy where Luxia could find her brother."

Dargrin looked at me with wide eyes.

"How do you know any of this?" He asked.

I clenched my hands a bit and took a deep breath.

"I've... *seen* it.." I said. "I've been having visions of Luxia... and I-I know that something horrific has happened to her..."

Dargrin put on his glasses and stood from his stool.

"Sit down," he said as he gently gestured me to the stool before sitting himself in another, "and tell me everything that you've seen."

I nodded and told Dargrin everything about my visions of Luxia up to that point, everything from the first passing glimpse in the mirror at the barracks to the dream about Luxia and the Morgenstern prince. Dargrin hummed in thought at the information, holding his chin as he let himself think deeply. To my interest, he was not focused on the visions themselves, but on the melody.

"An old nursery rhyme from the Outskirts... within these visions of Luxia..." He muttered. "How peculiar..."

"Wait, that song is a nursery rhyme?" I asked, an involuntary shudder prickling up my back. "But... it's so... *creepy*..."

Dargrin looked up at me from his postulating state.

"Oddly enough, it's based on a tragic event that happened in the Outskirts nearly a century ago." He explained. "Five young women were murdered in the Outskirts, a rather gruesome occurrence to speak of. When they found the murderer, he was publicly executed by the Ebony Guard. At least that's what we all had been told. There were a lot of rumors around the incident." He spoke and shook his head as he crossed his arms. "But as far as your visions of Luxia are concerned, it should go without saying that you shouldn't tell anyone about them, least of all Esilas. And don't mention it to Elderik."

His voice was so serious that all I could do was nod, but there was a singular question that conquered my thoughts as he let me go back to my room: what was Dargrin not telling me? As I walked back to my room, I found Esilas leaning against the windowsill, looking out as the courtyard illuminated with soft rosy light. He seemed to be in a state of contemplation that puzzled me, and with hesitation, I approached him.

"Esilas?" I asked. "Are you alright?"

The dhampir looked at me before looking back out the window.

"Yeah..." he said. "Just thinking..."

“What about?” I asked, tilting my head a little. “If you don’t mind me asking—”

“A lot of things are on my mind.” He said, standing from where was leaning and then turning to me, the moonlight causing his face to be covered in shadow with only his red-amber eyes glinting softly. “I’ve been thinking about my sister... about you... and most recently about why I could smell that *he* had been here in this apartment.”

His eyes were so piercing that I felt frozen in place, as if he were a hunter stalking his prey.

“What was *that man* doing here, Lux?”

I bit the inside of my cheek as I held my trembling hands behind my back.

“He... wanted to speak with Dargrin.” I lied. “But he wasn’t here, so I offered him some tea while he waited. After a while, he said he’d come back to speak to him another time.”

I didn’t enjoy lying to Esilas, but at the same time, I didn’t have the right to tell Esilas what Ailgraym had told me about his mother; it needed to be something that the two of them talked about themselves.

“Did he tell you what he wanted to talk with Dargrin about?” He asked, his eyes still watching me.

“No.” I shook my head. “He didn’t tell me anything.”

Esilas approached me, and I stood incredibly still. I flinched a little as he put his hand on my head. He leaned his head close to my ear.

"Don't trust that man." He whispered, his voice dampened by a mix of hatred and despair. "I won't let him take you to the Courts."

Before I could say anything, Esilas gently pat me on the head and then left to go to the guest room that he, Elderik and Ephrem were using. He held so much resentment towards his father, but telling him his father's reasons for what he had done wouldn't absolve him in Esilas' eyes. I exhaled softly through my nose and pinched the bridge of my nose.

'Surely... there has to be something I could do...' I continued to my room; 'but the two of them are too alike... it would be difficult for them to even discuss anything.'

I sat on my bed and looked at the mirror. Recalling my first vision, I whispered a question that I knew would never be answered

"What would you do if you were in my place... *Luxia*?"

8

Visions of Blood, Sorrow, and Trickery

As it turned out, there was more to the monthly visit to the Mid-City of Obsiditourma; this month marked the peak of summer, and Elderik had obligations to attend an annual social gathering because of his family's status: the Summer Soiree. Esilas had also been invited to the gathering, and I suspected that Captain Ailgraym was the one to send the "anonymous" invitation. Because the two of them were given an extended stay in the Mid-City for the event, Ephrem was sent back to the barracks with the supplies, much to his disappointment.

"So, why am I getting my measurements taken if this party is meant more for Low-Bloods and Aristocrats?" I asked as Dahliah measured around my waist.

"This year's hosts for the Summer Soiree are the Carkwrights." She explained. "And it would seem that René wants you to be there."

There was amusement in her tone, a near playfulness. I felt a bit embarrassed; Lady Carkwright *had* said that her son was smitten. A part of me believed it was because of my nature as an *Aster-Blood*, the ability we have to attract things toward us. Thankfully, this was the more positive outcome of that ability.

"It's also an opportunity for apprentices and businesses to be recognized for their work." Elderik said as he finished with Tana's measurements. "Eshrik was able to become the research assistant to a prominent scholar in the Archives."

"Exactly." Dahliah smiled and looked at me, finishing my measurements. "Businesses all over the Mid-City are invited. Make a good impression and you'll receive favor and requests for patronage. It's why events such as these are important."

"And Watch-Keepers can be recruited into the Ebony Guard or the security detail for Nobles," Elderik added, "which is why Esilas was invited because of his rise through the ranks at the barracks."

Esilas wasn't with us in the room; Dargrin had wanted to talk with him, probably to see how he'd been faring in the month since his last attack. I must have had a gloomy expression on my face, because Dahliah tapped my nose in her motherly way.

"Don't worry about Esilas, dear." She smiled caringly. "He'll be fine as long as you're with him."

I blinked at her, confused.

"With me?"

"He's going to be your escort for the Soiree." She elaborated. "Elderik insisted on it."

My cheeks warm with embarrassment as I snapped my head to look at Elderik, who was hiding his smile behind his hand.

From the look in his eye, I could tell that he was scheming something mischievous.

With the Summer Soiree fast approaching, the clinic didn't receive many patients. In fact, many businesses were slow because of the preparations, according to Dahliah. This down time was filled with lessons on etiquette, which she and Elderik readily provided for Esilas and me, everything from posture and stride to dance lessons. It was the dance lessons that were awkward for Esilas. Elderik was teaching me to dance while Dahliah was teaching Esilas in the cleared dining room.

"Esilas, you're too tense." Dahliah stopped their waltz for the fourth time with a sigh. "Dancing is meant to be fluid and delicate."

"Who am I even going to be dancing with at this posh party?" Esilas said, frustration lacing his tone. "I'm not even supposed to be—"

Dahliah immediately stopped him with a *thwack* to his forehead.

"*You* were invited to the Soiree, boy." She lectured. "That invitation was sent to you, which means you have the right to be there."

Dahliah was using her stern, motherly tone, which meant that you weren't supposed to argue with her. When Esilas wouldn't let up on his own degradation, Dahliah let out a sigh as she pinched the bridge of her nose.

"Let's take a break." She said, and at this suggestion, Esilas fled the dining room. Dahliah put her hands on her hips and shook her head at his attitude. "I swear, that boy is so stubborn."

"He's been even more stubborn since our visit last month." Elderik said as he stopped our waltz for the break. "He's not comfortable with how far up the ranks he's risen. He's still getting used to the concept that he has value."

I looked at him, and then down slightly; Esilas had gone through such a change... all because I gave him my blood so that his hunger could be sated.

'Does... Does Esilas hate me for giving him my blood?'

"Am... Am I to blame for him being frustrated?" I asked hesitantly.

"Not at all." Elderik said as he looked at me, gently putting his hand on my head. "I think he's more hesitant because this gives him a chance to find his sister... and he's afraid."

"But of what?" I hid my fear from my voice.

"He... has it in his head that Luxia forgot about him." Elderik said after a long pause. "And that thought has been eating at him."

Despite the comfort of Elderik's hand, I felt guilt eat at my stomach; only Dargrin and I knew the truth about Luxia, and keeping that truth from him was cruel. I took a deep breath and then looked up at them.

"I'm going to talk to him." I said, leaving the dining room.

Dahliah had been about to say something, but Elderik stopped her.

"I'll leave him to you, Lux." I heard him as I left the dining room.

I found Esilas in the back courtyard, sitting beside Ash and picking at small clumps of grass and weeds that had popped up between the mud-caked cobblestones. He didn't even look at me as I approached him.

"Did Dahliah tell you to bring me back?" He asked. "Or did Elderik say something to you? Probably the latter, if I had to take a guess."

Esilas' tone was harsh and cold.

"Well, he said something..." I said as I sat next to him, gently petting Ash's side. "But I want to hear what you have to say. I... want you to know that you can talk to me about what's on your mind."

Esilas paused from his onslaught on the sprouted greens and closed his eyes, exhaling through his nose.

"Fine." He said simply, finally looking at me. "What if I find out that my sister has lived this fulfilling life, and that she forgot about me completely?" He then looked down at his hands, before running them through his hair and grabbing at the roots. "It's killing me... to think that my twin sister, my own flesh and blood, wouldn't even want to see me... even after all this time apart..."

His body trembled and his voice shook; he was trying not to break down into tears. I put my hand on his, gently prying it from his head.

"Esilas…" I whispered.

He looked at me as tears threatened to spill from his eyes. It broke me, and I gently pulled him towards me. I couldn't say anything to comfort him; if I opened my mouth, then I would end up letting slip everything I knew. I didn't want to tell him like this, his mind nearly driven mad with each likely scenario getting worse and worse.

'I need to distract him, including myself.'

I took a deep breath and then looked at him, gently taking his hands in mine.

"Dance with me." I said, the only thing really coming to mind.

He looked at me with his eyebrows arched upwards in shock.

"Wait, what?" He asked. "Y-You're not serious…"

I smiled and stood up, gently tugging on his hands to get him to stand with me.

"Come on." I said, my cheeks slightly warm in the light of dusk. "Let's dance."

Esilas just stared at me, but nevertheless stood up.

"Geez, what has gotten into you?" He looked at me. "What's the point of dancing out here?"

"You're my escort, remember?" I reminded him, keeping a smile on my face to keep my secret. "Besides, I'm also trying to distract you from your thoughts."

Esilas stared at me, and then after a moment, he stood with me.

"Alright, fine." He looked at me. "But as you already know, I'm not really much of a dancer."

I chuckled.

"I'm not either." I said honestly, as I put my hand on his arm, gently guiding his hand to my waist.

He tensed immediately from the touch to my waist, and I looked at him.

"Esilas, relax. It's just me."

"It's because it's you that I'm nervous." He muttered.

He still seemed hesitant, but he took my other hand in his anyway and led a bit of a clumsy waltz. The air was silent as we focused on each other, and as we danced, it became smoother and smoother. Esilas had finally relaxed, much to my relief. But he stopped then suddenly, looking at me with his piercing red-amber eyes that had now become a soft scarlet-honey hue.

"Esilas?" I looked at him. "Why'd you stop?"

The dhampir didn't answer me; he just stared with those soft eyes. Heat gathered in my cheeks, and I opened my mouth to speak when there was a soft brush against my forehead. My heart skipped a beat when I realized he was kissing the space just below my hairline. He gently pulled me closer to him, resting his chin atop my head and softly weaving his fingers through the wavy tresses of my hair.

"I'm sorry." He said, his voice a simple whisper. "I'm... not used to anyone caring so deeply the way you do... especially about someone like me..."

I gently wrapped my arms around him, placing my hands on his back as he whispered in insecurities. As I listened, his fingers curled slightly in my hair. He was silent afterwards as he slowly pulled away.

"You dance very well." He mumbled, just above his whispering before.

All I could do then was softly smile, hoping that my tears wouldn't fall from the emotions I felt from him.

"You dance very well, too, Esilas."

With the whole of the Mid-City preparing for the Soiree, no one was roaming the streets, and I could convince Dahliah to let me walk around outside, given that I was mostly confined to the clinic and the apartment to keep my secret safe. She agreed to let me explore, her only condition being that either Esilas or Elderik accompany me on the walk. With Daliah still giving etiquette lessons to Esilas, it was Elderik who walked with me. As we walked along the streets, I admired the architecture of the shops and businesses. Elderik asked me a startling question.

"Lux," He addressed me; "I've noticed that you've been in your head a lot as of late. Is everything alright?"

His query froze me in my steps; I honestly didn't know how to answer him without telling him the truth. Elderik stopped and turned to me, waiting for my answer. Dargrin had told me not to tell anyone else about my visions, but I needed someone to confide in, someone who knew Esilas better than anyone else. I clenched my hands into fists at my sides, gathering my courage in the street's silence.

"Have..." I started, swallowing a lump in my dry throat; "have you ever heard of anyone like me... having visions of another?" I asked, looking at him. "Like... seeing a past that doesn't belong to them, but to the person they're seeing?"

Elderik was silent, my query seeming to have equally startled him.

"Lux..." He said, his hand trembling at his side. "What exactly do you mean?"

I bit my lip, considering what I was about to say and how I should phrase it; when I found those words, finally, I spoke in a voice that only he could hear.

"I... I saw her, Elderik..." I whispered, watching as Elderik's red eyes grew wider; "I saw Luxia..."

Not a moment after those words had left my mouth, Elderik took my hand and dragged me behind him as he walked hastily through a series of alleyways. We reached a small courtyard, a hidden little space amidst the two and three-story buildings of the Mid-City. It was here that Elderik turned to me and put his hands on my shoulders, his eyes filled with desperation.

"Tell me everything." He said, urgently. "Right. Now."

I'd never heard him speak so anxiously, and it was because of his tone that I told him everything. At the end of it all, he stumbled back and leaned against a wall. His prolonged silence unnerved me.

"E-Elderik...?"

"And Esilas knows nothing about this?" He asked, suddenly. "Nothing about your visions or the fact that Luxia is–"

He couldn't bear to finish the question, and he rubbed his forehead. I swallowed in my dry throat once more and shook my head, gathering the will to speak.

"No..." I breathed. "He doesn't..."

"Good." Elderik said, taking deep breaths as if to stop himself from panicking. "He doesn't need to know any of this. You can't breathe a word."

He was adamant about it, but considering the state Esilas was in, I wasn't so sure.

"But... Esilas will suffer if he doesn't know the truth–"

"And he'll suffer more if he does." Elderik's head snapped up to me.

I wouldn't deny that he was right, but I still felt that it was wrong to keep such information from Esilas. Elderik straightened and then stood in front of me.

"Lux, you have to realize how perilous this newfound ability of yours is."

"Wait... perilous how?" I asked, my nerves prickling like pins and needles in my skin.

"You're the *Aster-Blood* of the Gods' Tree, remember?" He reminded me, his voice lowering to an urgent whisper. "You told us that the Tree gave you an apple, giving you your abilities to empathize, your compassion, and care for others. These are typical powers for *Aster-Bloods* because they are pure of spirit." He put his hands on my shoulders, his red eyes staring into mine. "But things are different now. You can see the past life of Luxia, the only *Aster-Blood* before your spontaneous appearance in the Pale Woods... and I don't think it's a coincidence that your Heart-Mark is the Gods' Tree."

"Elderik... what are you suggesting...?" I breathed the words, my heart hammering against my ribs.

"If Luxia was murdered, along with her child, then *that* was the imbalance that was created." He said. "I think... you were created by the Gods' Tree to correct it..."

At his words, my head began to spin, and a strange pulse pounded against my skull. I grabbed at my head in pain and lurched over.

"Lux!" Elderik put his hand on my back. "Lux, what's wrong?!"

"M-My head..." My voice cracked under the pressure. "I-It feels like it's splitting...!"

My vision phased rapidly from the courtyard to a tall hallway of white and dark blue and then back again. "A-A hallway..."

"What?"

"It's a tall hallway! A white and blue hallway!" I shouted as my sight blurred and the pain in my head ebbed at my strength to stand. I lost my footing and Elderik kept me from falling further. His voice sounded far away, as if it were an echo. My sight spotted black as I was pulled into another vision.

It felt as if I were floating in a pool of still water, but as I lifted my eyelids open to find that I was, in fact, laying in a rather plush bed. I sat up, my sight coming into focus on tones of gray-white and blue. What I had thought to be a hallway was actually a large bedchamber. I stood up from the bed, but before I had the chance to really take in my surroundings, I heard weeping behind me.

"*Luxia...*" I turned around to find the Morgenstern prince holding a pale hand, stained with blood, to his forehead. "*Why, my starlight...?*"

I followed the hand up its pale arm and to its body, and at the sight, I covered my mouth for fear of my stomach emptying itself. Lying in the large, luxurious bed was the body of a familiar woman, her abdomen sliced open. Her eyes were glazed silver and her light tan skin was a sickening white. I turned back and squeezed my eyes shut.

"*Why?!*" The prince screamed in mournful agony. "*How much must be taken from me?!*"

I hurried from the room into the hallway and leaned against the wall, trying to breathe deep to calm the horrific anxiety in my stomach.

"*The prince has lost his* animae nexum *and his unborn child.*" There was a woman's voice at the end of the hall. "*He'll mourn himself to death at her deathbed.*"

I snuck towards the corner as the woman continued commanding another.

"*Get rid of her existence from the Estate. No trace of her must be found. Understood?*"

My heart rate became erratic, but it wasn't out of fear. It was a different emotion altogether.

"*I'll erase her from the memories of the young prince and of everyone she interacted with.*"

The subordinate was a male, and it was a familiar voice that made the emotion in my chest even more rampant.

"*It'll be as though she never existed... I'll even rewrite your memories.*"

"*W-Wait, what are you–?!*"

There was a struggle, and I heard the woman's voice muffled.

"*Shh, shh.*" That sinister voice soothed menacingly. "*Don't worry,* Mother... *I won't make you forget everything... just a few minor details regarding her murder.*"

My entire body was seething with unspeakable rage, a fire that threatened to consume my sanity.

'He's the one...' I nearly growled aloud. 'Luxia's death... Esilas' suffering... he caused it all!'

Before I could round the corner to get a look at that man's face, I heard a voice calling me back to the waking world.

"Lux!"

It was muffled, but I could make out that it was my name.

"Luxahliah!"

The surrounding vision faded, and I fought to stay, to see who this dastardly mastermind was. I reached out my hand to grasp onto the dream, but my focus became distracted by a flash of color. A single, ruby-red leaf fluttered down and landed on the back of my hand. My mind cleared, and with that newfound clarity, I felt myself coming back. When I awoke, it felt as if I had resurfaced from underwater, adrenaline surging through my veins. My breath was heavy, and I couldn't find my bearings. A pair of slightly cool hands cradled my head, and I was met with the worried, red-amber eyes of Esilas.

"Lux, it's okay." His voice was soft. "Shhh, you're okay. You're okay."

He gently ran his thumbs over my cheekbone, and I felt a tranquility as the adrenaline in my system slowly ebbing away.

"E-Esilas..." I breathed.

The dhampir breathed a sigh in relief and then gently wrapped his arms around me, holding me close as tenderly as he could.

"You're alright." He whispered, gently petting my head to soothe me.

As my breathing calmed, I could recognize my surroundings as my room.

"What happened..?" I asked, my throat feeling slightly raw.

"Elderik said you'd collapsed while on your walk." He said, pulling back to look at me. "When he carried you in here... I thought that you'd–"

He didn't finish; he just brushed my hair from my shoulder and laid his head there. I slowly recalled the events before I'd been pulled into the vision, and out of the corner of my eye, I saw Elderik leaning against the doorway. His eyes were pleading in such a protective way, silently begging me to not tell Esilas the truth.

"I'm sorry, Lux." Esilas spoke softly, his hold tightening slightly. "I should have been there with you."

I frowned a little and gently pet his head, which seemed to calm him as I ran my fingers through his ebony-to-ashen hair.

"I'm sorry for worrying you." I whispered, leaning my cheek against his head and closing my eyes.

'For now... I won't tell him anything...' I thought reluctantly. 'If I told him about my visions now, especially what I just saw, it would only break him even more.'

I continued to gently comb Esilas' hair with my fingertips. However, I knew that this lie would only be a temporary measure to protect; he needed to know about his sister at some point... and I knew that *I* would have to be the one to tell him. I owed Esilas that much.

9

The Summer Soiree

THE DAYS LEADING UP to the Summer Soiree seemed to pass us by hastily after that, and I was filled with anxiety; my last vision had put a lot of things into perspective and was a constant reminder of the dangers of being an *Aster-Blood*. My mind constantly reeled with the possibility of getting caught; I couldn't live with myself if Dahliah and her family were in danger because I was discovered. The punishment for that crime was death… and it scared me to think that I could be the cause of it.

"You look like you've seen a ghost." Dahliah's voice brought me out of my thoughts. "Are you alright? Any light-headedness from before?"

I looked at her and shook my head.

"No…" I said. "I… guess I'm just worried about keeping my nature hidden…"

Dahliah stood up and brushed my hair from my eyes with her fingertips.

"You won't be there alone," She reassured. "Esilas and Elderik will be with you."

She smiled slightly. She then turned me towards the full-body mirror to let me have a look. My dress was an off-white gold with a gold silk ribbon around my hips. The skirt was made of several layers of thin fabric of the same color with bright red leaves embroidered into it. The dress's dark red ribbon neckline hid my Heart-Mark and its growth, lightly draping off my shoulders, and the sleeves were made of a thin red fabric, billowing to stop below my elbows. Dahliah had lent me a choker necklace with thin gold chains from which small red jewels dangled and shimmered in the light. My long red and amber hair was woven into a braid and wrapped around itself in a bun held in place by a metal hair ornament. Dahliah gently put her hands on my shoulders, looking at my reflection with me.

"Don't think of tonight as a business opportunity like everyone else is," she advised. "Just be yourself and have fun. You've worked hard and have earned a break."

Dahliah's words were lost on me as I stared at myself. My thoughts weren't on having fun at the event to come, but of the past that I had seen not too long ago.

'Luxia had also once been dressed so beautifully.' I thought, looking at where my Heart-Mark was covered. 'I can't let myself be discovered. She won't be at rest if I become a target...'

I couldn't investigate without drawing attention to myself, and I couldn't ask anyone else for help without revealing the truth about my visions or that I was an *Aster-Blood*. The quandary was maddening.

"H-Hey, Ms. Dahliah," I asked, still staring at my reflection. "Might I ask a question?"

"You never call me 'miss' unless you're so deep in thought." Dahliah noted. "Are you okay?"

"Are *Aster-Bloods*... dangerous?" I asked, my heart beating anxiously.

Dahliah's eyes widened in shock as she stared at me.

"What brought this on, child?" She asked.

I looked at her in the mirror.

"I've been thinking about Luxia...." I spoke carefully. "If *Aster-Bloods* are so treasured, then why take them away and keep them hidden?"

The vampire woman looked at me and then gave a soft sigh.

"I guess it's a way of thinking similar to the humans during the Trials." She started. "Back then, those who were free-thinking or too beautiful were thought of as unnatural, and it was viewed as a threat to their higher authority." She turned and leaned back against the vanity. "When the *Aster-Bloods* were created, these beliefs of humans gave rise to zealotry, and long-lived ones such as we were driven to protect them when they were slaughtered."

"Elderik said that the Trials were when *Aster-Bloods* were slaughtered—"

"Well, what he said was half true." Dahliah said, shifting her weight a bit. "*Aster-Bloods* and their families weren't the only ones to perish. When Lucien got a hold of the humans who slaughtered their own, he killed them with no hint of remorse, and those who weren't responsible but still as guilty were made to serve him and his closest disciples. It was how he became known as a demon." She looked at me. "For those as long-lived as us, we are drawn to those who are pure of spirit and rich with innocence. We do anything to protect them, even if it would mean locking them away from the eyes of the world."

Her words brought to mind the vision of Luxia and the prince; their relationship didn't reflect that mindset at all. The prince had been so attentive to Luxia, and it had appeared that he didn't care that she was an *Aster-Blood* at all.

'He loved her so much that he had been willing to reshape the system so that the hierarchical ridicule no longer had a place to set its roots.' I thought to myself. 'But Luxia wasn't killed for her world-views... someone wanted revenge, but why? What did Luxia do to deserve such a horrible death?'

I took a deep breath and smiled at Dahliah, pushing my thoughts to the side for the moment. My mind was made up, and a goal was firmly set in my heart. It was a goal that Luxia was adamant about, and so I felt I should take it upon myself as well.

"Who knows?" I spoke up, drawing her attention once more. "Maybe, one day, everyone will be free."

I decided then that if I was going to be targeted, then I wouldn't go down without bringing the mastermind with me.

'If what Elderik said was true, and the Gods' Tree created me to correct the imbalance,' I thought, 'then I will fight to correct it with everything I have.'

True, I was still afraid of being caught and bringing danger to those who had helped me, but things needed to change. And what Dahliah had told me in that moment only made it all the more clear; it seemed as though my path was firmly laid out before me. I just hoped that I would not walk it alone.

The night of the Soiree had already started off rather amusingly; Dahliah had insisted that my dress be kept secret so she could be the one to present me to the others. She had a playful smile as she brought me from my room to the dining room.

"Gentleman," she said, drawing their attention, "may I present the beautiful lady of the hour, Luxahliah."

"Dahliah, don't be so dramatic," Esilas said as he straightened his tie while looking in a small decorative mirror in the dining room. He sighed as he moved to turn towards us. "I mean, this isn't—"

When his red-amber eyes met mine, he became incredibly still. He looked as though that one well-placed gust of wind would have knocked him over. His stare made heat rush to my cheeks.

"Lux, you're—" Elderik had started, but Esilas uttered a single word to finish him.

"Beautiful." He said, his light tan cheeks becoming darker with a blush.

Dahliah smiled softly and put her hands on my shoulders.

"See? Told you the surprise would be worth it." She giggled as she looked at me.

Esilas was still trying to maintain his composure, but his eyes and blush were failing. Dargrin chuckled softly.

"Truly breathtaking, child." He gently tapped my chin up. "Keep your chin up. Show that you're an equal."

I smiled shyly at his advice, and I straightened my posture.

"You three should get going," Dahliah said. "Don't want you to be late." She sang, leading the three of us down the stairs and to the front where a cool-black carriage before he and Esilas followed.

"Have fun, you three," Dargrin said.

It was strange that they weren't coming with us, even if Elderik was supposed to be their family representative and I the clinic representative. I waved to them as the carriage drove off to the inner districts of the Mid-City.

Esilas and Elderik were both silent during the ride, and I took that time to look closely at what they were wearing. Esilas' suit was black and his red waistcoat embroidered with gold stars, his shoulder-length hair was tied in a low ponytail at the base of his neck which was probably Dargrin's doing. Elderik's suit was a dark gray with a blue waistcoat embroidered with flying swallows, the colors of the Passor Family Clinic.

"Y-You both look very handsome." I nervously tried to prompt conversation in the awkward silence.

Esilas flinched a little, and Elderik tried not to smile at his comrade's flustered reaction.

"Thank you very much, Lux." Elderik said, though he was rather flustered himself.

He nudged Esilas, who looked at me and looked back out the window.

"Y-Yeah." He muttered. Elderik sighed with a tired smile.

"For the Gods' Tree's sake, Esilas," he reminded, whispering urgently. "You're her escort. You're going to have to look at her to dance."

I felt sorry for the awkwardness this whole situation was putting them through. As the two quietly argued in hushed tones with each other, I was reminded of the short time I'd spent with them before I came to the clinic, and those times of brotherly banter brought a smile to my face.

The carriage came to a stop outside the Carkwright Estate, a beautiful mansion of sterling gray masonry with veins of black crawling through the black stone columns. I was reminded of the magnificence of that courtyard I'd seen in my vision. The door of our carriage was opened by a footman dressed in black and gray. Elderik was the first to disembark, then Esilas was next, and then the latter turned to me.

"If you'll allow me, my lady," he offered me his hand, a bashful look in his eye.

I gently put my hand in his, and he gently helped me out of the carriage. As my small-heeled slippers touched the stone walkway, it was as though the eyes of every coachman, butler, and guest were on me. I was tempted to lower my head, but Esilas whispered in my ear the very words Dargrin had spoken.

"Hold your head up high, Lux," his words were soft like feathers; "you are a guest here, same as everyone else. An equal."

I smiled softly and then looked at him.

"The same goes for you as well," I said. "You have every right to be here as well."

Esilas' lips curled into a slight smirk, and he gently put my hand on his arm.

"No promises," he whispered as we started walking, Elderik walking ahead of us onto the Soiree, and we were met with beautiful music and candle chandeliers.

The ballroom of the Carkwright Estate was warm hues of golden light against silvery-white walls, black marble floors, and ornamented columns. The other guests were dressed extravagantly in hues of red, gold, black, and gray, and some were dressed in dark blue or dark green. A familiar boy wearing a dark red suit and a gold tie came running through the crowd and latched himself to my waist, startling Esilas.

"Miss Luxahliah!" René smiled up at me. "I'm so glad that you came!" I chuckled softly and gave him a gentle pat on the head.

“I was happy to receive the invitation,” I said. “These two are friends of mine, Elderik Passor, and my escort, Esilas—”

“Solani.” I turned to see Captain Ailgraym dressed in a black uniform with gold trim. “Miss Luxahliah, I’m happy to see you here at the Soiree.”

“Captain Ailgraym.” I curtsied. “Dahliah asked me to be the clinic representative... she thought I could use some time to relax.”

“That sounds like her.” He spoke with an amused chuckle. “If you wouldn’t mind, could I borrow your escort for a moment? We shan’t be long.”

I looked at Esilas, worried about his reaction to the request.

“Only a brief conversation,” the dhampir said as he turned to me. “After all, I was promised a dance.”

I blushed softly as he gently pressed a kiss to my fingers. He then let go and then turned to leave with his father.

“Well, that was an interesting interaction.” Elderik leaned over and muttered to me. “You wouldn’t have anything to do with that, would you?”

“I’m not sure, to be honest,” I muttered back. “And... I will admit that I’m worried about how it will turn out.”

“Well, he’ll be fine, I’m sure,” Elderik said and then looked at me. “He has you, after all.”

I smiled softly. René took a step back and then looked at me. He looked a little nervous.

"Miss Luxahliah," I looked at the young Carkwright as he held his hand out to me. "M-Might I be your first dance for the evening?"

Despite my unease, I smiled at the young Aristocrat and curtsied.

"Of course, though I hope you'll go easy on me," I said before gently putting my hand in his. "I'm still a little new to dancing, but I know the basics."

"She's too modest," Elderik chuckled, looking at René with a smile. "She's a natural."

The Aristocrat boy smiled at me and slowly guided me onto the dance floor while Elderik went to socialize. He put his hand on my waist, though he seemed very tense. His slightly pale cheeks were tinged pink.

"Relax, René," I whispered with a smile. "Just follow the music."

He looked up at me and smiled shyly before guiding the waltz. It was a bit of clumsy footwork because of the height difference, but René's awkwardness made way for a bright smile; he was enjoying himself, and that was all that mattered.

"How dare you humiliate me?!"

The moment was ruined as music and socializing came to an abrupt halt at the disruption, and I turned to see a shocking sight; there was a woman dressed lavishly in dark blue and gold, clenching an empty wineglass in her shaking hand, and Esilas was standing between her and the captain, red wine dripping from his face and staining his clothes. I gently pulled away from René and ran over to pull Esilas away.

"Esilas—" I said, gently putting my hand on his arm.

"And who are you? Are you one of my son's bastards too?!" The woman shrieked as looked at me; she looked as though she was foaming with rage like a rabid hellbeast.

"Mother, please, calm down—" The captain tried to soothe the erratic woman, but she wouldn't relent.

"No, Ailgraym!" She slapped his hand away. "Tell me, how much more dishonor must you thrust upon the Solani Family?!" She then jabbed a sharp, ruby-nailed finger at Esilas. "I will not acknowledge him as your so-called first born! The son of some common *human* whore!"

"Why does it matter what blood he has in his veins?" I asked, my anger getting the best of me at the woman's bigotry. "Blood shouldn't dictate status. He was invited here, so he has every right to be here."

"And who are you who are *so wise* in the ways of politics, girl?" She sneered at me.

"Luxahliah, the human physician at your daughter's clinic," I answered.

"I have no daughter!" She screamed. "She abandoned her family for some lower-class poor man's doctor!"

"Look back through any family bloodline in this room, and you'll find that everyone here has human ancestors!" I shouted, rage searing through my entire form. "Your social hierarchy is nothing but poison to the Gods' Tree! You look down on those with 'impure' bloodlines when who bears what blood shouldn't matter! Everyone here is equal, whether or not you want to believe it!"

The entire room was silent as my anger flared. I felt Esilas' shaking hand on my arm.

"Lux, stop—"

"How *dare* you speak to me in such a disrespectful tone!" She raised her hand back to strike me. "You impudent little cow!"

Before she could slap me, she was stopped by a tall man with silver-gray hair and fierce red eyes full of anger, and beside this man was Lady Carkwright.

"Duchess Mareene," the man spoke with a warning tone, low like a refined growl. "You may be a member of the Courts, but you only gained that position from your remarriage. You are a sixth-generation vampire, and I will not stand by and let you harm the woman who treated my son for his ailment."

Lady Carkwright looked at me, her eyes soft with apology.

"Miss Luxahliah, why don't you take Esilas and dry the wine from his clothes?" She asked, bowing her head. "You can use one of the guestrooms upstairs. René will show you the way. I do apologize for our guest's distasteful behavior."

"Why, you treat her as though she is a Noble!" The duchess chuckled with befuddlement. "Or even a Morgenstern! She's just a human!"

"A human who cares deeply for anyone, no matter their rank." The captain spoke up against his mother. "This woman is more of noble blood than you are, you who behave like a first-generation who lacks self-control."

René came over to me and Esilas, gently taking my hand and leading the both of us away from the crowd as they murmured about the human guest who had been invited and was supported by the Carkwrights.

Esilas was quiet on our walk to the guest rooms, and when we arrived, he walked inside ahead of us, closing the door behind him and leaving René to talk in the hallway. I turned to the little Aristocrat.

"Could you tell Elderik that we're alright?" I asked. "He'll be concerned after that incident and come looking for us."

The boy nodded, though his eyes told me he wanted to say something but couldn't find the words.

"René?" I whispered, kneeling to look at him. "What's wrong?"

"I'm sorry..." he said in a soft voice. "I did not know that the duchess would be here... I don't know anything about the other families in the Aristocracy... b-but..."

He looked almost ashamed. I gently put my hand on his head, careful not to ruffle his neatly combed hair.

"René, you have nothing to apologize for," I reassured him. "I admit, I provoked the situation, but I wasn't about to let her berate Esilas like she was. All she cares about is status, and that alone makes her shallow."

The boy looked at me, his eyes still reflecting gloom, though there was a spark of curiosity.

"But... I don't understand..." he said; "why did you risk yourself for Esilas?"

His question was simple, and yet the answer was anything but. Instinctively, I answered with little thought.

"You do crazy things for the ones you hold close to your heart," I muttered. Before he could question me further, I kissed his forehead. "You should go back to the party and tell Elderik where we are."

He nodded and hugged me before leaving me alone in front of that closed door. I stood straight and turned toward the barrier between me and Esilas. I took a deep breath as I knocked on the door.

"Esilas, I'm coming in."

I walked in to find Esilas, his suit jacket, and waistcoat discarded on the bed and about to unbutton his shirt. My eyes widened as heat gathered in my cheeks at the sight.

"E-Esilas, what are you doing?!" I asked as I hastily closed the door behind me. He looked at me, his eyes dull.

"What, are you expecting me to wear these while I get the wine out of my hair?" He asked.

I clenched my shaking fists, trying to calm my sudden anxiety.

"I-I'll take care of the stains..." I stuttered as I walked over to the bed, sitting down to dry the stains on his clothes.

The room was silent except for the splashing of water against the ivory china wash basin as the now bare-chested Esilas washed the wine from his hair. Droplets of water snaked trails down his neck before he was satisfied that the wine was out. I finished drying the stains and stood to return his clothes to him.

"H-Here..." I said. Esilas looked at me and quietly took the clothes. But he didn't get dressed; he just stared at the embroidery on his red waistcoat.

"E-Esilas—"

"Why did you do that?" He muttered, not looking at me as he spoke.

"W-What do you—?"

"You know damn well what I mean, Lux." He looked up at me finally, and I froze at his steely red-amber gaze. "Why did you provoke that harpy of a woman?"

I bit the inside of my lip as I clenched my hands, trying to calm myself.

"I didn't like the way she was treating you," I answered. "She—"

"*She*," Esilas said, his voice heavy with anger, "is a duchess of the Courts." He took a step toward me, grabbing my arms. "Do you not realize the danger you've put yourself in? The danger you've put Elderik and his family in? Damn it, Lux."

"W-Why are you so angry with me for defending you?" I asked, my anxiety slowly making way for anger.

"Lux, the law dictates that those who hide an *Aster-Blood* will be punished." He lowered his voice in case anyone was listening from the hall. "That is more important than how this damned society sees me."

"Why is it so hard for you to accept that you have value?"

"Because I don't, Lux!" He raised his voice at me. "I am a bastard and a dhampir! All I am is something for Elderik to take pity on! Even you take pity on me!"

"I do not take pity on you!" I yelled at him. "Are you really so ignorant to see that there are people who care about you?!"

"You have no right to care about me!" He returned, bearing his fangs as though it would scare me. "Don't you dare say that you care about me when you know nothing!"

"Why can't I care about you Esilas?!" I asked as tears formed in my eyes. "Is it so wrong for me to love you?!"

Esilas was silent then, and it took a moment for me to realize what I had said. My entire form shook.

"E-Esilas, I–"

The dhampir dragged me to the door, the anger in his eyes replaced with panic. He didn't say a word as he promptly pushed me out of the room.

"Don't you dare say those words again." He said, his voice almost pleading. "You can't... never again..."

"Esilas–!"

"Go back to the party." He said before shutting the door in my face.

There was a heaviness that I felt in my heart, and it threatened to crush it in a firm hold. I covered my mouth as my mind went over every moment that I shared with Esilas, how each one had made my heart flutter with a flighty warmth. The words I had spoken were from my heart, and it was becoming clear that I was rather impulsive when it came to what I believed in my heart... and in my heart, I knew I loved Esilas.

And he had just forbade me from ever telling him those words again.

I fought back my tears despite my shattered heart, and I walked away from that room and down the hall.

10

The Attempt on the Morgenstern Heir

I DIDN'T HAVE THE courage to go back to the Soiree; my heart was still fragile at that moment, and I didn't want to risk any more of a scene than before. So, after some wandering around, I found myself in the gardens of the Carkwright Estate. I felt a little more at peace, even if it wasn't by much. I walked along the gardens' stone paths and then sat on a stone bench. I looked around the ethereal nature-scape, trying to distract myself from thoughts of Esilas, though with very little avail. Small glass globes of light flickered in the hedges and flower bushes, seeming to dance to the music of the ballroom.

'They must have continued the Soiree after that woman's outburst...'

I looked in front of me. There was a small water fountain—a small child with feathered wings and horns curved back like a ram's holding a watering jar—poured murmuring water that lulled me into a deep sense of thought.

'Why did I tell him that?'

I looked down at my hands in my lap.

'Do... I really love him?'

Everything was still for me, and I wondered if my silent promise to Esilas to find out what had happened to his sister still meant anything.

'I still want to fulfill that promise... but will it do him any good?'

Doubt had taken root in my mind, and that unfamiliarity caused me to curl a little where I was seated.

'Will... will he hate me for not telling him the truth? Will he think that I'm smothering him?'

I squeezed my eyes shut as I felt tears build in my eyes.

'What do I do? What *can* I do?'

"What is a sterling lily doing here by herself?"

I froze at the familiar voice, and I looked up to see a silk handkerchief being held out to me. I lifted my eyes further to be met with a pair of gentle gold eyes framed by neck-length black hair. The man before me wore an elegantly made suit of black with a dark purple waistcoat and a black tie. When I didn't take the handkerchief, he knelt at eye level and gently dabbed the cloth at the corners of my eyes to collect the tears.

"Why does she cry such precious tears?"

That voice.

That delicate touch.

Those golden eyes I'd seen gaze so lovingly at another.

Before me stood the form of a man I recognized from my visions.

The Morgenstern Prince.

"I-I'm sorry..." I said as I stood from the bench. "I-I need to go—"

I was stopped by a gentle hand wrapping around my wrist.

"Why do you apologize?" He asked me. "You've done nothing wrong, not that I have seen." The gold-eyed man gently slid his hand down to hold mine. His touch felt so foreign compared to Esilas'. "The incident before was not your fault. You were in the right in that situation."

I froze at his words, and I turned my head back to look at him.

"What... what do you mean?" I asked, my voice barely a whisper.

"You supported the dhampir Watch-Keeper when that callous duchess Mareene made such a disgraceful scene." He elaborated. "You are certainly an interesting one."

He'd seen everything, and my mind swirled with questions.

'Does he know what I am?' My heartbeat quickened in my chest at the implication. 'What will happen to Dahliah and her family? To Elderik? To Esilas...'

What he did next surprised me; the demon prince held our hands between us, gently running his thumb over my knuckles. It was a calming gesture.

"Might I have the pleasure of your name, my lady?" He asked, his tone kind.

"If you saw everything before..." I said hesitantly, watching his eyes, "then you should already know my name..."

My response garnered a chuckle from the prince, and his smile revealed slightly sharpened canine teeth. Fangs.

"While that may be true, sterling lily," he said; "it would be rude to call you by your name without a proper introduction." He then bowed low, still holding my hand. "My name is Cassius."

His words and actions were elegant, as if they were made of intricate silver, and I took note that he didn't say his last name.

'Why did he introduce himself without his family name?'

Even after a few moments, he didn't move or say anything to prompt a response from me; he was waiting patiently. I was still hesitant to go along with anything, but I remembered my vow to Luxia; that vow did not waver in that moment.

"Luxahliah," I said finally. "The human physician employed at the Passor Clinic."

The prince finally looked up at me, his lips curling into the kindest of smiles.

"Well, my lady Luxahliah," he said as he pressed a soft kiss against my knuckles. "Might I have the honor of a dance?"

The music from the Carkwright ballroom was a gentle melody playing in the background, and we were completely alone in the gardens. I willed my heart to ease itself of its anxiety, and I took a deep breath; this was an opportunity to investigate Luxia's murder, a fleeting chance that I wasn't about to let pass. I curtsied and nodded.

"If you'll have me, my lord," I accepted humbly.

Cool fingers gently brushed against my cheek before he dropped his hand to my waist and guided me in a slow waltz. I contemplated the questions I should ask, fear of letting my curiosity make the interaction awkward.

"If... you don't mind me asking, Lord Cassius," I asked after much contemplation, "what brought you to the Summer Soiree?"

He chuckled softly as we twirled on the stone path.

"Who knows?" He said simply, a carefree smile on his face. "Social obligation, perhaps, or maybe it was my curiosity at the mention of your attendance."

I raised an eyebrow at him.

"My attendance?" I asked. "Why was that a factor in your decision for you to attend?"

"Because you are the only human here," he answered. "A lamb in the den of lions, as ancient scholars would describe. I couldn't help but wonder what kind of person you were, a human physician whose reputation prompted Aristocrats to neglect their own personal physicians and then testify such praise."

"I... am hardly aware of such praise..." I said, "nor am I worthy of it."

"You truly are humble, sterling lily," he said, chuckling, "but you are worth every word of praise. Your kindness and your compassion for those who humans often see as monstrous are renowned, even in the Courts."

His eyes flashed with a familiar sense of melancholy, a somber familiarity that I recognized in the eyes of another. A longing for what had been lost. Cassius stopped the waltz and continued to stare at me.

"L-Lord Cassius...?" I asked, but he didn't answer my address.

My heartbeat quickened once more as he stared silently, looking lost within himself.

'Something is wrong here.' I realized. 'If the one behind all of this actually made true on his word, then why does Cassius look so lost, like he's having conflicting thoughts?'

It then dawned on me like a candle flame illuminating a dark corner.

'His heart still remembers what he felt for Luxia. The mastermind might have made him forget her, but he still feels those emotions for her. And the rewritten memories are causing the confusion he has.'

I was brought out of my thoughts by a panicked commotion from the ballroom.

"What's going on?" I asked.

"I don't know, but that definitely doesn't sound like entertainment." Cassius answered, taking a step closer to me.

There was a rustling behind Cassius, and I saw something glinting in the pink-hued ambience. Reflexes took over, and I pulled him out of the way.

"Get down!" I yelled as a crossbow bolt whizzed past our heads. I grabbed the prince by his hand and ran. "We have to get help!"

Cassius seemed to return to his senses, and he pulled me behind a tree.

"We can't put the other guests in danger." He said, his voice lowered.

"But either of us could get shot if we stay out here!" I whispered back urgently.

I clenched my hands, clutching the skirts of my dress as my anxiety was on the rise. Cassius looked as though he was caught between the two choices, and I wished that Esilas and Elderik were there.

"Lux!" As if by a miracle, I heard Elderik call out for me. "Lux, are you out here?! Where are you?!"

I looked out to see Elderik wandering the courtyard in a panic. I saw the glint again, and I panicked.

"Elderik!" I shouted. "Be careful! Someone is shooting at us!"

I saw Elderik duck behind another tree.

"Friend of yours?" Cassius whispered, looking at me.

"He and Esilas both." I nodded.

"Someone attacked the Soiree too!" Elderik said. "Captain Ailgraym is assembling the Ebony Guard and evacuating the guests!"

"Where is Esilas?!" I asked, my panic rising at the thought of him getting hurt.

"Right here." I heard his voice as wind rushed past us; I watched with wide eyes from behind the tree as Esilas made his attack.

Another bolt was fired, missing the dhampir as he lunged for the assailant.

"Gah!"

I snapped my head back to Cassius as he held his shoulder, the bolt having embedded itself. The demon prince fell to the ground, writhing in pain.

"Lord Cassius!" I knelt next to him and I froze as I watched the veins in his neck become a bruised purple. "E-Elderik! Something's wrong!"

Elderik came over to us, and even he was shocked at the sight.

"It's poison." He said simply. "Very advanced. It won't be easy to cure, even if we had the proper equipment with us."

"If he dies, we'll have the Courts coming after us." I said, looking at him. "He's a Morgenstern."

"Oh, well, aren't we screwed." Esilas spoke; I turned to see him, a waterskin in his hand.

Elderik sighed.

"There's only one way to stabilize him." I looked at him as he ran his hand through his hair. "Your blood–"

"Fuck, no!" Esilas said. "If he drinks her blood, then he'll know she's an *Aster-Blood*, Elderik!"

"And if he dies, we'll be to blame." I said, reaching to remove the metal hair comb from my head, letting my hair fall.

I'd been about to cut my palm when Esilas caught my wrist.

"Lux, *please*," he looked at me with pleading red-amber eyes. "Don't."

As much as the sight broke my heart, I jerked my hand away from him.

"I'm not about to let him die, Esilas." I said, pulling the bolt from the prince's shoulder, the demon yelling in pain.

I didn't say another word as I slit my palm and squeezed the blood into the demon's mouth. His eyes fluttered as he tasted my blood, and then his irises flashed from gold to blood-red. Before I could even react, he grabbed my hand and buried his fangs into my wrist. A fresh pain replaced the throbbing soreness of the cut in my palm, and before I could scream, Esilas quickly held me from behind and covered my mouth.

"Lux... you have to be quiet..." he whispered, his voice soft in my ear.

The dhampir continued to whisper in my ear, trying his best to distract me from the pain of the demon's fangs gouging my flesh. My heartbeat rang in my ears and I could feel my head become heavy as my eyesight spotted out black. A new question among many was the only thought in my mind as I slipped into darkness: Cassius was a victim of blood hunger.

11

The Royal Estate

Dahliah had once told me about the levels of disorientation associated with blood loss. Lightheadedness was always a symptom, but to have one's head throb with painful pulsations was definitely one sign that a lot of blood had been lost. I awoke with these very symptoms, along with my vision being blurry and my ears still ever ringing. The abundance of light in the room definitely didn't help with the pain. My entire body was stiff. My bones felt sore and heavy. I felt cool fingers touch my forehead., and I moved my head to lean into them.

"E-Esilas..." My throat was dry and crackly as I spoke out.

"Shhh, miss." Whoever answered wasn't Esilas, or even man; it was a woman's voice that I heard, but it wasn't Dahliah's either. "You might feel some nausea if you move too much."

My head was gently inclined, and a cup was gently pressed to my cracked lips. Cool water soothed my raspy throat.

"Where am I?" I whispered.

"His Highness brought you and your two companions here." She said, not really answering the question. "They refused to leave your side."

As I was slowly rehydrated, I gained some sense of my surroundings... and the first thing I noticed was that I was *not* in my Soiree dress.

"W-Where am I?" I asked again, panic prickling through my body, and the woman gently put her hand on my shoulder to calm me. "My clothes—"

"Master Elderik brought Lady Dahliah to dress your wound and change your clothing, miss." She said; "His Highness is indebted to you for saving his life. He wants you to be as comfortable as possible." I relaxed, humming softly as I laid my head back against the fluffy pillow.

"What's your name?" I asked. "I'm Luxahliah."

The woman caring for me smiled, a smile I could hear in her voice.

"A very pretty name, miss." She complimented. "My name is Lita."

My vision gradually cleared, and I could see the woman, Lita, a little better; she was as tall as me and had short white hair and dark pink eyes. She was wearing a black dress with long white sleeves. It had pockets, similar to that of the aprons that Dahliah and I wore at the clinic.

"I'm a maid here at the Royal Estate."

I felt my blood run cold at her words, and I fought the pain to sit up.

"T-The Royal Estate?" I looked at her with wide eyes. "H-How long have I been asleep?"

"Nearly a fortnight, miss." She answered, gently easing me back to lie down. "Masters Esilas and Elderik have been staying here since the night of the Soiree." My words were caught in my throat as she bowed. "Excuse me, miss, I need to inform His Highness and your two companions that you're awake."

She didn't leave me any time to ask any further questions as she left the room. I was then left alone with my thoughts.

'Asleep for nearly two weeks... and no visions of Luxia...' I took a deep breath through my nose as I closed my eyes. 'But why...? Then again, I only seem to end up with more questions than I do answers...'

I let out a sigh and opened my eyes again to look around the room I was in. There were tall windows adorned with black curtains drawn by gold cords. There was a small study desk, a wardrobe and a tall bookshelf. I slowly sat up, wincing slightly at the soreness in my bones. I was relieved that Dahliah had insisted on changing my clothes herself; she'd dressed me in my clinic uniform. I looked at my dressed palm, shivering a little as I remembered the pain from Cassius' bite.

'Cassius is part vampire... but he doesn't seem to have had any of the medicine to curb the blood hunger... I wonder why...'

I was brought out of my thoughts when the twin doors to the guest room opened, revealing Cassius Morgenstern, Esilas and Elderik.

"Lux." Esilas breathed and was sitting at my bedside within a moment. "What the hell are you doing, sitting up like that?"

I flinched a little as he gently put his hands on my cheeks. "Please, lay back down." Before I could even say anything, he lowered his hands to pull me close to him. "Why must you risk yourself so much? You scared the shit out of me."

"Esilas, that's enough." Elderik put his hand on Esilas' shoulder. He looked at me. "We're glad you're awake, despite the circumstances."

Esilas pulled away, and I looked at them.

"What do you mean?" I asked. "What circumstances? What happened?"

Esilas and Elderik looked at each other.

"Well–"

"Their comrade is missing." Cassius spoke. "A first-generation named Ephrem."

I looked at the three of them as shock gripped me.

"Ephrem... is missing? But how can that be?" I looked at Elderik. "I thought you sent him back to the barracks, and that was nearly a month ago."

"We *did*." Elderik confirmed as he crossed his arms, his stature tense with uneasiness. "But we received word from the barracks captain that he disappeared a few days after he should have returned. We couldn't do anything with us being on leave."

"Why didn't either of you tell me about this?" I asked, looking at him frantically.

"We didn't want to worry you."

"There's something else." Esilas added with a sigh. "The waterskin I snagged from the assassin that night... it belongs to Ephrem..." He looked at me. "The kid has gotten himself involved in something... it could get him killed..."

"He'll be caught and interrogated." Cassius spoke up. "He could tell us who put him up to it."

"According to *your* law." Esilas said in a rather hateful tone. "The same law that separates children from their families."

The two of them seemed one word away from being at each other's throats.

"Esilas, don't." I gently squeezed his hand, trying my best to calm him, but it seemed to have very little effect on his demeanor.

"For the last time, Mr. Esilas," Cassius spoke with a sigh; "your sister has never been in the Estate. You've seen the records for yourself."

"Yeah, I saw a rather shitty clean-up job." Esilas was nearly feral. "I will find my sister, even if I have to dig up the foundations of this damn building."

"Will you two just stop?!" I shouted, feeling uncomfortable with how intense the situation had become. "Geez, what exactly has the two of you in such a quarrel? This isn't just about Esilas' sister... so spit it out."

I was justifiably irritated. Silence ensued as I looked between the two of them, neither one of them giving up an answer. It was Elderik who then answered me.

"It would seem," he spoke, breaking the silence rather hesitantly; "that you've been found out by someone."

My blood ran cold, my hand tightening on Esilas' as anxiety tightened my chest.

"B-But how–?"

"We don't know." Elderik said softly. "We're going to have Eshrik look at the substance in the waterskin. The poison in it was lethal, enough to deteriorate the body's circulatory system."

The waterskin was a mystery, but it really wasn't my concern at that moment. Esilas gently pet me on the head as my form shook.

"W-What will happen to me?" I muttered. "If the Courts know about me–"

"They don't, Luxahliah." Cassius spoke up. "No one else in the Estate knows about you other than myself, and I've not told anyone."

"Astonishing." Esilas muttered sarcastically.

"I've *not*." Cassius said, punctuating his point. "All I've done is offer you three sanctuary, and the Passor Family is being protected as well. It was the least I could do, especially for you, my lady."

He looked at me. Relief washed over me, realizing that Dahliah and her family would be protected, but anxiety still prickled at my nerves.

'What was the purpose of the assassination? If the mastermind was confident in his ability to rewrite memories, then there shouldn't be a need to kill him... so why?'

"In any case," Cassius spoke up again with a deep breath; "I would like to offer you further protection, Luxahliah, so that my debt to you is repaid."

I blinked a little, watching with confusion as the prince walked over to the bed and knelt at the side of my bed.

"Wait, what do you mean?" I asked.

"As the next head of my family, I have the authority to protect you," he looked at me; "you saved my life at the risk of your secret, Miss Luxahliah, so allow me to do this for you."

He cradled my hands, and I could feel Esilas grow tense as the prince touched me with familiarity, as if we were courting.

"W-What are you suggesting?" I asked. Cassius took a deep breath, gently running his thumb over my knuckles.

"To safeguard your life, Luxahliah," he spoke, looking up at me; "would you marry me?"

I was momentarily rendered catatonic because of Cassius Morgenstern's proposal. The irony of the situation hadn't escaped me; he and Luxia were supposed to be married, and even she couldn't be protected from whoever was behind this horrendous plot. Elderik kindly asked the Morgenstern prince to leave so that the three of us could talk. Cassius obliged the request and left the room. When he was gone, Esilas stood up and paced a bit before he turned to me. He folded his hands, his fingers touching his chin pensively as he took a deep breath as he tried to remain calm.

"Tell me you are not considering this, Lux." he said, looking at me with a baffled expression.

Before I could answer, Elderik let out a breath.

"Gods' sake, it's basically subterfuge! A lie!"

"There are more pros than there are cons to this arrangement, Esilas." Elderik spoke, holding his chin deep in thought.

"I fail to see what good could come from this." Esilas' head snapped towards Elderik. "It's basically a prison sentence for her!"

"It would give us a chance to search for Luxia." He elaborated, looking at his comrade. "That's been what you've wanted from the beginning—"

"But at the cost of Lux herself?" He looked at Elderik, befuddled by his comrade's suggestion. "Elderik, I didn't know that you could be so diabolical."

I clenched my fists as the two continued to argue. I took a deep breath and then looked at the two of them.

"Something happened to Luxia." I spoke up to draw their attention. "I saw it."

Elderik looked at me with wide eyes.

"Lux, don't—"

"Elderik, he needs to know." I looked at him. "He needs to know what I saw of Luxia."

I was only going to tell fragments of the truth; it was a kinder way of telling him.

"Lux..." Esilas breathed shakily, looking at me; "what do you mean by 'see?' What do I need to know?"

I shared a look with Elderik, silently asking him to not stop me. I then looked at Esilas.

"Luxia and Cassius... they were supposed to be married..." I answered carefully. "And something has happened that has made him forget her."

"Wait, what do you mean?" Elderik asked.

His surprise was genuine, and for good reason; I hadn't told him about my vision from that day in the hidden courtyard.

"It was the last vision I had before the Soiree." I said, looking at Elderik. "Luxia was looking for Esilas in the Outskirts, but she didn't know that he had been taken to the Watch-Keeper's barracks." I looked at Esilas then. "Captain Ailgraym told me that he had told the guards who had come looking for you where to find you, but in the vision, Cassius mentioned that the guards never told them. I think that the same person who made him forget about her also made the guards forget about what they had learned."

"But why...? Why would anyone want to keep us apart?" Esilas asked, his voice shaking.

"I... don't know yet," I spoke truthfully. "But this arrangement with Cassius gives us the opportunity to further investigate what happened. To find the truth about what happened to Luxia." Esilas looked at me.

"Why..?" He breathed. "Why the hell would you risk everything for this truth?" His hands were shaking. "Whatever happened to my sister could happen to you as well."

"I know..." I said, stopping to take a deep breath as I looked between the two of them. "That's why I want you both to be here with me."

Esilas sat down at my bedside once more, running his fingers through his hair. His throat looked tightened, as if he was trying not to cry.

"I guess... asking you for your reason is moot... yeah?" He whispered, knowing what my answer would have been had he asked me why I was helping him find his sister.

He was hesitant as he gently touched my hand. I smiled sadly at him as he looked at me. He gave a dry chuckle and then exhaled.

"Alright, Then I'll stay by your side."

"As will I." Elderik added. "If you're going to go through with this arrangement, then you'll need bodyguards. And who better to protect you than those who know you best?"

I nodded and then nervously bit my lip.

"I... also have a request if you two are going to do this..." The two of them looked at me rather quizzically as I continued. "If you're going to risk your lives like I am... then I want you both to drink my blood."

"Lux, why would you make that request?" Elderik asked, shocked at my suggestion. "You've only just woken up–"

"Esilas grew stronger after drinking my blood." I cut Elderik off as I looked at him. "It was only a drink. You should be just as strong as he is now, especially with the unknown enemies we have ahead of us."

Elderik and Esilas both looked at each other, seeming to weighing the options. Elderik let out a tired sigh and then turned to me.

"Alright." He said, kneeling at my bedside with a tired smile, and Esilas followed him.

"If he's getting a drink, then I want another, too." He said, his face blank of expression. "If that's alright with you, Lux..."

I blushed a little and nodded before giving them both my hands. They touched the back of my hands to their foreheads in a gentle gesture of fealty before they pierced my skin with their fangs. Like Esilas' bite had been before, it was more comparable to the pin-prick of briars. A moment later, they both pulled away and Elderik dressed his and Esilas' bite marks.

"Any lightheadedness?" He asked, looking at me like his mother would. "I felt like I took more than I did."

I smiled softly and shook my head.

"None at all." I said, smiling softly. "I feel fine."

Esilas silently stood, still holding my hand before he let it go and turned to leave the room. Before I could even ask where he was going, he declared his intention.

"I'm going to get you some food." He said simply, opening the door and then closing it behind him.

Elderik looked at me and smiled. When this seemed to confuse me, the vampire explained.

"Don't mind him." He looked at my newly bandaged hands. "He's—"

"Conflicted." I finished his sentence with a sad smile. "Yeah… I know…"

"He feels the same way about you, you know." He said. "He's.. having a hard time finding a way to apologize for what he said to you… he's already lost someone so close to him. He doesn't want to lose another."

I blushed a little; it didn't surprise me that Esilas had confided in Elderik about our conversation in the guestroom of the Carkwright Estate.

"I… I somehow doubt that he holds me as dear as you believe he does." I spoke as I looked at the dhampir's bite mark on my hand.

"I'm not wrong, though," he countered. "Because Esilas wouldn't have confided in me about you, nor would he have demanded that he stay by your side while you recovered. He *does* care about you, Lux. I think he's just afraid of himself."

I was silent. Elderik seemed to so wholeheartedly believe that Esilas cared for me. I didn't know if Esilas had told him the whole truth of what happened between us, but I wasn't about to argue. Even if what Elderik said was true, I couldn't tell Esilas the truth that I had told him in the Carkwright guestroom.

Not until I had given him some closure for Luxia.

12

A Cruel Dream

Because of Cassius' marriage proposal—as well as my acceptance of the offer—I was quickly thrust into the world of the Royal Estate and Courts; officially, I was his guest and most prominent suitor, which garnered a lot of looks from servants, guards and the other Nobles at Court, looks ranging from shock and awe to absolute disgust. This arrangement also forced a certain dhampir to accept his father's surname; dhampir or not, he was still the son of a seventh-generation.

This technically made Esilas an eighth.

An Aristocrat vampire.

As bodyguards, Esilas and Elderik were given lightweight black uniforms, a more elegant version of the Watch-Keepers' uniforms, with the Ebony Guard crest embroidered in gold thread over their hearts. The two of them stood on either side of me as Cassius presented me to his parents in the throne room. Despite the sneers and looks of prejudice from the Lords and Ladies, the Morgenstern Family didn't seem to bleed with malice, and I realized why when I saw them. The king and queen of Obsiditourma, the Morgenstern Family heads, were Claustus

Thaddeus and Elaine Maye Morgenstern. The queen mother had long black hair that was tied in an intricate bun on her head with two silver streaks in her bangs, and her eyes were a familiar soft red.

'That explains Cassius' blood hunger.' I thought to myself. 'The queen is a vampire... but I can't tell her generation. But either way, that means Cassius is a—'

"Father, Mother," Cassius addressed with a bow. "May I present Luxahliah, my chosen suitor, and her devoted friends and guards, Elderik Passor and Esilas Solani."

Malice seemed to reverberate from one particular corner of the throne room; I didn't have to look to know it was Duchess Mareene.

"Luxahliah," the queen mother repeated, "a name with roots that mean 'flower' and 'light.' A very fitting name for such a virtuous lady." She smiled, and it was a warm and comforting smile. "Lady Dahliah has chosen a very promising protégé."

"You saved the life of my son." The king spoke up. "You have our thanks, Luxahliah of Passor Clinic. If you have any wish, we shall grant it."

I smiled softly and shook my head.

"You're very welcome, Your Graces," I curtsied, "but there is no wish that I want granted, though the offer is very much appreciated."

The throne room echoed with soft murmurs, and then a familiar haughty voice spoke up.

"Yes, the *famed* human physician from the Passor Clinic." Of course, it was the duchess Mareene who had spoken up. "This is the one who spoke so distastefully of our society. She is only humble because she is of such inferior status, but I bet if *she* was a Noble, then she wouldn't want to liquidate the rank system."

"Ah yes, I heard about that little incident." Queen Elaine spoke. The duchess had a smirk on her ruby lips, but it was fleeting once she saw the smirk the queen mother had. "You caused quite the scene, Duchess Mareene. Rather unbefitting of a member of the Courts."

Before the duchess could defend herself, the king father held up a hand, causing the air in the room still with a heaviness. Everyone seemed to hold their breath as he spoke next.

"Duchess Mareene," he spoke, his voice firm and sharp as steel. "You only have your position because of your late second husband. You hardly have the decorum to be a Noble-rank."

He narrowed his fierce gold eyes, making the duchess tremble.

"If you act out of line toward Miss Luxahliah or any of her associates, you *will* be dismissed from the Royal Estate and sent back to your home in the Mid-City. Is that, in any way, unclear to you, Mareene Solani-Ahdaghast?"

The duchess was rigid with shame, and she bowed her head as she curtsied.

"Y-Yes, Your Grace." She said simply, her voice slightly trembling. "We are all bound by your commanding rule."

The king then turned his piercing eyes to me, and his gaze softened.

"You are most welcome here, Luxahliah of Passor Clinic." He declared, his tone full of dignity. "If you require anything, do not hesitate."

I didn't object to how he had clearly rephrased his offer; I simply curtsied, thanking him for his welcome.

That night would be the only time I would be able to share a meal with Esilas and Elderik during my stay at the Royal Estate. We discussed the events of my presentation to the Courts.

"So, the prince is a demon-dhampir..." Elderik said. "That explains Lord Cassius' hunger when you healed him at the Soiree, but I honestly didn't think it was possible."

"And here I thought regular dhampir were rare." Esilas huffed before drinking from a glass of wine.

I blinked and looked at him.

"Wait, dhampir are considered rare?" I asked. "I thought they made up the population of the Outskirts."

"Not exactly." Esilas said. "Not that many dhampir children survive their childhoods."

"There are actually very few dhampir in the Outskirts." Elderik added.

"The blood hunger usually kills us by age three, slowly losing ourselves the longer we fight it. It eats us from the inside out, starving us to death." Esilas said.

"And that is why the medicine Eshrik makes is so important." Elderik nodded as he looked at me. "Dhampir children could live full lives with a perfected dose of the medicine."

"Well, as full of life as they can live in a place like the slums of the Outskirts." Esilas sat back and crossed his arms.

"Okay... but what does this situation mean for Cassius?" I asked as I ate a bit of roasted pheasant we had been given.

"It's unknown." Elderik sighed in defeat. "Lord Cassius is more than likely the only one of his kind. The strain passed on from the vampire parent violently reacts with human blood on its own, causing the hunger, but for it to somehow have coexisted with demon blood? It's been thought to be impossible."

"Because the vampire strain would react violently with demon blood?" I asked.

"That doesn't even begin to describe it." Elderik said. "The combination of the two bloodlines is volatile, nearly toxic to one another. The child would have been either miscarried before it could be brought to term... or it would be stillborn."

"In other words, the prince is a bona fide miracle." Esilas said, rather disenchanted with the revelation; I, however, was pulled into my thoughts as I recalled my visions of Luxia.

'Was Luxia's baby miscarried? Or was it murdered by the mastermind?' A chill prickled up my spine at another possibility. 'Or... was her baby the intended target?'

After we shared our meal, I was left alone in the room I'd been given. While left alone, I realized that there was a particularly disturbing feature in this room; it was the very room where Luxia had been found murdered in her bed, butchered like an animal.

'Well, this isn't creepy at all...' I shuddered as I slept near the very edge of the bed. Sleep didn't come easy to me, and after about an hour of tossing and turning, I finally gave up and sat up. I gave a frustrated sigh.

'This is ridiculous.' I threw the covers off and lit the lantern on the bedside table.

I touched my bare feet to the soft rug on the floor and walked over to the bookshelf at the other end of the room. I set the lantern on the table and ran my fingers over the spines of the books. Suddenly, I felt a slight breeze as I reached the end of the shelf. Curiosity gripped me at the sudden occurrence, and I felt for where the back of the shelf met the wall. I found a small crack; the air was coming from there. I went to grab the lantern to further investigate the wall. The crack seemed to open up into a larger space, and I looked back at the shelf.

'Was this how the mastermind got into the room to kill Luxia?' I tried to push against the shelf to move it, but my efforts were to no avail. I sighed and put a hand on my hip; the shield was definitely too heavy to move. 'I'd have to get Esilas or Elderik to take a better look.'

I was still rather puzzled by this recent development, but it didn't seem to deter a yawn from escaping my lungs; the shelf would have to be a mystery I'd solve in the morning, though it was going to be a busy time for me. I sighed in defeat as I sat on the bed. I blew out the lantern flame, and I was about to turn and lie back down when a chill prickled at my nerves, freezing my entire body.

Standing in the room's corner, there was a chilling silhouette, not too far from the bookshelf.

It was barely visible, but I could tell that someone was standing there. The only thing I could make out from the darkness was a pair of glowing, pink-gold eyes. My heart hammered in my chest as panic squeezed my lungs. The eyes blinked at me, and I slowly curled up in the bed.

'Esilas...' I wanted to scream for him, to feel some semblance of peace.

"W-Who are you?" I breathed.

The eyes blinked again, no sound emanating from the shadow. I was afraid to even close my eyes for fear of the eyes not being a vision.

I nearly jumped out of my skin when there was a knock at the door. My head snapped towards the door and then back to the corner. The glowing eyes were gone, and I hastily relit the lantern to look at the corner; no one was there. There was another knock at the door, this time more panicked.

"Alright, alright, hold on." I sighed before getting up.

When I opened the door, I was astonished to find Esilas, wearing his black under-tunic with the strings on his collar untied. He was out of breath, his hands gripping feverishly at the door frame.

"Esilas? What are you–?"

"What's wrong?" He asked. "I heard you calling my name."

Heat gathered in my cheeks as he stared at me.

"I-I didn't–" I paused when I saw how his eyes widened. He pushed past me and searched the room. "Esilas, what's wrong?"

"Someone else was in here." He said before turning to me. "Is that why you called me in here?"

"Esilas, I didn't call for you..." I stuttered. "I... did think I saw someone standing in the corner... but when I lit my lantern, there wasn't anyone there..."

I covered my arms, avoiding Esilas' gaze. I heard his footsteps as he walked up to me. I flinched a little, not expecting him to ever so gently caress my cheek.

"Lux..." He whispered, gently pulling me to look at him. His red-amber eyes seemed to search mine; they reflected conflicting emotions, like he was trying to reign in his feelings.

I remembered his words from the Soiree, and I broke eye contact, gently putting my hand on his.

"Esilas–"

"I can't..." his voice was low and soft; "I don't want to risk loving you... and then you suddenly disappear..." I looked up at him with wide eyes as he put his other hand on my check, gently running the pads of his thumbs along my cheekbones.

"And I fear you'll disappear… and I will have this regret that will slowly kill me from the inside…" his eyes then softened, his cool hues becoming warm with a tender affection.

He slowly leaned in, and as his shuddering breath brushed against my lips.

"E-Esilas… I–"

"Don't say the words." He whispered. "I… have no right to hear them… not after what I said to you before—"

"Esilas."

I gently held his hand while using my other hand to hold his cheek. His eyes wavered and became glossy, as if my whisper brought forth tears.

"Esilas."

My heart throbbed in my chest as I gathered my courage.

"I-I love you."

His breath shuddered against my lips once more before he closed his eyes and pressed his lips against mine.

His lips were soft like down feathers, but his kiss was filled with a heated longing. My eyes fluttered closed as my breath was caught, consumed by the dhampir before me. The kiss was over all too soon as he pulled away, his hot breath fanning my lips as we both fought to breathe normally again. I kept my eyes closed, terrified that it had been a dream.

"I love you too, Lux." I heard Esilas' barely audible whisper in my ear, and my entire body felt light with relief. "I love you more than the waking world, than life itself... and I want nothing more than to stay by your side forever... my purist, Lux..."

When I opened my eyes to return the sentiment, I felt my heart start to break and tears formed in my eyes; I was laying down in bed, and white sunlight was just streaming through the windows.

I was alone.

I covered my mouth as I fought to keep a heartbroken sob from escaping my throat. I curled up in bed and closed my eyes once more.

Esilas, his heartfelt confession, and his tender yet passionate kiss...

Everything about that night had been a dream.

A cruel dream.

13

Beware the Man in White

LIFE IN THE ROYAL Estate started early, and for me, it began with the introduction of my new handmaiden. Lita came in with a cart of morning tea and a young servant girl with long, mousy-brown hair tied into a braid at the bottom of her neck and green eyes trailing a bit behind her; these features told me that she wasn't a vampire, or if she was, at least not the same generation as Lita.

'Is she a first-generation like Ephrem? Or is she just a normal human?'

"My lady," Lita smiled as she gently put her hand on the girl's back. "This is Avaline, and she'll be your maidservant during your stay here at the Estate. His Highness picked her from Her Grace's staff."

Avaline looked at me and then immediately looked down; the poor girl looked to be only twelve years old—maybe a little younger—and her body trembled as if she were terrified. I walked over to her and knelt to her level, gently taking her hands with a smile.

"Avaline, huh?" I said in a gentle tone. "That's a very pretty name."

When she looked at me, I saw a long scar across her neck; the poor girl, much to my horror, looked as though her throat had been slit open from ear to ear. I looked at Lita, and she smiled sadly.

"She was sold by her family to a Noble, nearly killed by him, miss," she explained. "The Noble's son took pity on her and turned her into a vampire. When the queen discovered the girl's abuse at the Noble's hands, he was dismissed and executed. The son is the head of the family now, and Her Grace took her in."

The girl's story was surprising considering that it had been my understanding that first-generations were sent to the Outskirts by their sins. I turned to Avaline and smiled softly.

"Well, either way, I'm glad you're safe." I placed a soft kiss on the girl's forehead. "Don't overwork yourself, okay? Just do what you can."

The girl nodded and coughed a little, the scar on her throat seeming to irritate her. I looked at Lita.

"Could you go and get me some honey and milk? It'll help to soothe her throat."

The woman nodded and left the room. I gently brought the girl over to my bed and sat her down.

"Some honey will do you some good—"

The girl suddenly grabbed my arm, her eyes frantic; I could feel her panic as if it were my own, my nerves jolting with a fight-or-flight response.

"You're in danger." She whispered, surprising me. With the severity of her scar, I would have thought that her vocal chords had been cut. "Don't trust the man in white. He hurt the other nice lady."

My eyes widened, wondering how she could remember Luxia when no one else seemed to.

"The nice lady?" I whispered. "You knew Luxia? You remember her?"

The girl had been about to answer when Lita returned with a cup of warm milk and honey. It was an old remedy to help sore throats that Dahliah and Dargrin had taught me. As she slowly sipped the drink, my mind hung onto the girl's warning.

'Don't trust the man in white.'

During my short time at the Royal Estate, I had seen no one dressed in white. After I had finished my morning tea, Lita left with the cart and, and Avaline helped me to dress. I'd just fixed the brooch pin on my bow when there was a knock at the door.

"Come in." I said, turning as the door opened to reveal Esilas and Elderik.

My cheeks flushed with heat as I remembered my dream from earlier in the morning.

"G-Good morning." I smiled softly, trying to hide my embarrassment.

"Good morning to you as well." Elderik said before noticing Avaline. "And who is this?"

"Oh, this is Avaline." I knelt next to her as the girl grasped my hand nervously. "This is Esilas Solani and Elderik Passor, dear friends of mine." I said. "Esilas... is Luxia's twin."

The girl's eyes widened and looked at the dhampir.

"The man in white hurt the other nice lady." She whispered as she looked at me. "He did something very wrong."

"She knows Luxia?" Esilas' voice sounded full of hope. "But how–"

"I think she couldn't be made to forget her." I said. "That or whoever did this didn't think that she'd be able to tell anyone because of the scar on her neck."

At the mention of this, Elderik knelt and held out his hand to the girl.

"May I see?" He asked softly.

Avaline looked at me, and I nodded, smiling a little.

"Go on," I whispered. "Elderik only wants to see your scar."

She nodded silently and hesitantly stood from the bed and walked over to Elderik. He was gentle with her as he checked the scar, giving her some simple exercises to see how well she could speak.

"She's healing," Elderik said, sounding rather puzzled.

"But how can that be?" I asked.

“The strain from when a vampire turns a human mutates them, also healing any ailments or injuries they received.” Esilas explained.

“The strain is still working through her system.” Elderik added.

“But doesn’t that mean she would have to have been turned recently?” I asked. “The last anyone saw of Luxia was–”

“I’ve seen her.” The girl whispered. “She walks around the corridors of the Estate. She’s smiling even though she looks so sad.”

Her cryptic words sent chills down my spine, and I looked at Esilas and Elderik; they were just as puzzled and on edge as I was. My visions had given me the impression that Luxia had been murdered, and there was even evidence to support it.

‘Could it be... that Avaline can see Luxia’s ghost?’

Even with the discovery of Avaline and her strange ability with the information it gleaned, the three of us still had to keep up appearances, and it didn’t help that we were late getting to the dining hall for breakfast. Even with how late we were, Cassius’ parents—particularly Queen Elaine—greeted us warmly.

“Ah, Luxahliah, my dear,” she smiled at the three of us, “and Sers Esilas and Elderik, good morning.”

I curtsied.

“Good morning, my lady.” I answered.

“Did you sleep well?”

I tried not to flinch at the question, fighting the heat rising in my cheeks; I was reminded of my dream of Esilas, and I couldn't mention it in front of them. There was also the fact that the bed had been the literal deathbed of Cassius' previous suitor and the mystery opening behind the shelf.

Nevertheless, I smiled as I answered her.

"Very well, Your Grace," I said as Esilas pulled out my chair for me.

I sat beside Cassius and put my napkin in my lap. Esilas and Elderik stood at the back well as servants walked in, rolling carts with a variety of food. Before me was placed a plate with poached eggs on thick slices of toast and a side of thick succulent ham. Other dishes included potatoes roasted with herbs and spices, flaky scones glazed with the sweet butter, and bowls with different kinds of fruit, and there were pitchers of freshly squeezed orange juice and lemonade. To put it simply, it was a feast, and one that I wished everyone in the city could indulge in.

'The farms' crops most primarily come to the Royal Estate and the Nobles, leaving the Outskirts with scraps...' I thought to myself.

"I hope you enjoy the breakfast, child," the queen said with a smile. "The vegetables and fruit were grown in the Estate Gardens. Let us eat and converse. Don't be shy."

"They were grown here?" I asked, looking at her with surprise.

"Indeed," Cassius said; "Mother tends to them herself, and I help too."

I looked at him and then at the queen mother, who smiled with a rather human modesty.

"Cassius has taken more charge of it in recent years." She spoke modestly. "I used to have a garden where I used to live, though I could only ever grow strawberries for my sister. She loved strawberries."

She was rather reminiscent. I looked at the food again and picked up my fork to eat. The poached egg ran golden as I cut into the white. As it touched my tongue, an exquisite flavor filled my mouth. I smiled softly and closed my eyes, and I heard Cassius chuckle.

"You look like you've entered ecstasy." He said, causing me to look at him with heated cheeks "Is it that good?"

I swallowed the bite I'd taken and nodded.

"I-I'm a bit embarrassed now—"

"Nonsense, child," Claustus spoke in a playful tone. "Please, request anything you wish from the kitchen staff. Your companions are free to eat with us as well."

It was a warm welcome that I hadn't expected. I looked over at Esilas and Elderik, and the two hesitantly joined us at the table, sitting on either ends with the latter next to me and the former next to Queen Elaine. The queen looked at the dhampir with a reminiscent melancholy that didn't escape me. It was only a moment, but I could see a sense of familiarity flash across her face.

'Does the queen... somehow know Esilas?' I wondered. Her eyes were ones I'd seen before, a single emotion that I recognized whenever Esilas thought of his sister or the expression Cassius had during the Soiree: heart-break.

After breakfast, Queen Elaine invited me to go with her to the library. Her invitation was odd; from what I gathered, she knew nothing about me, especially not of my nature as an *Aster-Blood.* As we walked down the corridor to the library, I noticed several portraits along the walls. It was one of the larger portraits that caught my eye. It was the portrait of a tall man with black hair and gold eyes, standing with a young woman with white and gold hair and blue eyes. The two of them were equally beautiful.

"That is Lucien Morgenstern." Queen Elaine explained. "And with him is his sister, Adelaine."

"The progenitor of this noble family." I said.

"That's right." She nodded.

"He... almost looks like a woman with features like those." I said absentmindedly.

The queen chuckled and stood beside me as she looked at the painting as well.

"He does, doesn't he?" She said, "I had the same thought when I first saw this portrait." She looked at me. "Tell me, what do you know of the first head of the Morgenstern Family?"

"Not much." I answered. "Elderik told me that he was given his powers by the Gods' Tree, and that he gifted others with his knowledge."

"And what of the *Aster-Bloods*?" Her question startled me a little, and I looked at her. "What do you know of the first *Aster-Blood*?"

I honestly didn't know how to answer, though something in my heart skipped as she mentioned the first.

"All I know is that they were hunted by their own people." I said, cautiously. "And that a law was passed that would protect them from those who wished to harm them."

That familiar spark of melancholy flashed in her eyes, and she looked back up at the painting.

"Adelaine was one of the first to be murdered by the religious zealots in their village." The queen frowned then. "So overcome with grief, Lucien used his power to subjugate the humans who had killed her, and he decided it would be his bloodline and his followers that would lead them from their self-inflicted damnation by serving the vampires and the Morgenstern Family." She turned and continued walking towards the library, speaking as I followed her. "*Aster-Bloods* are so rare that the discovery of one drives us mad with the need to protect them. In a way, Lucien's first commanding law is a curse for us all."

I'd been about to ask her something when she stopped at a pair of large storm-gray doors. She opened them to reveal a massive trove of bookshelves. There were two floors to the library; the first held a seemingly extensive labyrinth of shelves, while the second was a partial floor with its shelves standing like dominoes. A flash of the white caught my eye on the second floor, a blur that ducked behind one of the shelves.

'Is someone else here? A librarian, maybe?' I thought to myself before Queen Elaine brought me out of my headspace.

"Miss Luxahliah, I have a question for you." She addressed me, making me turn to her. "Has my son been acting strange in any way?"

It was another question that I didn't know how to answer without telling the truth about what I knew. I turned to face her; I needed answers as well.

"If I answer your question, Your Grace," I said, considering what I was about to ask, "could you answer one for me as well?"

The queen's eyebrow rose slightly when I didn't directly answer her question.

"You're rather brazen, aren't you?" She spoke, almost defensively.

"I would say it's a fair trade, wouldn't you?" I asked. "We both get information."

It was a risk, but there was a gut-feeling I had; only she could answer this question. The queen looked at me, her eyes analyzing me, before she let a sigh escape through her nostrils, and she nodded.

"Very well," she said. "I will answer your question if you answer mine."

Her tone as she agreed to my conditions made my palms slightly sweaty, and I answered her question.

"Cassius spaces out, at times." I answered, cautious with the information I was giving her; "He seemed to space out when we first met at the Soiree. I simply just thought that he had a lot on his mind."

The queen's reaction was a curious one; she seemed to relax at the answer I had given, almost as if she were relieved.

"Alright," the queen said, "and what is your question, child? I did agree to your terms, after all."

I clenched my fists, fighting not to wring my hands at my anxiety. I took a deep breath and straightened my posture.

"How do you know Esilas?" It was at this question that Queen Elaine seemed petrified.

"W-What makes you think that I know your dhampir companion?"

"I saw the look in your eye at breakfast this morning." I clarified. "It was rather fond, as if you were looking at family–"

"I can't answer your question." She snapped. "I-I apologize, my child, but I don't know what you think you saw, but I do not know your Esilas." She then turned on her heel to leave the library. "Come, I have a few more places to show you before noon. The ladies of the Courts are meeting for a garden luncheon, and you should get to know the others."

Her behavior was hasty; it was obvious that she was frightened of something.

'What could have terrified her so that she couldn't answer my question?'

I followed her, watching her carefully. I stopped at the door to look at the library, and as I did, I noticed another flash of white. I remembered Avaline's warning, and I wondered if the man in white was what had Queen Elaine scared so terribly. Around the corner of one of the shelves, a glimpse of white cloth disappeared.

Queen Elaine seemed to return to normal as she showed me around the rest of the Estate. Her initial panic in the library was puzzling, and it raised more questions in my mind.

'It was almost as if the white blur had been some sort of trigger for her.' I bit the inside of my cheek as I ruminated. 'Has the mastermind done something to her? A countermeasure, perhaps?'

I was brought out of my thoughts as a sweet perfume filled the air. I looked up from my thoughtful gaze to find that Queen Elaine had brought me into a large conservatory. Around us were a variety of gorgeous flowers of numerous colors. There were roses, lilies, irises, and snapdragons, and there were several large pots where citrus and fruit trees and vines of vegetables.

"These were the plants Cassius mentioned." I said allowed. "The garden you planted because of where you grew up, right?"

"Yes," the queen said. "He's taken quite gracious care of them."

Her tone was pensive as she seemed to gaze at the flowers with reminiscence. She said nothing else, and soon a small gazebo came into view as we walked past a few tall rose bushes.

"Lady Elaine!" A well-dressed woman was already sitting at the table under the gazebo. "Oh, and you've brought Lady Luxahliah with you!"

She was thin, wearing a dark red dress, and her long blonde-white hair was tied in a luxurious bun. I recognized the style; it was how Dahliah had styled my hair for the Summer Soiree.

"Lady Cecilia," Queen Elaine smiled softly. "Your hair is styled so beautifully."

"I styled it after Lady Luxahliah and her heroic efforts."

I blinked at the Noble lady's upfront admiration. The queen looked at me and smiled softly.

"Luxahliah, this is Lady Cecilia Michaelson, one of my more trusted Ladies at the Courts." Elaine introduced. I curtsied at the Noble lady.

"It's nice to meet you, ma'am."

"Oh, you're such a jewel!" Lady Cecilia squealed with delight. "Please, call me Cici."

I was surprised by her friendliness, remembering what Ephrem had said about his experience with Noble-rank vampires.

"Then... you can call me Lux." I smiled softly. "Everyone I know calls me that."

I sat beside as a familiar callous woman arrived as she froze when she saw me, her eyes hardening into a fierce glare.

"Ah, Duchess Mareene." Elaine's tone was as cold as the white sun, which made the aforementioned duchess compose herself. "It's so good of you to join us."

"Look, Mareene!" Lady Cecilia—or rather, Cici — spoke excitedly. "Lux is here to dine with us as well! Isn't that lovely?"

I saw the duchess swallow a lump in her throat and she nodded.

"Yes... very lovely indeed..." she quietly sat down between Cici and Elaine; the duchess seemed on edge, but I attributed it to Elaine's authority and the commanding word King Claustus had used.

Elaine seemed a little too pleased with the duchess' discomfort.

"Well, ladies, let us delight in conversation." She said, which surprised me; at a place where six people could be seated, only four of the seats were taken.

The luncheon was a delicate spread of small sandwiches, mini strawberry tarts and rose tea, which I recognized from the aroma. I wasn't in the mood for sweets, but the floral flavor of the tea seemed to have been specifically paired with the mini tarts.

"Are you enjoying the tea, dear?" Elaine asked me, smiling softly as she set her teacup down.

"It's delicious." I nodded. "Rose goes very well with the taste of strawberry. It... feels like springtime."

"There's not been a fruitful springtime in nearly a decade," Duchess Mareene muttered pessimistically. "And I doubt that there will ever be another."

"Now, now, Mareene," Cici soothed. "Let's not talk about such gloomy affairs. Instead, let's keep the mood like springtime." She then turned to me as she dabbed at her mouth with a napkin. "How many children are you and Cassius going to have once you're married?"

Her innocent question made me choke on my tea as heat flooded my cheeks. I snapped my head towards Cici.

"W-What brought that on?!" I nearly shrieked.

"Don't be so shy!" She giggled. "You and Cassius are such a perfect match! I cannot wait to see the size of the wedding!"

She started to excitedly talk about every tradition from the wedding feast to the bedding ceremony, which made my face feel like it was about to burst into flames from the embarrassment I was feeling.

"C-Cecilia, I'm not sure—"

"Oh, please," the duchess said, nearly shattering her teacup as she set it forcefully on the table; "she's no more a better match for the prince than—"

I looked at her as she paused, and she looked confused. She put a hand to her forehead.

"Funny... I had a thought... but I can't remember what I was going to say..."

The woman closed her eyes as her brow furrowed with discomfort.

"Are you okay, Mareene?" Elaine asked, looking at her; "you look awfully pale."

The queen's tone was not one of concern; it was the same warning cadence as before.

"I-I'm fine, milady." She said as she ate a bit of tart. "F-Forget my outburst from before."

Her behavior was concerning, and my instincts as a physician and an *Aster-Blood* were crackling as if trying to alert me to her distress.

"What were you going to say, dear?" Elaine said, trying to return us to the topic at hand. "Are you excited about your wedding?"

I bit the inside of my cheek; in all honesty, I had never thought about marriage or any prospects that came with it, and it didn't help that my engagement to Cassius was only a farce so that Esilas, Elderik and I could investigate what had happened to Luxia.

"I... I don't know, to be honest," I said, carefully speaking the truth. "I never once imagined that I would be married..."

"You haven't?" Cici asked, rather shocked; "I would always dream of my wedding day as a child!"

"You were born into Nobility, Cecilia." Elaine chuckled. "Speaking from experience, I never thought I would be married, either, so I understand Luxahliah's thought process a bit."

I looked at her as she calmly sipped her tea.

"Wait, you do?" I asked.

She nodded as she set her cup down once more.

"Yes, you see, I was—"

Before Queen Elaine could further explain, Duchess Mareene grabbed the table with one hand, causing the china tea set to clatter at the disruption, while her other hand clutched at her chest as it heaved with ragged breath. She looked as though she was having trouble breathing.

"Duchess, are you okay?"

I set my teacup down and had been about to reach my hand out to help her when she slapped my hand away. She glared at me with eyes red with painful tears of blood.

"Don't touch me, you filth!" She roared, her voice raspy and dripping with venom; "I-I don't need your—''

The duchess abruptly tumbled out of her seat, dragging the tablecloth with her and spilling the food and breaking the tea set. Cici screamed in horror, and I immediately went to the duchess' aide as she foamed at the mouth. Her blood vessels turned a bruised purple, a symptom I fearfully recognized from the assassination attempt on Cassius.

"It's poison." I muttered. "B-But I don't know what kind..."

"Can you save her?!" Cici cried girlishly.

"Not without knowing exactly what was used." I said.

I was caught at a crossroads; either I could save the woman who hated me and reveal my nature as an *Aster-Blood* at the same time... or I could do nothing, keeping my promise to Esilas to not be reckless.

'But... if I can't save her... then can I even call myself a physician..?'

Frustration festered in my nerves, producing tears as I held the woman's hand.

"Please, Duchess Mareene, hold on!" I said before turning to Cici and Elaine. "Call Lita from the infirmary! I can't heal her here!"

The woman grabbed me by the shoulder and turned me back to face her. The whites of her eyes were turning red with blood. She pulled me down, and I feared she was going to bite me; however, she was speaking with gasping breaths in my ear.

"Y-You... will die here... just like *her*..."

There was another word caught in her throat as she choked on her vomit.

"E-... E-..."

She never finished what she was trying to tell me; her grip on my shoulder loosened as her breath faded, and when I pulled away to look at the duchess, her face was forever molded into a visage of horrific pain, tears and blood leaking from her eyes and bile dribbling down either side of her ruby-lipped mouth.

Cici screamed in terror as I turned to the other two women with me, tears streaming down my cheeks.

"S-She's dead..." I breathed. "I-I'm sorry... I couldn't..."

I choked on my words as they turned into sobs. Cici turned and ran screaming out of the conservatory. Even in my devastation, I noticed the look on Elaine's face; her eyes didn't reflect panic or sorrow... but an expression of terrorized befuddlement. A terrifying thought crept into my mind like a worm in the dirt; did the queen suspect that someone would die at the luncheon... or did she plan it?

14

The Passage in the Wall

Time was slowed in my catatonic state; I barely registered the arms that wrapped around me to pull me away from the corpse of Duchess Mareene or that I was carried out of the conservatory and brought back to my room. My chest was heavy, and I could barely breathe at the realization of my failure.

‘I couldn’t save her...’ my thoughts echoed. ‘N-No... I *didn’t* save her... I spent too much time thinking about what I should do instead of doing what I needed to do... regardless of what I promised Esilas... I-I should have—’

“*Lux...*”

‘What do I do?’

“*Lux...!*”

‘I can never face Dahliah or Captain Ailgraym again... she was their mother—’

“Lux!” I was brought out my thoughts and nearly jumped out of my skin as I was forced to look at the urgent and concerned red-amber hues of Esilas.

“You’re alright...” He soothed, gently caressing my cheeks. “You’re alright.”

"No..." I whispered. "I'm not."

"What?"

"I'm not alright, Esilas." I repeated. "I didn't save her... I should have saved her... I—"

"You promised me you wouldn't risk yourself, Lux." Esilas said, his eyes going from concerned to serious as he dropped his hands to grasp my shoulders. "You *promised*—"

"And it was because of that promise that I was second-guessing myself!" I raised my voice as my frustration got the better of me. "I could have saved her! I *should* have saved her, Esilas!"

"That harpy of a woman hated you, Lux!" Esilas argued. "She hated anyone that wasn't a so-called *Noble* vampire! She wouldn't have cared if you had saved her! Do you really think that your skills or your life matter to the Nobles or the Morgenstern Family?!"

"It doesn't matter!" I cried out. "I could have saved her! I'm a physician! It's my job to save lives! And what's more is that she knew something about Luxia! Her memories were overwritten like everyone else's! She was even about to say your sister's name before she collapsed!"

Esilas let out a groan, and he stood up. He paced around a moment before he turned to look at me.

"What the hell is up with you, Lux?" He asked, more of a demand than a proper question. "I'm starting to wonder if all of your people are like this. Your lack of self-preservation is astoundingly mortifying."

"You think I don't know that I have to hide my nature?!" I nearly shrieked. "I bet you're the expert when it comes to hiding things."

"What the fuck does that mean?" He put his hands on his hips, flabbergasted.

"I practically have to pull your fangs for you to even talk to me about anything or somehow be put in danger for you to show any emotion toward me that isn't anger or contempt!" I raised my voice once more, my frustration once more getting the better of me as tears built in the corners of my eyes and threatened to spill. "You're so difficult to read, and whenever I feel like I'm getting close to getting you to open up to me, you shut yourself away!"

There was a silence as Esilas just stared at me, his hands dropping from his hips in shock.

"Do you really think that's all I feel towards you?" He asked. "Anger and contempt?"

"Well, you sure as hell don't love me!" I said as I wiped my eyes, my voice cracking as I fought the sobs in my throat. "You only show concern for me because I'm an *Aster-Blood* like your sister! You won't even let me tell you that I—"

"Of course, I love you, you damn idiot!" He shouted as he held me by the shoulders. "Don't you get it, Lux?" He moved his hands to gently cradle my cheeks. "I do love you. So terribly and deeply... but I don't deserve it. Don't you get that, Lux?" His eyes swirled with an emotion that I'd never seen in him before.

Fear.

His hands trembled with it.

Before I could even say his name, he let go of my shoulders and stormed out of the room. My heart hammered against my chest as I collapsed on the bed, gripping the sheets in my fists as I played Esilas' words repeatedly in my head. I clung to his every word; Esilas said that he loved me. Elderik had been right about his dhampir comrade when he said that he had been afraid. I'd witnessed the fear that he felt as it made his entire form tremble, his hands shaking because of it. Esilas' touch had even been delicate, as if I would shatter like glass. Tears streamed down my face as I let a shaky breath escape my throat. I heard another set of footsteps enter the room, but I didn't look up as I was still coming to terms with Esilas' confession.

"Lux?" It was Elderik that had come in. He'd walked over to me, slowly kneeling beside me and wiping my tears; "Lux, what is it? What's wrong?"

"E-Esilas..." It was the only word I could manage without breaking down into hysterical sobs.

After the incident in the conservatory, I'd locked myself in my room for a few days before Dahliah and Captain Ailgraym came bursting through the door, the former frantically calling my name. The two of them had been informed about the duchess's untimely death, and not surprisingly, they were more concerned with my safety than the funeral arrangements of their own mother. I looked up from my place on the window seat as the two of them came into my room. Dahliah wasted no time in practically running over and embracing me.

"Oh, my sweet child."

I felt my chest tighten as she gently stroked my head, and I wrapped my arms around her as tears formed in my eyes once more. I realized then just how much I needed her particular dose of motherly affection, someone to talk to that understood my plight. She looked at me, gently wiping my tears.

"Shh, shhh. It's alright, dear." She soothed, trying to calm me.

"Elderik told us what happened." Captain Ailgraym said as he came over and gently put his hand on my head. "Your heart truly is pure."

"I-I tried to help..." I whispered. "B-But I... Esilas and I..."

"Shh..." Dahliah hushed tenderly. "You did all you could..."

"B-But..."

"You promised Esilas that you would stay hidden." She said, gently brushing a lock of my hair behind my ear. "Knowing you as I do, you didn't want him to worry."

"But... I-I couldn't save her... she–"

"You can't blame yourself, Luxahliah." Captain Ailgraym said, his tone gentle; "our mother... she—"

"She was poisoned." I said abruptly as I looked up at him.

"Wait, what?" Dahliah asked, pulling away to look at me with wide eyes.

"It was the same poison that Cassius was afflicted with when he took the crossbow bolt in the shoulder at the Soiree." I explained as I looked at her. "Her blood vessels were bruised the same way that his vessels had."

"And you're sure?" The captain asked in a whisper.

"There was no mistaking it." I said. "A-And... she said that I would die here, too..."

Dahliah gently put her arm around my shoulders and looked at her brother as he spoke.

"I'll have the Ebony Guard investigate this further—"

"No." I said, looking at him. "I want Esilas and Elderik to investigate it."

"They can't investigate this case and protect you at the same time." The captain said.

"I'll investigate with them." I insisted.

"Like hell you will." Dahliah said, her motherly voice serious. "I'm not about to let you involve yourself any further in this. If you make even one wrong move, you could lose your life."

It had been similar to what Esilas had reminded me of numerous times, but I couldn't bring myself to argue with her. Captain Ailgraym knelt and looked at me.

"Please, let me and the Guard investigate this. You and the boys will be kept in the loop on what we find. You have my word, Lux."

Once again, my promise to Esilas kept me from saying anything else, warning them of what I knew; telling Dahliah and the captain about my visions would only worry them, and he would be bound and determined to find the conspirator that killed Luxia. I let out a shaky breath and nodded in defeat.

"Okay."

Thanks to the visit from Dahliah and Captain Ailgraym, I'd felt a lot more sociable; Dahliah had helped Avaline prepare my bath and made sure that I was actually getting clean from my week-long self-isolation. After the smaller vampire helped me dress, Dahliah insisted on doing my hair, choosing to pull the top of my hair and braid it into a fishtail braid. After a well-balanced meal that was prepared by Dahliah—that I thankfully could eat at my leisure in my room—Elderik accompanied me on a walk in the Estate's outlandishly large courtyard. I was feeling a little better thanks to the care of Dahliah, but I was still demoralized from the incident at the conservatory. I looked at Elderik.

"Thank you." I spoke, feeling the tranquility of the gardens.

"For what?" Elderik gave an amused smile, looking at me as we walked.

"You're the one who brought Dahliah and Captain Ailgraym here to help me." I said, smiling a little. "Dahliah's company was exactly what I needed, and not to mention that it was nice to feel like I had a mother to look after me."

Elderik chuckled a little as he clasped his hands behind his back.

"I can't exactly take credit for the idea. I just told them about what happened once they got here." He said before looking at me. "It was Esilas who left the Estate to visit with them and talk about your emotional state."

My smile faded, and I stopped, causing him to stop a few steps ahead of me and look back.

"Esilas did that...?" I muttered. "He did that for me?"

"He did." Elderik said, a brotherly smile on his lips. "He was concerned about you, even more so than I had ever thought possible for him. I've never seen him care so deeply—"

"That day when he brought me back to my room," I said, looking at him as I gently hugged my arms; "he... he told me that he loved me... and I could see that fear you were telling me about..."

Elderik's face didn't show any sign of revelation of that fact; it seemed as though he had known all along.

"He told me." He said. "But... I have to wonder what drove you to snap like that. It wasn't just the trauma of the duchess's death." He gently took my hand and led me over to the fountain to sit on its ledge. "So, tell me what else is on your mind. What happened?"

My throat suddenly became tight, as if I was forbidden from saying anything. Nevertheless, I fought through that sudden fear, and I looked at Elderik as he knelt in front of me.

"I... had a strange dream my first night before I was presented to the Courts." I said. "I was in my room, and I thought I was awake because I couldn't sleep. I got up and went over to the shelf to find a book to read... and I thought there was something behind the shelf. I tried moving it but I gave up. I went back to lie down, and as I blew out the lantern..."

I shuddered a little at the memory.

"Lux?" Elderik whispered. "What is it?"

"I saw pink-gold eyes." I whispered back as I leaned in closer to him. "They were glowing in the dark... I could have sworn that there was someone in the corner watching me like a predator... and then suddenly there was a knock at the door. I lit the lantern once more to find that the figure was gone, and when I went to open the door, Esilas was there and—"

I cut myself off as I felt my cheeks flush red with blood. I didn't want to mention the fact that Esilas had also confessed his love for me in the dream; it honestly didn't seem relevant. I looked at him. I then recalled an interesting detail as I replayed the dream in my head.

"The eyes..."

"I'm sorry...?" Elderik looked at me questioningly.

"Those eyes... the ones I saw in my dream..." I elaborated. "Elderik, they were the same eyes I saw in my vision my first night at the clinic."

The detail about the eyes drew his interest, and he stood up.

"If that's true... then I don't think that dream of yours was really a dream." He said. "It might have been a vision." He looked at me and held out his hand. "And if it is a vision, then I think we should take a closer look at that bookshelf."

I watched as Elderik examined the bookshelf; I'm not sure if I was relieved or even more terrified when he had found that there was indeed a space behind it. He tried moving the shelf, and I let my thoughts speak for themselves.

"I don't get it." I said as I crossed my arms. "What does the mastermind have to gain from killing Duchess Mareene? Or attacking Cassius at the Soiree? They're not the same rank, but they both were targets for the poison."

"I don't think they were targets." Elderik said as he took a step back from the shelf after a sigh of defeat. He put his hands on his hips. "I think they were experiments to see how the poison works on different bloodlines."

"But why? And what is it even made of that would cause the blood vessels to bruise like it did?" I asked.

"Eshrik has been busy with the Archives." Elderik said. "He hasn't had the time to even examine the poison from the waterskin that Esilas got from the assassin. But I *did* have Father investigate the matter as well. If it's pharmacological, then he'll find something."

That bit of information was a relief; I learned everything I knew about medicine from Dargrin, so I had faith that he could discover something about the poison. Elderik ran a hand through his hair. He then looked at me.

"But if you want my hypothesis, I think that poison is being tested for another target."

Now, it was *that* thought terrified me. It made me rethink all that I had thought about the mastermind; if Esilas' sister wasn't the true target of the mastermind's revenge, then who was the actual target?

"Dammit, it makes no sense." Elderik cursed lightly as he looked at the bookshelf. "This thing shouldn't be that heavy, but I can't get any purchase on it. It's not bolted to the floor..." He looked at the shelf from the front before turning and looking at me. "Where did you say you saw the eyes in your dream?"

I looked at him and then walked over to the corner, shuddering a little at the memory of those predatory eyes.

"In this corner." I said as I turned to look at my bed. "It was right–" I stopped as I suddenly felt my heel sink into the floor.

"Lux?" Elderik asked.

I looked at him and then moved my skirt aside to notice a depressed floor tile. I pressed down on the tile with my foot, causing it to sink a good inch from the rest of the floor, and the sound of clanking gears could be heard behind the wall, almost as if it was a clockwork counterweight system that had been keeping the shelf in place. Elderik took a step back as the bookshelf suddenly shifted, sliding across the wall to reveal the opening behind it to be a narrow passageway. Elderik and I shared a wide-eyed expression at the discovery.

"Here." I finished, my voice a whispering breath as I looked at the foreboding passageway.

"And here I thought it was going to be the cliche of a book that was the key to opening the door."

Our heads snapped towards the door to my room at the voice, and we saw Esilas standing there as he leaned against the closed door. Neither of us had heard him enter the room or close the door behind him.

"E-Esilas..." I stuttered, still not sure how to address him after the rather heated conversion we had had.

He walked over to the passageway entrance and sighed.

"You're staying here. Elderik and I will investigate this." He said.

"Like hell I'm staying here." I said, looking at him as I gained courage of indeterminate origin.

"I thought we agreed that you wouldn't be reckless." He looked at me. "Please, Lux. Stay here."

He had lowered his voice, pleading with me to stay put.

"This passageway is in *my* room, Esilas." I argued lightly. "If my dream was really a vision, then I want to know what it was trying to show me."

"You saw this in a dream, too, huh?" I thought I heard him mutter.

"I'm sorry?"

"It's nothing." He said and then he sighed as he ran a hand down his face. "Alright, fine. You can come along." He turned to me. "*But* you stay close to me. No zoning out or wandering off by yourself. I will hold your hand if I have to."

There was a seriousness in his eyes that scared me; it was as if his confession had renewed his motivations. He held out his hand to me.

"Do we have a deal, Lux?" I bit the inside of my cheek and nodded.

"Okay... deal..." I said, making Elderik sigh as he walked over to my bedside table and lit the lantern.

"You two really need to find time to talk about this new step in your relationship," Elderik said as he walked over to us.

"And you're bringing up the obvious *now*?" Esilas said as he took the lantern from his comrade.

He had wordlessly implied that he would be the one leading us. Elderik simply returned this implication of authority with a lighthearted smile. Their back-and-forth banter brought some relief to my heart despite the perilous unknown that we were about to face, and as we three entered the foreboding corridor, the only comfort that kept me from panicking in that uncomfortable darkness was Esilas' hand.

15

The Ghost in the Passageway

THE BOOKSHELF EERILY CLOSED behind the three of us as we cleared the doorway, and after twists and turns in the corridor, we came to a crossroads. Literally. We were stopped at a fork in the corridor, and we looked at either path before us.

"Well, this is going to be a problem." Esilas let out a sigh as he looked at either path, shining the lantern down either corridor. He turned to look at me. "Which way do we go? There aren't any recent scent trails for us to follow."

I shook my head, at a loss; both paths were equally creepy, and I hadn't had a vision to even show which way was the best to take.

"Lux..."

I heard a familiar feminine whisper, and my heart skipped a beat. I turned my head to look down the left corridor, and there was a faint glow of a hazy white figure at the end of the path. The figure became clearer, and my breath caught in my throat.

"Lux? What is it?" Esilas whispered as he gently squeezed my hand.

"This way, Lux..."

The figure at the end of the corridor was Luxia; she was wearing a familiar white dress, similar to the one I'd woken up in.

"We go left." I whispered as I tugged on Esilas' arm to lead him that way.

"Lux, this really isn't the time to be guessing—"

"I'm not guessing." I quietly protested as I pointed at the figure. "She's showing us the way. Don't you see her?"

\Esilas and Elderik both looked down the corridor.

"Lux, there isn't–"

"Who are you seeing?" Elderik interrupted Esilas as he put his hand on my shoulder.

"I think..." I breathed as I turned back to look at the figure at the end of the darkness; I realized then that only I could see her apparition. "I think it's Luxia... she's showing us the way..."

Esilas' form stiffened, and he gently squeezed my hand tighter.

"You... see her?" He breathed in query, his throat tight with emotion.

I silently nodded and gently led them forward as Luxia started guiding us.

Luxia's long hair flowed behind her as she walked in front of us. She never spoke a word other than to gain my attention to keep following her. Esilas seemed anxious at the prospect of his sister being there with us but being out of reach at the same time.

"I-Is she saying anything?" Esilas whispered. "Does she know we're here? T-That I'm–"

My heart broke at his desperation; he wanted so badly to see his sister, even if she was dead. I gently squeezed his hand.

"She's not said a word." I whispered. "She's only telling me which way to turn."

After a while of twists and turns through the hidden passageways, the apparition stopped and turned to us, putting her hand on the wall where candlelight could be seen flickering through a sizable crack. I stopped as Luxia nodded to me before fading.

"Lux?" Esilas whispered as he looked at me. "What is it?"

I looked at him and then slowly stepped forward, letting go of his hand to take a closer look. I put my hands on the wall and leaned to peek through the crack, and upon seeing the room on the other side, I felt my heart leap into my throat, my chest heaving with panic.

"Lux?" Elderik addressed. "What do you see?"

I couldn't answer as I tried to control my breathing; on the other side of the wall, I recognized the worktable that I had seen in my visions, and there was the sound of liquid bubbling inside glass beakers. A sickeningly sweet and coppery perfume wafted through the crack, making my stomach churn with disgust. I covered my mouth and turned away from the wall. Esilas gently held me against the wall, and his cool hands gently caressed my cheeks.

"Easy, Lux." He whispered. "Breathe."

He soothed my panic attack, making me look at him. The faint glow of the lantern and his red-amber eyes helped to calm me from what I had seen.

"What did you see in there?"

"M-My vision..." I whispered back as Elderik took a peek through the crack for himself. "I *know* that table, Esilas... I saw him sitting there, sharpening that knife..."

"It's a laboratory of some sort." Elderik whispered. "Along with quite the collection of alchemical equipment. I smell blood, as well... and something else... I can't place the scent though—"

"He's coming."

I turned toward the whisper, and I nearly jumped out of my skin at the sight of the wide-eyed, frantic apparition of Luxia inches away from my face. A scream caught in my throat at her face; where it had been a normal face before, her eyes were gone, just empty bleeding holes and blood dribbling down either side of her mouth with her fangs cut from her jaws.

"Hurry, Lux! You need to go! He's coming!"

"Lux, what is it?" Esilas asked, gently turning my head back to him to calm me once more. "What did she say?"

"She... says he's coming..." I whimpered in fear, trying to keep my eyes off the face of her corpse-like apparition.

"*Who* is coming?" Esilas asked, urgently.

As if to further punctuate the severity of the situation and Luxia's warning, the sound of footsteps echoed from the other end of the corridor... the very direction from which we had come.

"Oh, shit." Esilas cursed under his breath.

"*Lux!*"

I turned to look at Luxia again; her face had returned to how it had been before and had disappeared before her apparition reappeared at the other end of the passageway, glowing faintly like a beacon.

"*Quickly, Lux, this way!*"

I grabbed Esilas' hand.

"She's leading the way for us." I said urgently as I pulled him along with Elderik following in due haste.

Luxia's hazy white form seemed to phase out and then materialize again at corners to guide us out of the corridor. My heartbeat rang in my ears as anxiety ate away at my nerves at the prospect of being caught, the ominous footsteps seeming to echo louder and louder after us and the sounds mixing with our own. We followed Luxia's apparition to a dead end, and Esilas and I both put our hands on the wall.

"Lux, I thought you said she was leading us out of here!" Esilas looked at me urgently, his eyes glowing in the flickering lamplight as he tried pushing on the wall.

The footsteps were getting closer, this time at an agonizingly slow pace.

"She was." I breathed, nearly hyperventilating from my anxiety. "I-I don't–"

"Guys, we need a way out of here." Elderik said. "We can't spin a tale in this situation."

"We're trying, dammit!" Esilas shouted in frustration.

"*Lux.*"

I turned my head towards his sister's whisper. Not three feet away stood Luxia. She slowly put her hand on a single particular brick in the wall. With a single nod, Luxia faded away.

"Here!" I shouted before moving to the brick.

The moment I pressed my full weight on it in my haste, an entire section of the wall seemed to push on a swivel. Esilas and I shared a look and then the former looked at Elderik. The three of us escaped through the revolving wall section, the three of us landing on a rug covered marble floor as the wall swiveled back to its closed position. The three of us lay on the floor beside each other, breathing heavily at our narrow escape. Esilas laid his head back against the rug.

"Alright..." He grunted as he sat up and looked at me; "what the hell is going on?"

The passageway had led us into the library, and we were lucky enough that it was in a secluded part of it. Elderik helped me stand as Esilas got up himself and looked at me.

"What was that in there?" Esilas asked.

"Trust me," I took a deep breath to calm myself, "that's what I want to find out just as much as you do."

I looked around the library and then peeked out from the bookshelves. The library had a cool air about it, completely deserted.

"Seems like we're alone... just like before..."

"What do you mean, 'before?'" Elderik asked. I turned and looked at the two of them.

"Before the incident in the conservatory, the queen brought me here to ask a question," I explained. "I told her I would only answer her question if she agreed to answer one of my own."

"What did she ask you?" Elderik asked.

"And what question did you have for her in return?" Esilas added in his query. I took a deep breath.

"She..." I started; "she asked me if Cassius had been acting strange... and I told her he would sometimes zone out. She almost seemed relieved at that answer. When I asked her my question, she told me she couldn't answer it... something here scared her."

"What did you ask her?" Esilas pressed as he took a step closer to me.

"I... I asked her if she knew you."

"Wait, what? What brought that on?" Esilas' eyes widened a little as he looked at me. "Why ask about me?"

His eyes then widened at the realization of the same possibility that I had thought of before.

"Do you... think she remembered Luxia?"

"From the way she looked at you, I would say she knows something." I confirmed. "She looked at you as though you were familiar to her, like she knew who you were."

"The hell she does." Esilas scoffed in disbelief. "I've never seen the damned woman before in my life."

"Sometimes that means nothing." Elderik suggested as he looked at me. "But... given everything we've seen, I think it's safe to say that we're missing something here..."

"I agree." I nodded.

"Well, for one, Lux can apparently see Luxia's ghost now." Esilas pointed out as he crossed his arms.

"Avaline mentioned she could see Luxia, too." I recalled. "Maybe there's something else she knows."

"Whoever killed Luxia and made everyone forget about her didn't think that the girl would be a threat." Esilas looked at me. "And it's clear that she trusts you."

"But where do we find her?" I asked. "The Estate is huge–"

"Let's check the scullery and the servants' quarters." Elderik suggested. "Someone must have seen her today."

"I'll go with Lux to check the servants' quarters to find her." Esilas looked at his comrade. "Check the scullery?"

"Will do." Elderik nodded. "I guess it goes without saying to be careful?" He queried as he looked from Esilas to me. "That goes for the both of you."

"Yeah..." I let out a sigh; "I figured that warning would have been more for me."

Elderik chuckled and put his hand on my head.

"Well, you do seem to accidentally make our jobs of protecting you harder." Esilas scoffed with a smirk.

"Okay, even if that's supposed to be a joke, that's hurtful." I pouted at him.

"I guess you'll have to find out whether or not it's a joke."

"Alright, you two, enough." Elderik chuckled. "You two can flirt when this is all over."

"We are *not* flirting." Esilas and I both said simultaneously.

Elderik simply chuckled, shaking his head with a knowing smile before leaving us to check the scullery.

The servants' quarters were located at the farthest side of the Royal Estate, separated by gender. Esilas and I asked the servants that weren't too busy to get directions, and we were led to the room that Avaline shared with Lita. Esilas had been about to open the door to their room, but I stopped him.

"Esilas, manners." I reminded him before knocking on the door.

The knocks reverberated through the quiet hallway but were followed by silence; there were no sounds coming from behind the door. Esilas and I shared a concerned look before I knocked on the door again.

"Lita? Avaline?" I called. "It's Luxahliah. Can I come in?"

Again, we were met with silence from the room.

"I don't get it." Esilas shook his head. "The other staff told us that we could find Avaline here. They both know you and your voice, so they should know it's safe for them to talk to us."

I knocked on the door again, this time a bit more frantically.

"Lita?! Avaline?!" I tried to turn the doorknob, but it wouldn't budge. "It's locked."

"Stand back." Esilas put his hand on my shoulder to gently pull me back.

He stood in front of the door, and with a swift kick, the door was blown off his hinges. I jumped a little and looked down the hall as Esilas entered the room. I looked back at Esilas.

"Was kicking the door down really necessary?!" I whispered urgently as I followed him inside.

I had just reached the threshold when Esilas put out his hand to stop me.

"Wait." He muttered. "Something isn't right."

"Esilas?" I watched as he looked around the room. His nostrils flared as he sniffed the air.

"I smell blood... but there's not a trace of it anywhere..." He muttered as he looked around again.

His head suddenly snapped towards one of the two beds in the room, and he immediately walked over to the bed and knelt down. He looked under the bed and then he shot back up.

"Lux, over here!" Esilas stood and violently flipped the bed out of the way.

I stepped closer, and I immediately covered my mouth to keep myself from screaming; underneath the bed was the lifeless body of Lita, clothed in a tattered, bloody, maidservant uniform.

"W-Wait..." I looked at Esilas, though he didn't look at me; "if she's dead here... then where is Avaline?!"

My query was not met with an answer as Esilas hesitantly turned her body over to see an expression of terror petrified on Lita's face, and there was the most nauseating detail that couldn't be ignored.

Lita's eyes had been carved out.

Just like the form that Luxia had taken when she was warning us.

As my heart pounded in my chest, pounding against my ribcage like a drum and throbbing in my ears, I let out a horrified scream.

16

Murmurs of the Butterfly Killer

THE DISCOVERY OF THE horrific murder had prompted a meeting of the Courts. Captain Ailgraym's men were to investigate the discovery of the murdered Lita, and since she was the chief nurse in the infirmary, I volunteered to take her place until they found another head nurse to take her place. Cassius was immediately concerned with my safety and that of Avaline.

"On top of a murder in the Royal Estate," Cassius looked pensive. "Avaline is missing. Could she have been kidnapped by the perpetrator?"

"Or she could be the killer." A noble suggested, which made me flinch at the implication.

But before I could say anything, Elderik spoke up.

"No, this is not a modus operandi a girl her age would be familiar with."

He looked around the Courts; the other Nobles weren't thrilled by him speaking up, but that didn't seem to be the whole of it. At Elderik's ominous words, the air seemed to become heavier and colder.

"You have no right to speak here, little Watch-Keeper." The Noble sneered.

"Silence." King Claustus' calm-yet-commanding voice sliced through the confidence of the Noble who had called out Elderik. "Please, continue with your testimony, Ser Elderik."

"Thank you, Your Grace." Elderik bowed his head in gratitude before continuing. "This signature has only been seen in one other place... the Outskirts of Obsiditourma... and it is one that my father is *very* familiar with."

The Courts erupted with murmurs at the realization, and a single name crept through the tense air of the throne room.

"It couldn't be... the Butterfly Killer?"

The Nobles whispered of the gruesome events and my skin went rigid with goosebumps; I was reminded of what Dargrin had told me of the murders, and more specifically, the creepy nursery rhyme that had been inspired by it. I rubbed my arms at the uncomfortable feeling that crept up my spine. I felt a cool hand touch my shoulder, and I nearly jumped out of my skin.

"Easy." Esilas whispered, and in his presence, I relaxed a little.

He wouldn't admit it, but he had become rather attentive.

"If this murder is like those unfortunate events," King Claustus started, silencing the Nobles once more, "then we need to confirm whether this is the original or simply a fanatic. Could you summon your father to autopsy the body and compare notes with Captain Ailgraym, Ser Elderik?"

"Of course, my king."

"What about Avaline?" I stepped forward, speaking up. "Whether this is the original killer or a deranged fanatic, she could be in danger."

"Fret not, child." The king reassured me. "We will search the Estate for the girl and secure the grounds for yours and my son's safety. And as such, Sers Esilas and Elderik are to not leave your side."

All I could do was thank the king for his consideration, and I could tell that Esilas was a bit relieved with the declaration; however, my mind swam with thoughts revolving around the gruesome murders and the nursery rhyme from my visions.

'Is the mastermind the same psychotic killer, or is he a disciple? And why would he restart his killing spree now?'

My blood then ran cold at another possibility.

'Was Luxia's murder part of his pattern?'

I looked at the Morgenstern monarchs, and my thoughts of the killer were replaced with a startling observation; while the king was stern in his declaration of improving security, Queen Elaine looked as pale as death, as though she had seen a ghost. If I hadn't known better, I would have thought that she was on the verge of a panic attack.

After the meeting of the Courts, Esilas and Elderik escorted me back to my room, and on the way, we conversed about the information conveyed.

“The queen looked as though she was about to drop dead.” I looked at Elderik. “I think we can rule her out as a suspect. We’re back to square one.”

“Every woman was scared to death of the Butterfly Killer back in those days.” He let out a sigh. “Even though all of his victims were women from the Outskirts, he still scared women, no matter their blood or race.”

“Are we really considering the possibility that the one who killed my sister is the Butterfly Killer?” Esilas asked. “Or even a disciple or a fanatic?”

“We can’t really dismiss it.” Elderik looked at his comrade. “It’s too coincidental that she was killed and then everyone was made to forget her.”

“But why go after Lita?” I wondered aloud. “She didn’t have any connection with Cassius or Duchess Mareene. And what about Avaline?”

“I’m not sure,” Elderik put his hand on my shoulder; “but we’ll find her.”

“I hate the possibility that this could either be the Butterfly Killer himself or his protégé.” Esilas spoke up. “He was one of the most ruthless monstrosities in the city, and either possibility is disturbing to think about.”

“Agreed.” Elderik nodded.

I had a question in my mind that I was afraid for them to answer, but I needed confirmation. I stopped walking, and they stopped, looking at me questioningly.

"Why... Why was he called the Butterfly Killer?" I asked as I looked at either of them.

The two comrades shared an uncomfortable look before Elderik looked at me.

"The moniker refers to what he called his victims." He explained. "He mocked the Guard and the Keepers of the Watch, calling his victims 'little butterflies'."

I shuddered as I once again recalled the dreary lullaby from my visions. I took a deep breath and gathered my thoughts.

"Alright," I started; "so, the mastermind might be a serial killer or his protégé, killed Lita and then kidnapped Avaline, and on top of all that, is experimenting on the Nobles and the Morgenstern Family with a poison made of unknown components—"

"And you're under the watchful eye of the Ebony Guard for your safety." Elderik added.

"Right... and that..." I hugged myself and rubbed my arms a little. "How would you describe the situation, exactly?"

"Well, that's all wrapped up in a nice little morsel, isn't it?" Esilas said nonchalantly. "If I didn't know any better, I would say we're fucked."

"Language, Esilas." Elderik muttered to his comrade before he looked at me. "So, what do you want to do now, Lux? What's the plan?"

I honestly didn't know how to answer his question; there were no strategies that came to mind, and certainly no thoughts on how to proceed. I shook my head, letting a sigh escape my nostrils.

"I don't know..." I whispered.

We continued walking to my room, and I half-wished that Luxia could come and help us solve this mystery, but I knew it would never be that easy.

Because of the Estate's security lockdown, Esilas and Elderik were charged with standing outside my door while I slept. I tried so desperately to sleep, but I was having a hard time doing so as I tossed and turned on the plush mattress that had seemed to turn into a stone slab. I let out a sigh of frustration and opened my eyes, looking at the pink moon that shone through the window. It was only a sliver of rose pink now, a sign that it was only a few days from leaving the night sky a lonely void.

'Elderik once told me that the stars disappeared when the *Aster-Bloods* were killed during the Trials.' I remembered. 'I wonder if those stars will ever return... or if they are gone forever...'

I closed my eyes once more, turning onto my back to get comfortable, but it didn't help. I tried to imagine the stars in the night sky so that I could dream, and I exhaled through my nose to center myself. So caught up was I in my thoughts that I didn't realize that there was another person in the room.

Not until a hand clamped over my mouth.

My eyes popped open as panic raced through my nerves. In the fading pale light of the crescent moon, I saw a pair of glowing eyes, the eyes of a first-generation.

"Lux, will ya stop your squirming?" I froze at the familiar voice, and I slowly made out the assailant's face. "It's me, Lux."

I nodded, though my body was still trembling. He withdrew his hand and quickly retreated from the bed, retreating to the shadows of the curtains that shone on the floor. I sat up and looked at him.

"Ephrem?" I whispered. "Where have you–?"

"Look, I don't have a lot of time." He whispered urgently, looking at the bookshelf with fear. "He'll call me back if I take too long with my task."

"Who, Ephrem?"

"Lux, you *have* to leave the Royal Estate." His head snapped back to me, his eyes wide with panic. "You can't look any further into Luxia's death. He'll kill my little sister if you don't leave!"

"But, Ephrem–"

"Lux, you don't get it!" He seethed as if he was strained. He clutched his head, his fingers grabbing at his hair. "It's *you* he wants!"

"But *who*, Ephrem?! Who is after me?!" I practically leapt from my bed to approach him, but he crawled backwards to keep his distance.

"Y-You don't understand!" He said, his voice raised, alerting Esilas and Elderik outside.

They struggled to open the door. It was locked.

"T-The man in white..." Ephrem struggled, grasping his head in pain. "H-He's a half-breed! T-This is a demon skill..!"

"Lux?! Why is the door locked?!" Esilas called from outside the door.

"Ephrem, please! Tell me who is behind this!"

Ephrem couldn't answer me, a cry of pain tearing from his throat as he threw his head back and his body rigid. Ephrem's cries suddenly went silent and his body seemed to loosen like he was a marionette. His eyes then locked onto me, glowing with a familiar pink-gold glow over his red hues.

"E-Ephrem.." I stepped back fearfully as I whimpered, tripping over the rug and falling onto my rear.

The first-generation looked at though he didn't see me but was looking at feeble prey. He pulled a dagger from his belt and moved to prepare a lunge.

"Death to all the High-Bloods."

"Esilas!" I screeched as I squeezed my eyes closed.

I heard the door break off its hinges as I waited for the pain. However, the air was silent. I peeked an eye open at the door, and I saw Esilas and Elderik standing frozen in their strides. I looked back at Ephrem, and my blood ran cold as tears formed in my eyes and threatened to spill over. Ephrem had foregone his attack on me and stabbed himself in the abdomen. The abnormal glow faded from his eyes as he looked at me, sweat forming on his brow.

"H-Heh… finally… I broke free…" He struggled to speak as he fell to his side. Esilas was quick to action, catching his comrade before he bled onto the floor.

"Ephrem, why?" He looked at him.

"She's important to you… i-isn't she, boss?" He looked up at the dhampir. "A-And she's one of us… w-we look out for each other…" The first-generation coughed up blood and I rose to my feet as he looked at me. "R-Right?"

"You're not dying on me, you idiot," Esilas made his younger comrade look at him. "So don't you dare talk like you're dying."

"And he won't die." I declared.

Esilas and Elderik looked at me, the former looking at me with wide eyes.

"Lux–?"

"Get him to the infirmary, and make sure no one sees you leave from here." I commanded. "I'm not losing another friend."

Esilas and Elderik looked at me with what seemed like awe, and then their eyes hardened with determination. They nodded and hastily left the room, Esilas carrying Ephrem in his arms. I grabbed my robe from the wardrobe and quickly followed them as I tied the sash around my waist.

'Ephrem was trying to warn me… he hurt himself trying to save me from the order he had been given.'

I broke into a run.

'And he broke himself free of whatever mind control he had been put under.'

I found myself filled with renewed determination; I was going to save Ephrem, and I would not give up on him.

17

An Important Clue

I FINISHED STITCHING EPHREM'S stab wound and placed a poultice to ward off infection. I carefully wrapped bandages around the first-generation vampire's waist to keep the poultice in place. I gently laid the unconscious Watch-Keeper down on the infirmary cot and let out a sigh of relief, proud of my somewhat hasty work.

"He'll be out for a while, thanks to Dargrin's sleeping tonic." I said as I looked at Esilas and Elderik with a soft smile. "He'll probably wake up tomorrow afternoon."

"While that is a relief," Esilas looked from his bedridden comrade to me. "We need to discuss the actual issue here. What the hell was Ephrem doing in your room?"

I looked at him and then at Ephrem, watching his chest rise and fall steadily.

"He was warning me." I answered. "He was telling me to leave the Royal Estate."

"And the knife to the gut?" The dhampir asked.

"He was fighting the mind control he'd been put under," I explained; "but he stopped himself from hurting me."

"It takes some serious mental restraint to fight hypnotic suggestion." Elderik mused as he held his chin in thought.

"There was something else." I mentioned as I looked back at the two of them. "Actually... there were two things."

"And those would be?" Esilas asked, crossing his arms.

"He mentioned that if I didn't leave, he'd kill her..." I said. "He was talking about Avaline... he mentioned her being his younger sister..."

"He must have seen her while he was under suggestion." Elderik said. "So, she's his younger sister... that's the reason she was taken... whoever did this knew how attentive you were to her."

"What was the second thing he mentioned?" Esilas asked.

"Ephrem gave us a clue about the mastermind... *the man in white...*" I took a deep breath and looked at them. "He said that he's a half-demon... and given that clue, it means that the prince must be the one who killed Luxia."

The two comrades looked at each other with wide eyes before looking at me in shock.

"Lux... are you absolutely sure about this?" Elderik asked, his voice low as a whisper.

"You said it yourself... half-breeds are rare..." I pointed out.

"We have to be sure... and considering Ephrem has been missing for nearly two months, his reappearance now immediately makes him a suspect."

Elderik's words were heavy. I knew the gravity of the situation, especially for Ephrem; if Cassius was the mastermind, he would know that Ephrem failed in his mission, and the first-generation vampire's failure would be the perfect scapegoat to throw the investigation off of the true identity of whoever was responsible.

"I know that we have to be sure..." I muttered; "but... Ephrem risked his life to keep himself from hurting me."

I rubbed my forehead a little; something still wasn't right.

'What is Cassius' motive? He and Luxia were so in love... I saw it myself... so why would he kill her?'

"We need to be careful." Esilas suggested. "I doubt that this will be the only threat sent to you."

I rubbed my arms, feeling an uncomfortable chill creep up my spine. The dhampir then sighed.

"But let's not worry about that right now." He walked over to me and took my hand. "You need to get some sleep."

"Esilas, we can't take her back to her room!" Elderik whispered urgently. "The door is off its hinges and not to mention the passageway—"

"It'll be suspicious if she's not found in her room," Esilas said as he gently pulled me behind him; "that being said, she can sleep in the guest room we were given. You can inform the guards that we fought off an assailant that attacked her and that we put her in our room to keep her safe, as is our duty."

"And what exactly are you planning, Esilas?" Elderik looked at him.

"I'm not taking any chances, so I'm staying in the same room with her." At his nonchalant declaration, my cheeks flushed red. When Elderik didn't—well, it was more like *couldn't*—say anything, Esilas continued to pull me behind him to the other guest room.

When Esilas and I arrived back at the guest room they'd been given, the dhampir let go of my hand and walked over to the window seat. I looked around the room the two men shared; it was similar to mine, though it was sparing in furniture and had two beds instead of one. I looked back at Esilas, my cheeks still red from his declaration.

"E-Esilas—"

"You can sleep in my bed." He didn't look at me as he pointed to the messier of the two beds. "I'll sleep on the window seat."

"Esilas, that isn't fair to you. You need your sleep as well, and the window seat can't be all that comfortable—"

"Don't argue with me."

"I'm not arguing. I—"

"Then what are you suggesting, Lux?"

"Sleep beside me!"

The words escaped my mouth with little thought on my part, and his head snapped towards me. Our frustration towards each other's stubbornness disappeared in the silence that filled the room, his eyes so wide that it appeared they would pop out of his skull at any moment and my cheeks becoming redder.

"Why would you suggest that?" He stood from the window seat. "This situation is slightly more precarious than at the barracks, and that is a drastic understatement."

I looked down a little, a bit embarrassed by my abrasiveness. I heard Esilas let out a sigh as he walked over to his bed.

"Come on." He said. "I'll only stay by your side until you fall asleep."

I looked at him as he sat down on one side of his bed and discarded his boots. I took a deep breath, hesitating a little before I took off the robe and climbing into the bed with Esilas. I pulled the covers up to my chin, but once again, I tossed and turned in frustration.

"For the Gods' Tree's sake, will you relax?" Esilas sighed. I looked at him over my shoulder; his back was to me.

"S-Sorry." I whispered as I turned back around, curling a little.

The air was so tense that I could barely breathe. I closed my eyes, trying to clear my mind. I then felt the mattress sink with Esilas' weight as he moved, and I turned a little to look at him, only for his arms to wrap around my waist and his head nuzzled at the nape of my neck.

"Don't look at me like that." I felt Esilas' warm breath against my skin, causing a ripple of goosebumps to erupt across my skin. “No matter how much I try, I can never seem to say no to you.” He whispered.

“Esilas...?”

“Shhh,” he whispered. “Just... go to sleep...”

I was reminded of that night in the barracks when Esilas’ hunger struck him and I offered my help. The memory brought a bashful smile to my face. I reached my hand down to gently hold his hand around my waist.

“Thank you for this, Esilas.” I whispered. “I’m sorry for making things difficult at times.”

The dhampir moved his hand to intertwine his fingers with mine and sliding it to beside my head.

“It’s only difficult because you have no sense of self-preservation.” He chuckled lightly as he nuzzled my neck. “But it wouldn’t be love if I didn’t want to be there whenever you need me.”

I gently squeezed his fingers in between mine and closed my eyes.

“That’s rather poetic of you.” I mused.

“Well, I was tutored by someone with an expensive education.” He joked back.

I felt the smile on my lips widen to the point my cheeks were sore as a giggle escaped my throat. A thought then came to mind, one that made me bite my lip.

‘Should I—?’

I thought no more about it; I chose to act. I turned a little to face him.

"Esilas—"

I was never able to completely turn around or finish my sentence; the dhampir had moved faster than I could register to pin the hand he'd been holding above my head as he hovered over me, his lips pressed against mine. I closed my eyes, surrendering myself to the kiss as his other hand held the small of my back and lightly played with the strings at the back of my nightdress. He pulled away, his breath fanning against my lips as he looked at me with his glowing red-amber eyes. His pale tan cheeks were dusted with a bit of red; whether it was from embarrassment or from the sudden heat in the room, I wasn't sure. The hand that had been holding mine gently ran feather-like touches down my arm to my shoulder, and he stroked my cheek.

"Lux... I wish so much that I could take you away from this place." He whispered, gently running his thumb over my lips. "I don't think that I could continue living if something happened to you."

I reached up to caress his cheek, his black-to-ashen hair tickling my fingers and knuckles. His eyes fluttered closed, and he held my hand once more. He turned his head to press his lips against my palm and soon pressed more kisses down the inside of my wrist up to my forearm, warming my skin as it prickled with excited chill bumps. I gently ran my fingers through his hair as he continued pressing kisses against my skin. He stopped then and looked at me.

"I have no right to ask this," he murmured as he nuzzled my skin; "but I want you to consider it."

I looked at him and tilted my head a little.

"Consider what?" I asked, my voice just above a tender whisper.

Esilas hovered over me once more, his eyes staring into mine and reflecting every ounce of seriousness and passion in his being.

"Marry me." He whispered, almost pleading. "When all of this is over... I want you to marry me."

My heart skipped a beat at his words, my chest swelling with warmth. I smiled and nodded, ecstatic tears forming in my eyes.

"Yes." I breathed. "Yes, I will marry you."

Esilas smiled as a shaky sigh of relief escaped his lungs, and he gently wiped the tears from my eyes. He feverishly pressed his lips against mine in a passionate kiss.

"Say it again." He whispered in between kisses as his lips trailed down my neck, his fingers working to untie the strings at the back of my nightdress.

"I'll marry you." I breathed as I ran my fingers through his hair, entangling them as his hot breath warmed my skin.

"Again." He whispered as he kissed my pulse point, the night dressing loosening.

"I'll marry you."

Every time I repeated it, he breathed sighs of relief against my skin as he pressed feather-like kisses with his soft lips. As clothes were discarded, we explored each other, his touches burning ardent passion against my skin as he nestled between my legs.

Touches became squeezes and caresses.

The gentle raking of nails against skin became subtle clawing, which caused minor scratches that elicited hisses of pleasure from either of us.

Muscles constricted against muscles, and sighs lightly echoed through the darkness of that room as we surrendered to each other's embrace.

We lay in the room, illuminated by faint pink moonlight, the dhampir at my side still laying gentle kisses against my skin and his fingertips tracing patterns on my bare hip and upper thigh. I could feel the curve of his lips at my reactions to his touch. He was smiling. It was the first happy smile I had ever experienced from the man.

"I don't know if it's because of your nature or just you being you," he murmured before looking up at me, his eyes glowing faintly in the faint light, "but I don't think I could resist you after tonight."

My cheeks flushed with color, and when I'd been about to turn my face away in embarrassment, he turned my head back to look me in the eye.

"Don't turn away." He muttered, gently wrapping his arms around my waist and laying his chin on my bare sternum. "I want to keep looking at your beautiful face."

"Even if I fall asleep?" I asked, shyly.

"Either way," he chuckled softly, his fangs protruding in his smile, "I get to see that face of a goddess, my precious star-fire."

It was odd to hear Esilas be so poetic in his words, but it was a sentiment I enjoyed. And only I would be the one to hear such words from his lips. I ran my fingertips over the contours of his face. The dhampir's eyes fluttered closed and leaned against my touch, pressing his lips against my palm.

"Will you say the words again?" I asked.

His lips curved into a smile once more.

"I love you." His words were soft in the air, but they echoed ever so loudly in my ears, and I could feel my heart warm with those words' truth.

He loved me. He truly loved me.

"I love you, too." I whispered in return, relieved that I could finally say the words that had been on my heart since I first realized what he meant to me.

Esilas looked at me and then nestled into my side, nuzzling his nose into my hair and inhaling my scent.

"I've kept you up long enough, my star-fire." He murmured. "Go to sleep. I won't leave your side."

"Promise?" I asked, feeling sleep begin to take hold of me just as tightly as Esilas' arms around my torso.

Esilas gave a tired chuckle.

"I promise with every fiber in my being." He confirmed as one of his hands slid into mine, intertwining our fingers as we both fell into a loving and well-deserved sleep.

18

New Confidence

THE NEXT MORNING, I awoke with the white sun glistening through the windows, softly brightening the room in a delicate light. I turned my head towards the light, and at one of the windows, Esilas sat at the window seat, wearing everything except his uniform coat. The way he stood reminded me of the portrait of Lucien Morgenstern, and I smiled at how proud he seemed to hold himself as compared to before. I sat up a little, holding the covers over my naked chest.

"Good morning." I broke the peaceful silence of the room, and the dhampir turned to me. His lips widened into an amused smile.

"Well, you certainly look like you slept well." He chuckled softly as he walked over to the bed and sat on the edge. "How are you feeling this morning? You seemed to sleep rather blissfully."

He gently reached to tuck a lock of hair behind my ear, and I leaned against his hand as I smiled bashfully.

"No dreams or visions, so I slept well." I whispered as I moved to kiss his palm.

Esilas' gentle hand slowly crept to the back of my head, and he leaned in, touching his forehead to mine.

"You should get dressed before we're found out." He said teasingly.

"Oh, you're way too late for that."

We snapped our heads towards the entrance of the guest room to find Elderik leaning against the door with his arms crossed.

"You two should be thankful that *I* was the one to find you like this and not another, like a guard or a gossiping maidservant."

My eyes widened as I shyly pulled the covers up closer to my chin to hide myself.

"E-Elderik—"

"A lecture will come for *you* later." He pushed himself off the door, not letting me continue. "For now, get dressed so we can escort you to breakfast."

He laid a set of my clothes at the foot of the bed. I'm not sure if Elderik was disappointed in me or angry with Esilas, but I had a feeling that it was both. Elderik looked at Esilas.

Elderik wasn't smiling; it was a bit unnerving to see the usually kind man not smiling.

"Let's leave her to get dressed. We need to talk."

Esilas stood from his spot on the bed and joined his comrade outside the room for their talk. Despite the embarrassment of Elderik discovering us—along with the muffled lecture I could hear him giving Esilas outside the door—I couldn't help but smile, remembering every tender and loving touch that we had shared as they lingered on my skin. I filed those memories away, but made sure that I could easily recall them whenever I needed a smile. Esilas told me he loved me, and I was able to say the words back. I fixed the pin on my bow and tied my hair in its signature bun before I turned to leave the guest room. I opened the door just as Elderik was speaking.

"All I'm saying is that when I told you to finally admit your feelings for the girl, I didn't mean to bed her!" Elderik whispered frantically.

Esilas was calm compared to his panicking comrade. I blinked and then cleared my throat.

"Am... am I interrupting something?" I asked, the two turning to look at me.

Elderik composed himself with a tired sigh.

"No... it was just a conversation," he rubbed his eyes, letting an exhale escape his nose. "But, enough of that. Let's go before we're late."

He walked ahead of us, and I looked at Esilas.

"You're... I didn't get you in trouble, did I?" I whispered as we walked side by side with Esilas after Elderik.

"No, nothing like that... well, not really." He chuckled. "Let's just say that he's more concerned about the risk we're taking than he is actually being upset about the risk itself."

"Well, you did say that we needed to be cautious moving forward, Esilas." I mentioned. "And... last night wasn't exactly us minding that caution..."

"There's that... and there's the fact that he thinks of you as a little sister." He whispered.

"Wait, what?" I looked at him.

"It's true. He is rather protective of you, and you're like family to him." He explained in a whisper. "So, he's still a bit... shocked."

"I would say shocked is an understatement." I muttered, making the dhampir beside me chuckle.

"Well, you're not wrong."

"You *do* realize that I can hear you both, right?" Elderik looked back at us. "Don't make me separate, you two."

His brotherly behavior made Esilas laugh while I fought to control mine. The banter was just as lively as it had been when I first met the three Watch-Keepers in the Pale Woods.

'Is it wrong for me to wish that things stay like this forever?'

For the first time since I'd woken up in that field, I found myself thinking and dreaming of a future where Esilas and I were married with a family, a child growing up in a warm home with Dahliah and Dargrin to dote on them and no doubt spoiled by Elderik. I felt a warmth in my heart, a desire to see that wish come to fruition, not just for me but for Esilas as well.

"All joking aside," Elderik said, "I informed Captain Ailgraym and the king and queen about Ephrem."

I looked at him in surprise.

"Elderik—!"

"It's not what you think, Lux," he said. "I did not name Ephrem as your attacker, but rather the one who had been tracking the assassin and took the hit for you."

His elaboration made me feel better about how Ephrem would be treated, but only a bit; the first-generation vampire would still be under suspicion because of the failed attempt on Cassius' life, but for now, he would be given sanctuary.

That was my hope, anyway.

"My father is also here. He met with me before I came to find you for breakfast." He looked at me. "He's going to be performing the autopsy on Lita's body, and he's agreed to keep us in the loop about what he finds out."

At the mention of the autopsy, I felt a chill run up my spine; I hated the idea of having to cut her up even more to find out how she died, but I knew that if I left things as they were, then greater disasters could befall the Royal Estate. Luxia's spirit would never be at rest if I decided to give up now. I took a deep breath as we continued forward.

"Let's hope that the autopsy will provide us with the clues we need to catch the mastermind."

When the three of us arrived at the dining room, I was surprised to find that Cassius wasn't there, and his absence was only solidifying the possibility of him being the one behind Luxia's murder.

“Where is Prince Cassius?” I asked, looking at the Morgenstern king and queen.

“He requested to lead the investigation of the assassin that attacked you last night.” King Claustus informed. “He should be here soon to take a break with the family before returning to his work."

'Is Cassius leading the investiation... or is he covering his tracks?’ I wondered to myself as I looked at the queen; she was looking at us, too, though she said nothing.

“You, Sers Esilas and Elderik,” the king addressed my comrades, bringing me out of my thoughts. “You have our thanks for protecting Luxahliah and driving off the one who tried to kill her. The boy will have our thanks as well as soon as he awakens.”

“I was told that you mended the boy’s wounds, Luxahliah,” the queen finally spoke said. "He’ll make a full recovery thanks to your work.”

Queen Elaine still seemed rather distant, even though she was looking straight at us. She’d been distant since the meeting of the Courts and the discussion of the Butterfly Killer. Her fear of the name stemmed from more than just a fear that all women had around that gruesome time.

‘Why... does it seem like she’s—’

“Well, come and sit, you three.” The king’s invitation to sit broke me out of my thoughts, and Esilas pulled out my chair for me to sit down. "You seem in better spirits, Luxahliah. It is good to see you becoming more like your starling self again."

Elderik looked as though he was about to choke on air while Esilas calmly sat down next to me, not paying any mind to the king's words. Elderik sat next to the queen, though his eyes were adhered to the two of us as if begging us to not be conspicuous.

'Well, *that* behavior won't raise any alarms.' I thought sarcastically to myself.

I had been about to say something to answer the king when the prodigal prince walked into the dining room.

"My apologies for my tardiness, everyone." Cassius spoke, and then he noticed my presence and greeted me with a kind smile. "Luxahliah, I'm glad that you are feeling better."

His words were sweet, but they were nothing like Esilas', and at the memory of the night before, my cheeks dusted with a bit of pink.

"Thank you." I tried not to stutter as I straightened my back.

Cassius sat down next to me, and I felt Esilas become tense; I didn't have to be touching him to know that every muscle in his body constricted with the disagreeable circumstances.

"Well, now that everyone is here, let us eat." Queen Elaine said, clearing her throat as if she was trying to compose herself.

The king was the first to eat, and I had been about to take a bite of the delicious food as well when Esilas quickly stopped my hand from grabbing the silverware. I looked at him, his eyes seeming to glare at the food on my plate.

"Esilas?" I whispered. "What is it?"

"Don't eat anything from this table." He whispered as he leaned over to me; "something isn't right... this smell—"

The clatter of silverware and the gurgled sounds of choking immediately drew our attention to King Claustus as he fell from his seat, spasming on the floor. Queen Elaine leapt from her seat with a shriek, and time seemed to slow for me as my heartbeat throbbed painfully in my ears. All at once, the memory of my failure to save the duchess Mareene resurfaced in my mind.

"Lux...!"

A muffled voice called out, but I couldn't respond. I felt panic paralyze every nerve in my body.

"Lux..!"

My throat was so tight that I couldn't make a sound.

"Lux!" I was brought out of my recollection by Esilas as his voice now rang loud and clear.

The dhampir's cool hands gently cradled my face as he looked me in the eye.

"Lux, listen to me. Only you can help him." He whispered.

I looked at him with wide eyes.

"B-But... you said—"

"Fuck what I said before." He whispered. "It's in your nature to care so deeply about others... so I won't stop you anymore."

He leaned in close and pressed a kiss against my forehead, as if he was releasing me from a spell. I felt revived at his words and I looked up at him, as if to make sure that I was hearing him right. He nodded and then helped me stand from my seat. I took a deep breath and looked at the scene.

"Elderik, get Cassius and Queen Elaine out of here." I said as I rolled up my sleeves.

The vampire looked at me from the king's side, his eyes wide.

"Lux, what are you thinking?"

"I'm thinking that self preservation just took a swan dive out that window." I said as I took a knife from the table, shocking Cassius as he realized what I was about to do.

"Wait, Luxahliah, don't—!"

"Sorry, but I'm not going to listen to you." I held up my hand to him. "Elderik, get them out of here now, and tell Dargrin that I'll need help."

Elderik had been about to protest, but Esilas stopped him, kneeling beside him and putting a hand on his shoulder.

"Just do it." He said. "I'll stay by her side and make sure she doesn't do anything drastic."

Elderik gave a frustrated sigh of defeat and quickly ushered the queen and the prince out of the dining room. I quickly knelt by the king's side, his eyes bleeding red as he looked at me with fear. His blood vessels had already begun to bruise themselves in a sickly dull bluish-purple.

'He ingested the poison like the duchess had,' I realized; 'so pouring it into his mouth won't do any good.'

I looked at the knife and then took a deep breath to steel my nerves. I had to work fast.

"Just a warning," I spoke up as I took the king's hand in mind; "I'm not really sure this is going to work."

Esilas looked at me.

"Wait, what—hey, hey, whoa, whoa, whoa!" He raised his voice as I squeezed the king's hand in mind and then stabbed the knife through our joined hands.

I felt a small stream of blood dribble from my lip and down my chin; I had bitten my lip so hard to keep from screaming out that I had made myself bleed. Esilas looked at me with wide eyes.

"L-Lux... what the hell—?!"

"Ingesting the poison causes excessive bleeding, anaphylactic shock and subsequent vomiting and foaming at the mouth." I seethed through the pain as I looked at Esilas. "If I had tried to give him my blood through his mouth, he would have never gotten it into his bloodstream."

"And stabbing your hand is the route you went with?!" Esilas spoke frantically. "You really have thrown self-preservation out the window."

"I believe I said that it took a swan dive out the window." I pointed out, my voice strained from the pain.

"That's not the point, Lux!" He said, panicking. "How does stabbing your hand save him from dying from the poison?!"

"The adrenaline from his body trying to fight what's happening to him is forcing his heart to beat faster," I explained, feeling oddly calm as the sharp pain became more of a throbbing ache; "which will force the poisoned blood out through the wound, and my cut hand pressed against his will introduce my blood into his system, circulating it."

"Blood-letting and an improvised blood transfusion." He realized. "But you said that this may not work."

"At most, this will slow the poison until Elderik comes back with Dargrin." I elaborated. "I'll be able to help him properly in the infirmary."

King Claustus had long since been unconscious, and I had feared that we had been too late when I witnessed a miracle; the coloring of his blood vessels had begun to fade, but they hadn't disappeared completely. I gave a sigh of relief and I slowly pulled the knife out of our hands. It was slow and painful, and I couldn't help but whimper at the pain. Once I had pulled the knife all the way out and it clattered to the floor, Esilas quickly came to my side and held my injured hand.

"Dammit, Lux... you could have crippled yourself..." He scolded as he huffed.

I smiled softly at him despite the sweat on my brow, and I tenderly moved my fingers.

"There's a bit of pain, but I can still move them." I said.

Esilas chuckled with a tired sigh and then tenderly wrapped my hand, placing a tender kiss on my knuckles.

"You really are reckless." He said, a strained smile on his lips as he tried to chuckle.

He looked at me and then leaned in, gently licking the small stream of blood from my chin. I simply smiled, not minding the faint heat that flushed in my cheeks.

He helped me wrap the king's hand just as the doors were thrown open by Elderik, Dargrin, and Captain Ailgraym and his men.

"Luxahliah..." Dargrin breathed as I looked at them.

"It's the same poison that killed Duchess Mareene." I explained. "I had to blood-let him a bit, and thankfully, it slowed the poison, but we need to get him to the infirmary."

Captain Ailgraym acted quickly, ordering his men to lift the Morgenstern monarch gently onto a gurney to carry him out of the dining room. Esilas helped me stand, and I followed behind them. Dargrin stopped me, gesturing to my hand. I shook my head.

"I'll explain later." I whispered before we followed behind the captain's men.

I saw Queen Elaine's face as we passed her and Cassius on our way out of the dining room; there was a look of realization in her eyes. I knew very well that this risk might reveal my nature as an *Aster-Blood*, but it didn't bother me like it would have before. I'd saved a life, and that was what mattered.

And more importantly, if the mastermind of this plot was going to send messages, then I would, too.

My message was loud and clear.

Come and catch me. I am not afraid.

19
A Telling Detail

THANKFULLY, I WAS ABLE to stabilize King Claustus' condition with the help of Elderik and Dargrin; the Morgenstern patriarch was in a deep sleep, a hypodermic needle in his arm to transfuse his blood, cleansing it of the effects of the poison. I watched his steady breathing as Dargrin properly treated my hand.

"That was some quick thinking, child," Dargrin said as he finished cleaning the wound, the antiseptic stinging lightly around the cut. "Though, I do believe there might have been easier ways to improvise a transfusion other than stabbing yourself through you own hand."

"Yeah... Esilas thought the same thing..."

I flinched again and looked at him as he wrapped a thin poultice around my hand and secured it with a bandage.

"Still, it was that rash decision that saved the king's life." Dargrin said as he tapped my chin up with a smile. "Very well done."

"It was honestly just luck." I said, looking at my bandaged hand. "I didn't know if it would work... but I wanted to try..."

"And that courage to try is what makes us skilled physicians." Dargrin said. "We are not always going to be able to save them all, but we fearlessly move forward to do all that is in our ability."

I smiled at his philosophically inspirational words.

"That makes me feel better, at least." I thanked him.

Dargrin nodded, but soon after, his usually kind face turned serious. He leaned in a little.

"We need to talk about the girl's corpse." He whispered to me.

The last time I'd seen Dargrin Passor so serious was when I had told him about my visions. My back straightened on instinct and nodded my head.

"What did you find?" I whispered. "Was Lita... was she killed by the Butterfly Killer? And what about the poison that Elderik brought to you to analyze?"

"That's the odd thing," He answered cryptically; "I looked into the poison, but there wasn't anything pharmacological about it. No belladonna or deadly nightshade. As for Lita's body, that's an even more odd mystery."

"What do you mean?" I asked.

"That girl's body shows the same signs of heavy mutilations and assault, just like the other victims..." Dargrin paused.

"But...?"

"The original Butterfly Killer never took the eyes of his victims... and the amount of hemorrhaging would suggest that the poor girl was *alive* when he extracted them."

The thought of Lita's last moments made me sick to my stomach.

"So... this isn't the original?" I muttered, my voice shaking slightly.

"This had to be a disciple." He said. "My only question is... how did he stop her from screaming out? Her throat wasn't slit."

"Hypnosis." I immediately answered, coming to a rather chilling realization. "The one who killed Luxia... he's able to hypnotize and rewrite memories... it's why no one but Avaline remembers her. Because of the slit throat scar on her neck, she wasn't seen as a threat."

"Avaline is the missing girl, yes?"

"She is..." I confirmed and then looked at Ephrem's still sleeping body. "And... she's Ephrem's little sister... she's the reason Ephrem tried to warn me to get me away from the Estate... she was taken as a warning... a bargaining chip." I looked back at Dargrin. "Ephrem risked his life to give us a clue about the mastermind. He's a half-demon—"

Dargrin suddenly put his hands on my shoulders, startling at me a little.

"Lux, you have to leave this place."

"What? I can't just leave Avaline to—"

"If what Ephrem says corroborates what you and the others have found out, then could very well be coming after you next." Dargrin quietly argued. "You *have* to leave the Royal Estate."

His urgency scared me so much that I had no choice but to agree. I nodded without saying a word, and Dargrin put his hand on my cheek and kissed the top of my head. He let me leave the infirmary, and I walked with hurried footsteps to go and find Esilas and Elderik.

'I'm not running. There's something that isn't right.'

I couldn't shake the feeling that Dargrin knew something about this entire ordeal.

'Does he know who's behind this? Why would he tell us to leave when he could help us?'

I turned a corner and suddenly found the morning-lit corridor turned to pitch black. My body felt light, a sensation I recognized immediately; I was pulled into another vision at the worst possible moment.

In the still darkness of the vision, a single candle flame illuminated a familiar work table. I clenched my fists, gathering my courage to approach. The still air became cooler as the same sickening nursery rhyme fluttered in a haunting tune.

"The spider said to the butterfly;

'Let our love ensnare you

Like the threads of my beautiful web!'

And the butterfly said;

'I cannot stay,

For the wind is my love,

And I am destined to fly away.'"

Chill bumps prickled along my skin as fear continued to tap its way up my spine.

"And then the spider sighed.

'Oh, my beautiful butterfly,

Your destiny is to die,

My dead butterfly bride!'"

The silhouette of the mastermind was there, scraping his knife along the whetstone as he sang. He paused and let out a sigh.

"Aster-Bloods *are the purest beings.*" He stared, his voice sounding uncomfortably elated. "*It was believed for the longest time that only humans could be born with a Heart-Mark, but for a* dhampir *to be born with that trait! Oh, what a development!*"

My heartbeat pounded in my ears, and my stomach churned with nausea at the man's sickening ecstasy. I suddenly found my line of sight to be horizontal, and I couldn't move. The man got up from his worktable and turned to me. Shadows covered his face as he walked towards me.

Panic surged through my veins as my heart beat louder and louder.

"If I cut into this smooth flesh, I wonder what I will find."

'Stop it...' I tried screaming, but I wasn't able to move.

I couldn't even close my eyes to shut out the presence of the malevolent entity before me.

'Stop it!'

My heart thudded against my chest as it tightened with panic. The mastermind sang that creepy nursery rhyme once more, and the sound of cutting flesh — *my* cutting flesh — reached my ears.

'Stop it, please!'

"*Lux!*"

I heard a familiar voice, one that drowned out the nightmarish scene and sensations before me, even though the voice was an echo.

"*Lux, snap out of it!*"

'That voice... Esilas?'

"*Lux, please, wake up!*"

"*Pretty little butterfly*▯" The mastermind hummed, his voice far more sinister than before.

"Esilas!" I could finally scream, and I squeezed my eyes shut.

A feeling like electricity surged through my nerves, and I opened my eyes to blinding white light. I was frozen with panic, but there was a familiar warmth wrapped around me.

"Shhh, Lux." Esilas' voice whispered soothingly as his fingers combed through my hair. "It's alright, Lux. You're safe."

His presence eased my panicked breathing; the adrenaline that had been coursing through me ebbed away slowly.

"Esilas..." I muttered.

He pulled away and looked at me, moving his hand to gently caress my cheek. My vision cleared, and I saw Elderik, Captain

Ailgraym, and Cassius standing at the door of Esilas' and Elderik's guest room.

"We had been investigating in the kitchen about the poison, and Esilas just ran out towards the infirmary." Elderik mentioned. "It was as if he sensed your distress."

"And he nearly pushed me out of the way while he was running down the corridor." Cassius added.

I looked at Esilas, and I could see how worried he had been.

"I—"

"Don't even think about apologizing." Esilas whispered, seeming to have read my thoughts. "You have nothing to apologize for. Not for your visions or anything else."

"Wait, visions?" Cassius asked.

"What visions, Luxahliah?" Captain Ailgraym added.

I realized then that Cassius and the captain were the only ones who knew nothing about my visions. I looked at Elderik, who gave a sigh and then nodded. He had been about to answer when Esilas took it upon himself to answer their questions.

"She's been having visions of Luxia." He explained. "Someone in the Estate killed her and made everyone forget about her."

Esilas' blatant summary of the situation silenced the room. The captain looked as though he was about to crumble into rubble, but before he could even say anything, the Morgenstern fell to his knees. His pale skin seemed to turn completely white and his gold eyes trembled with recognition.

"That name..." he breathed shakily as tears formed and streamed down his face. "Say that name again..." He pleaded as if he had been trying to grasp at it in his mind.

"Prince Cassius?" Captain Ailgraym looked at the prince, concerned with his lost composure, and from the three of us who knew the most about the situation, I answered him.

"Luxia... she's Esilas' twin sister and the captain's daughter..." I spoke as I stood from the bed. "She was an *Aster-Blood...* and she and her unborn child were murdered."

My elaboration brought Cassius' entire world crumbling down.

Literally.

The Morgenstern prince grabbed at his hair, screaming her name over and over as he cried out in pain. After his display of intense mourning and anguish, Cassius' eyes rolled into the back of his head and he fell forward. Elderik was quick to catch him. All eyes turned towards me, and Captain Ailgraym finally spoke.

"Luxahliah, what the hell is going on?"

We made sure that only Dargrin was in the infirmary as we brought Cassius to him. The elder Passor looked at me with wide eyes.

"Lux, I told you to get out of the Estate."

"I can't, Dargrin." I said as I pointed to a bed for Esilas and Elderik to settle the unconscious prince in. "This confirms something that I've been thinking for a while now."

"Luxahliah, you still have to explain yourself." Captain Ailgraym said. "What is this all about?"

I took a deep breath and turned to the four men.

"Someone in the Royal Estate is behind the poisonings, Luxia's murder, and Lita's gruesome mutilation." I began. "They've been playing everyone as pawns. No one in the Estate remembers Luxia... no one except for Avaline, who wasn't seen as a threat because they thought she was mute."

"But I thought we suspected Cassius–" Elderik began.

"That's where we got it wrong... no, where *I* got it wrong." I looked at him as I corrected our previous assumptions. "Cassius remembers the emotions he had for Luxia even though he was made to forget her like everyone else had. He couldn't be the one behind all of this... and before Ephrem gave us the clue he risked his life for, I honestly thought that it could have been Queen Elaine..."

"Wait, why did you suspect the queen?" Dargrin asked, his crimson eyes wide at my confession of the queen's suspicion.

"I was suspicious because of something I noticed on the first morning that I had breakfast with the Morgensterns." I explained. "She looked as though she knew Esilas, but when I asked her about it, she seemed spooked. She was there when Duchess Mareene died, and when her husband was poisoned in the same manner, she had that same expression of fear. I don't think that she's that good an actress."

"But the queen and Cassius were the only two suspects we had," Esilas said; "and the only clues we have are Avaline's clue to beware of the man in white and Ephrem saying that the mastermind is half demon." He then blinked and then crossed his arms. "And from the look you have on your face, can I be correct to assume that you have another suspect in mind?"

"No, not a suspect." I shook my head. "I have a question." I said as I turned to Dargrin, whose eyes widened. "You know who the mastermind is... don't you, Dargrin?"

"L-Lux, what are you saying?" Elderik asked frantically. "Are you seriously accusing my father?!"

"No, I know he didn't do this." I explained. "What I *am* saying is that he knows who's behind this entire plot."

"That's absurd!"

"I told him about the Spider and the Butterfly nursery rhyme when it first showed up in my visions." I never took my eyes off Dargrin. "And when we exchanged information after he told me about Lita's autopsy, he panicked. I mentioned to him that the mastermind was able to hypnotize people and rewrite their memories. He told me that I needed to leave."

Dargrin looked as though he was close to tears.

"Dargrin, please... you told me to leave so that I would be safe... you did that because you know who killed Luxia and Lita, and is also behind the poisonings... didn't you?"

Dargrin was silent for a long time while Elderik kept saying that it was impossible for him to know anything. Before

Dargrin could even say anything to either defend himself or confirm my hypothesis, an Ebony Guardsman burst through the doors of the infirmary.

"Captain Ailgraym!" He cried. "The Passor Clinic is on fire, and it's spreading throughout the Mid-City!"

I snapped my head toward the guard.

"Dahliah... and Tana and Twiny..." I muttered, feeling panic tighten my chest.

"Luxahliah, stay here with the prince." Captain Ailgraym commanded. "We'll make sure that the citizens are evacuated."

"W-Wait, I can't just—"

Before I could finish my protest, a pair of lips pressed against mine. It took a moment for me to realize that it was Esilas kissing me in front of everyone, and when I finally did, my cheeks flushed bright red. The dhampir pulled away, gently stroking my cheek with his thumb.

"Stay here, Lux." He whispered. "You can treat any injured citizens we bring here to the Estate. You're the famed human physician, remember?" He smiled softly at me. He touched his forehead to mine, his smile fading into a concerned curve. "Please... just *stay* here..."

The pleading tone of his voice made it impossible for me to refuse him. I let a defeated sigh escape my nose, and I nodded.

Esilas sighed with relief before kissing my forehead as if he were a soldier going off to war, and without another word, he left with Elderik, Captain Ailgraym and Dargrin. I let myself collapse in a seat between Cassius' and Ephrem's beds, unable to do anything but wait.

20
Queen Elaine

Sitting still didn't last long for me, so I resorted to pacing around the infirmary in relentless worry. Apart from the imminent danger that Dahliah and the twins were in, Cassius showed no signs of waking up. I looked out the window, and it was there that I noticed something odd. The guard had said that there was a fire rampant in the Mid-City.

Fire produces smoke.

And I saw none.

There wasn't any smoke that could be seen from the window in the infirmary.

'Can I just not see the smoke? No, I should be able to see it.' I bit my lip. 'What the hell is going on?'

My heart skipped a beat in terror at a singular possibility.

'Wait... could this be—?'

In my frantic worry, I was trapped in my thoughts, so when the doors to the infirmary opened, I nearly jumped out of my skin.

My hopes of the doors revealing Esilas were sorely dashed as Queen Elaine showed himself.

"Q-Queen Elaine.." I addressed her.

The woman didn't answer me; she simply walked over to son's bedside and put her hand on his forehead.

"My dear boy... I never wanted you to be in such pain..." In response to her words, I was on guard. She looked up at me with sad eyes. "He remembers, doesn't he? He remembers Luxia."

My eyes widened, and I suddenly recalled a part of one of my visions, the silhouettes of two people talking in the corridor after Luxia's corpse had been discovered.

"You were the one who asked that everyone forget about her... even your own son—"

"And with good reason." She said defensively, snapping her head towards me. "He would have mourned himself to death over the loss of her and her child."

"You requested that he'd forget about her because he loved her so much?" I asked.

"It was more than just that." She said as she took the seat by her son's bed. "It was a fated bond. *Animae nexum.* You should know something about that, considering the relationship you and the Solani boy have."

Her defensiveness had become more apparent, and it confused me.

"Why are you suddenly so hateful toward me?"

"Because you're not supposed to know the truth."

"What truth?"

"Luxia's murder... the conversation you've implied that you overheard when her corpse was discovered..." She looked at me. "Do you know because you're an *Aster-Blood*?" I didn't even have time to answer before she spoke once more. "I've known about you since the incident at the Soiree... when my son came running to the Estate with you in his arms and those two Watch-Keepers behind you."

"And yet you told no one." I pointed out. "Even though it's law that anyone who keeps the existence of an *Aster-Blood* is sentenced to death." I narrowed my eyes at her. "This isn't just about your son, is it? If I didn't know any better, I would think that you hated Luxia... but why?"

"Hate her?" Queen Elaine stood up. "I *loved* Luxia! She was Mariam's daughter!"

My eyes widened at her declaration.

"Mariam...? But how do you—?" I paused as I came to a startling realization. "Mariam is your sister... the one that you grew the strawberries in your garden for."

Queen Elaine's shoulders slumped slightly from their elegant posture, and she once again sat back down.

"You truly are observant." She said. "It doesn't surprise me, in all honesty."

I sat down on the other side of Cassius' bed.

"But I don't understand..." I leaned in a little. "How did you come to be Claustus' wife?"

She gave a dry chuckle.

“Trust me, child,” she looked at me, a sad smile on her lips; “it was not by my free will.” She sat back in her chair, and she told me her story.

“Mariam and I worked at our father’s tavern as barmaids. We were fairly popular, too. She might have been a few years younger than me, but she had a spitfire spirit about her and made her very mature. She protected the other young barmaids that the drunkards often mistook for the prostitutes. However, just because we were barmaids, it didn’t mean predatory eyes didn’t want guilty pleasures. There was a particular Noble that had his eyes on me... and he kidnapped me, turned me... and then he defiled me. I’m not sure how much time had passed in my torturous imprisonment before he tired of me and threw me back into the streets of the slums. I couldn’t return to my family... not with my hunger as uncontrollable as it was. I was alone for the longest time, having to feed on small mammals so that I wouldn’t attack anyone. I wasn’t alone for long, however; I was found and taken in by a half-demon man by the name of Goshryke. He was kind to me, and he helped me to curb my hunger. I stayed with him for a number of years, and we were rather happy, even when young women were found butchered in the streets, drained of all their blood and even some organs removed. It was scary, but it didn’t matter to us; we were happy with each other. I... even find myself to be pregnant with his baby. I was so excited, and he seemed excited too. We were planning on getting married... but then I discovered a horrific secret.

"I came to meet him as he came home late one night... and found him covered in blood. Goshryke had been the one killing those women, mutilating them and draining them of their blood... blood that was given to me to curb my hunger as I carried his baby to term. I was so frightened that I ran... and I came across a physician by the name of Dargrin Passor as he was heading back to his family clinic in the Mid-City. He brought me back to the clinic and introduced me to his wife, Dahliah. I carried out the rest of my term there, and when the baby was born, I took care of him as well as I could. Not long after that, I found myself coveted by another man... Claustus. He was a prince about to be crowned as king. When it became clear that I could not shake his adamant affections, I asked Dargrin and Dahliah to care for my baby. I was terrified that he would be found by Goshryke somehow and that he would take my son. They agreed... and I agreed to marry Claustus in order to protect that baby boy. However, Goshryke's murders became even more sadistic and gory. He never relented in his desire for revenge against me for running out on him. He wanted to let me know he would be waiting for me in Hell. He was caught and committed suicide before he could be tried... and while the rest of the city returned to relative peace, I was still scarred by the experience. All of those young women died... the ones Goshryke called his *little butterflies*... because he loved me so obsessively... because I ran from him after all he had done for me..."

Queen Elaine's story filled in a lot of the blanks of my theory about the mastermind, and I recalled a lot of details that I had noticed but never thought about deeply. I was right about two things in particular; Dargrin *did* know the mastermind's identity, and in a roundabout way, the mastermind was a disciple of the Butterfly Killer.

The killer's own son, to be exact.

I looked at the queen as she tried to stop her trembling hands. She was still so terrified, and the current circumstances were particularly a valid reason to be so.

"Your Grace... no, Elaine..." I stood from my seat and walked over to her, kneeling in front of her and gently taking her trembling hands. "The one who rewrote Cassius' memories is also the one who killed Luxia and Lita, and he kidnapped Avaline to warn me away from the Estate." I whispered to her. "And... I now think that he is also the son you tried to protect by marrying Claustus."

She looked at me with wide eyes and then shook her head.

"N-No... that's not possible..." She whispered. "H-He shouldn't know anything about his birth parents... they promised to keep it from him..."

I gently squeezed her trembling hands.

"Elaine, please," I whispered; "tell me... what is his name?"

Queen Elaine was petrified, just like she had been in the library.

"Please..."

I needed to hear it from her, just so that I knew I wasn't mistaken even though I so wished that I was.

"H-His name... it's—" She stopped abruptly and pushed me out of the way.

I heard her choke, and when I looked back up at her, I found that she had been shot through the neck with a familiar crossbow bolt. I stared in horror as blood spilled from her mouth and neck onto her dress like a waterfall of wine, her veins turning a familiar bruised black. My eyes widened at the sight, my body rigid with fear.

'Poison...' I realized. 'The same as before... but—'

"You really should have left when dear old *father* told you to."

My head snapped toward the infirmary doors, and my blood ran cold in my veins; standing in the doorway was a familiar bespectacled vampire, his white hair still as feathery as ever and falling to just above his shoulders... and he was wearing white scholarly robes with scarlet designs embroidered along the hems.

A man in white.

"Eshrik..."

The vampire lowered the handheld crossbow with an audible sigh of disappointment, and he turned to me.

"You ruined my plans, Luxahliah... this reveal came too early for her. I wanted to see her eyes when she realized who I was. My... what a sad development."

He walked past me and to Elaine, gently cradling her cheek as she stared with fearful eyes that had lost their light.

"W-Where's Avaline?" I asked, slowly crawling back away from him.

"Oh, that little girl?" He didn't look at me. "I have no clue. She's very skilled at hiding, that damned brat. But, having her missing was the perfect leverage to try and get that imbecilic newborn to do my bidding, even with my... *persuasion.*" I felt a bit of relief then; Avaline was hiding, not kidnapped. "But, you shouldn't be worried about her... you should be more worried about yourself at the moment." I flinched as he turned to me. "You ruined my plans... oh, what should I do to punish you?"

My fight-or-flight response immediately went to flight mode, and I turned and ran, stumbling over my feet as adrenaline coursed through my veins.

"Ah, so a game of chase then." I heard him chuckle, his voice echoing as I ran through the corridors.

'I have to find Esilas and Elderik!'

My lungs burned as I hastily turned corners.

No matter how far I ran, it seemed as though Eshrik was never far behind me.

I felt that same fear I felt when I was running through the Pale Woods, and a familiar burn squeezed my lungs as my breath became ragged from my escape.

'Esilas and Elderik need to know who—'

"Gah!" I screamed in pain as I fell to the floor, pain crackling through my leg with fiery rage. I looked back, finding a crossbow bolt in my leg.

"You got pretty far, *little butterfly*," Eshrik's voice echoed from the end of the corridor, and I looked with tear-filled eyes to see him slowly sauntering over to me; "but not far enough, sadly."

I meekly tried to crawl away, only making him grin at my fruitless efforts to escape.

'E-Esilas... please... help me!'

"Lux!"

My eyes widened, and I turned my head back to see Esilas and Elderik running towards us.

"E-Esilas—"

"My, my, what a turn of events." Fingers curled around my chin, and my head was jerked to the side, where I was met with a familiar pinkish-gold glow. "Time for you to sleep... *my little butterfly...*"

I realized, then, that I had made a grave error.

Even if I hadn't known that he would use that ability on me, and even though I didn't know how it worked, I should have been more careful.

“Lux!” Esilas’ voice echoed in my head as I felt myself fall into a deep sleep.

My vision began to fade as I heard Esilas and Elderik soon succumb to the same trap, and my body felt numb against the carpeted floors of the Royal Estate.

21

The Truth Behind His Mask

I EXPERIENCED ANOTHER VISION in my unconscious state, and it differed from the others; it was calm, like a peaceful sleep, and it reminded me of the dream I had before I woke up in that muted-colored field. There was no anxiety like I had felt in my previous visions. I found myself sitting against the familiar wide girth of the Gods' Tree as its ruby red leaves fluttered above me in a nonexistent breeze. There were no golden apples on its branches; they had been replaced with small golden flowers. I stood, still looking up at the glistening buds as they seemed to glitter like jewelry.

"It's beautiful, isn't it?"

My eyes widened at the familiar voice, and I turned to find Luxia.

She was standing only a few feet away from me, wearing that same flowing white dress with her star-shaped Heart-Mark proudly on display while modestly covering her chest. She smiled softly at me, no sign of her morbid outcome about her.

"At last, we can speak to one another."

"Luxia..." I breathed, my eyes wide in my skull.

She chuckled and nodded once.

"That's right." She confirmed. "Though you learned a lot from my memories that we showed you. My brother and his friend are right. You are rather intuitive." She said as she folded her hands in front of her.

I furrowed my brows in confusion.

"Wait... 'we'?" I asked, though a nagging sensation in my chest told me I already knew the answer.

Luxia looked up at the tree with a nostalgic sort of smile.

"Every *Aster-Blood* is a part of the Gods' Tree," she explained, reaching up to touch the low-hanging branches with care. She looked at me with a kind and motherly smile on her lips. "They're a part of *you*."

"I-I don't understand..." I stuttered as I took a step back, the implication of her words making my heart race.

Luxia's Heart-Mark gave off a soft glow, and then other figures appeared behind her in the mist, silhouettes of men and women, each with Heart-Marks glowing on their chests.

"Did you really think that it was a coincidence that your Heart-Mark was the same as this very tree?" She asked as she slowly walked over to me and gently took my hands in hers. "With these hands, you received the apple, and it is with these same hands that life is given to others in the form of compassion and understanding, the hands of a healer."

Her explanation only raised more questions than it did answers, and even with the comfort of Luxia's hands around mine, I was terrified.

"W-What am I?" I breathed.

She smiled a knowing smile at me and raised one of her hands to put on my cheek. She leaned in and kissed the other, an affectionate sibling sort of kiss. She pulled away and looked at me, still holding my hands.

"You already know." She whispered.

Her smile conveyed many emotions.

Melancholy.

Kindness.

Comfort.

Regret.

"You are not alone, Lux." She reassured me before looking up at the tree, her smile conveying more melancholy now compared to before. "Our time is up, I'm afraid."

"W-Wait!" I fought to keep a hold of her hands as she pulled away to join the other fallen *Aster-Bloods*. "I still have so many questions! Luxia!" I pleaded with her as she pulled away.

"Avenge me and my baby." She smiled as tears tinted gold silently dribbled down her cheeks. "And tell my Cassius to continue living... and that we'll be waiting for him when the time is right."

The spirits of the other *Aster-Bloods* faded away, and as Luxia turned away, so did she. I was alone under the Gods' Tree, anxiety rippling through my nerves in my panic. I didn't know what to do. The leaves above me rustled with whispers.

"*Say your true name,*" The voice whispered, a collection of every *Aster-Blood* in the air; "*and you will correct the imbalance.*"

Their gentle tones gave me solace and encouragement, even though I still felt panic in my belly at the thought of what awaited me when I woke up.

"*We are with you.*" The leaves rustled once more. "*You will not be alone.*"

For the first time since my visions started, I felt a warmth in my chest.

The warmth of hope.

The vision was a pleasant dream of reassurance, that reassurance evaporating so abruptly with a few light slaps across my cheeks. I opened my heavy eyelids, my skin feeling cooler than it had been before. I'd been stripped down to my white underdress and was laid out on a worktable. My chin was jerked to the side, and my blurry vision cleared enough for me to see Eshrik with a satisfied grin on his thin lips.

"Wakey, wakey, *my little butterfly.*" He whispered. "We have an audience."

He moved out of the way a bit, and my heart skipped a beat in shock; Esilas and Elderik were tied to chairs by their ankles and wrists, and they looked as though they had been beaten. The four of us were in that same hidden room from my visions.

"E-Eshrik... you bastard..." Esilas growled, his bottom lip cut from a hard slap.

"*Tsk, tsk,* that's rather rude coming from you," Eshrik said as he took glasses off. "But I guess it does take a bastard to recognize a bastard."

"Eshrik, y-you're not a bastard." Elderik said, confused. "Y-You're my brother—"

"We are no more related than a butterfly is to a spider."

Eshrik's lips twisted into a wicked smirk, his fangs glistening in the light as he ran a hand through his hair.

"Why are you doing this?" Elderik asked; he was pleading, as if it was all a dream.

"You'll have to be more specific, *little brother.*" Eshrik hummed innocently. "Are you talking about why I murdered Luxia and her unborn baby? Or perhaps why I tested my poison on the Nobles and the Morgenstern Family? Oh, are you perhaps referring to rewriting everyone's memories?" He listed his crimes nonchalantly, as if they were items on a shopping list. "My, I've had a lot on my plate for the past several years—"

"Why the fuck did you kill my sister?!" Esilas screamed, seething with feral rage as he fought against his restraints.

"Oh! Oh, that!" Eshrik clapped his hands at the realization. "Well, simply put, I couldn't bear to see my *dear* little brother so happy." He answered vaguely, only confusing Esilas and Elderik more; only I knew the truth about his heritage, and I was having trouble trying to speak. "Plus, Luxia's blood provided some valuable information in my research. It soothes blood hunger, but, if taken in doses highly concentrated with inheritance powder, it can poison the blood of those who take it."

His nonchalant answer drove chills down my spine.

"The medicine for blood hunger..." I strained to speak, the realization squeezing my lungs in my chest as my heart pounded against my ribcage. "I-It was—"

"That's right!" He grinned maniacally, turning to look at me. "The so-called cure was made from Luxia Solani's blood!" He looked at me. "And *your* blood, Luxahliah. Oh, what a momentous find that was! I used twice the lethal dose—even mixing in some inheritance powder—to kill Claustus, but you saved him with your blood!"

"Inheritance powder..." I murmured. I knew the true name of that chemical. "A-Arsenic... y-you used arsenic..."

"Very good, Luxahliah. My 'father' certainly taught you well."

He brushed some hair from my face, a tender gesture that was made exceptionally creepy.

"But why?" Elderik asked, frustrated tears forming in the corners of his eyes. "Why try to kill the king? What was the aim? Why was he your target?"

"The king?" Eshrik looked at his adopted brother with a raised eyebrow. "What makes you think my target was the king? He was only a test subject for the final product."

"But... if he wasn't your target—"

“It wasn’t Claustus... that you wanted to take revenge on...” I breathed just above a whisper. “It was Elaine... because she’s your birth mother.”

Esilas looked at me with wide eyes.

“Wait, Lux... what are you—?”

“Very astute, as always, Luxahliah.” Eshrik confirmed with a mocking sense of pride. “That bitch, Elaine, is my mother, the sister of your whore mother, Mariam.” He turned and pointed with his knife at Esilas as he spoke.

“Your father... was Goshryke...” I continued. “The Butterfly Killer...”

“Correct again.” Eshrik chuckled, this time not looking at me. “One of Claustus’ many bastards in the slums. He was quite the womanizer in his youth before he married Elaine.”

“You did all of this because she was afraid of him and left him—”

A serrated knife embedded itself with a *thud* in front of my eyes, and I felt a bead of sweat roll down my neck.

“I don’t give a fuck about that sperm donor.” He hissed wickedly in my ear, his eyes reflected hysteric anger. “She *abandoned* me... left me with some disgraced family in the Mid-City while she became queen and gave that simpleton second born everything!”

Eshrik’s heart was so full of hatred for Elaine, but there was more than that under it all; he felt alone in the world.

Hurt.

'Esilas could have easily become like Eshrik had it not been for Elderik and the Passor family.'

Eshrik pulled the blade from the table.

"I ended up having to kill her before I could let her know the pain of being alone... because you made her realize the truth." He muttered. "She took that poisoned bolt for you. All because *you* couldn't keep your nose out of my plans."

He ran the tip of the knife down my cheek.

"Don't you dare touch her, you deranged lunatic!" Esilas roared as he fought against the restraints with greater fervor, and our eyes met briefly.

This didn't escape Eshrik's observation, and he looked between the two of us. After a moment, he burst into hysterical laughter.

"Oh, this is brilliant!" He cackled loudly. "Young love between an *Aster-Blood* and the bastard twin of another! *Animae nexum*!"

He pressed the blade against my neck, his wicked smile becoming a dangerously serious expression.

Hatred.

"How disgustingly touching." He spat.

Out of the corner of my eye, I noticed some movement.

"You, my pretty little test subject, are becoming all the more—gah!"

Eshrik let out a shriek of pain, dropping the knife and falling to the floor with a letter opener in his back. I could move again, and I sat up to see Avaline, breathing heavily at what she had done.

"Avaline..." I murmured as I hopped off the table, wincing from my hurt leg, and went to hug her close. "Thank heavens..."

"He hurt Ephrem..." she whispered. "And he killed the nice lady."

"The nice lady wasn't Luxia... you were talking about Elaine." I realized. "You only knew about Luxia because you could see her ghost."

She nodded and then looked at Eshrik as he struggled to reach for the letter opener.

I looked at him and then back at the little girl.

"Let's hurry and free the others." I urged, but as we were about to set Esilas and Elderik free, Eshrik grabbed me by my wounded leg and made me fall down.

"Go, Avaline! Free them now!"

Eshrik turned me over and pinned my hands on either side of my head.

"I'll kill you and that little bitch for ruining everything!"

Just as anxiety was about to grip my nerves with its ghastly tendrils, I felt as though soft flower petals brushed calmly against my skin.

'*You are not alone, Lux.*'

'*We are with you, always.*'

It was the collective voices from before.

Eshrik held both of my hands above my head as he grabbed the letter opener from his back.

"I wanted to take my time with cutting you up." He growled at me, his eyes furious.

'Say your true name.'

"But this will have to do." He raised the letter opened above my head.

"No, Lux!" I heard Esilas scream.

'Say it now, Lux!'

"My name..." I whispered. I remembered the name Dargrin had whispered in my ear. "My true name..."

"What?" Eshrik paused, surprised by my words.

"My name..." I repeated, looking him in the eyes with all the courage I could muster; "my name is not Luxahliah."

Eshrik's eyes narrowed.

"I think it's time for you to be quiet now." He scoffed dismissively, looking back into my eyes as his own eyes glowed with that hypnotic pinkish-gold hue.

However, I didn't feel his hypnosis take effect. No lightheadedness.

Eshrik's eyebrows furrowed in frustration, and he grabbed my chin as if to focus my eyes on his.

"Dammit, why won't it take hold?! It worked fine before!" He gripped my jaw harder. "What the hell is going on?!"

"My name..." I repeated once more. "My true name..."

Eshrik gripped the knife harder in his hand.

"I can't have you not bend to my will." He growled.

"Eshrik, stop!" Elderik screamed, pleading with him to see reason.

"Don't do it!" Esilas shouted, still fighting his bonds and causing Avaline to take longer to release him.

"Die."

He moved to plunge the letter opener into my chest, but I felt my name—two simple words—escape my throat in a calm breath.

My true name.

The lower part of my peripheral vision began to glow with an ethereal, lush green light, blinding Eshrik and giving me enough time to push him off of me. My push sent him stumbling back against his work table, breaking beakers and knocking books off his shelves. So stunned was he that Eshrik didn't notice Avaline finally getting Esilas and Elderik free from their restraints. Esilas practically ran over to me and helped me up.

"Lux, are you alright?" He asked as Avaline hugged my waist. "What was that?"

"They told me that if I said my true name, then I could correct the imbalance..." I muttered in shock. "I guess... that meant awakening my powers as an *Aster-Blood*..."

"'They'?" Elderik looked at me.

"Luxia... and the other *Aster-Bloods*..." I answered.

"Of course." Eshrik spoke with a smirk as he recovered, brushing his hair from his face. "Why didn't I realize it before?

You're the *Aster-Blood* of the Gods' Tree... and *Aster-Bloods* gain power from their true names."

He staggered forward, and Esilas pushed me and Avaline behind him as he brandished the knife that Eshrik had discarded from his fall.

"I'm going to have to ask that the both of you return my *newest specimen* back."

I could tell from his tone that he was trying to hypnotize them again, but Esilas and Elderik never moved to follow his commands.

"Yeah, that's not happening." Esilas retorted, glaring at an ever-frustrated Eshrik.

"Why the hell isn't it working?!" He roared in fury. "It worked before, so why not now?!"

'It must be my blood.' I realized. 'But why are they immune now? Is it because I've said my true name?'

"Fuck this!"

Eshrik brandished another knife from his disordered work table.

"I'll kill all of you!"

Esilas readied his knife, and Elderik pulled both me and Avaline back as the dhampir and the hybrid lunged at each other in battle.

22

The Final Blow

I NEVER ONCE DOUBTED Esilas' skill as a fighter, but to see Eshrik effectively block every move was surprising. Esilas was quick, striking his opponent in his arms whenever he dodged, but Eshrik was just as quick.

Strike after strike.

Cut after cut.

The two were evenly matched, their wounds healing as soon as they had been afflicted. Elderik kept pushing and pulling Avaline and me out of the way as their fight moved about the room.

And after several minutes, they stopped to catch their breaths.

"Ya know," Esilas smirked as a cut on his cheek healed, "for a *scholar*, you seem to be very skilled with a blade in combat. Something you picked up from Elderik?" He taunted.

"*Tch*, you're fast," Eshrik scoffed hatefully as he wiped his mouth. "That much I'll admit."

"I recognize that enhanced strength and stamina." Elderik informed Esilas. "It's the same change that you went through at the barracks."

"I know." Esilas' eyes narrowed at his opponent. "You've been dosing yourself with *Aster-Blood* blood. That's the only explanation for how you're keeping up with me."

My heart beat against my ribcage; Eshrik had taken vials of my blood for further experimentation, and I wondered if that was the reason for his abilities being the same as Esilas'.

'Or... is my blood the poison...?'

"So, the mongrel does have a brain." Eshrik took his turn to taunt Esilas. "No longer relying on Elderik or your pretty human whore to do the thinking? Bravo." He smirked. "Maybe before you die, you'll get to see me feed from her. I've always wondered what her blood tasted like. I wonder if I'll feel that same rush I felt in my veins when I injected myself with your whore sister's blood!"

"Shut up!" Esilas roared as he lunged at his opponent once more, this time his attacks fueled by anger instead of being calculated.

Eshrik seemed like he didn't have time to react as Esilas plunged his knife into the hybrid's shoulder with such force that I could hear the bones in his shoulder joint shatter.

"Gah!" Eshrik exclaimed, trying to fight the dhampir off, but Esilas forcibly took the dagger from him and turned to Elderik.

"Quickly, take this!" He commanded.

I couldn't shake this pit in my stomach.

"Can't have him attacking anymore before we bring him before the captain." Esilas continued.

Something wasn't right.

Eshrik's pained grimace turned into a smirk.

"Oh, that isn't the only weapon I have, mongrel." He dug around in his pocket, and at the glint of light against metal, my eyes widened.

Instinct immediately struck me.

"Esilas, it's poison!" I warned, and just as the words left my mouth and Esilas turned his head back, Eshrik moved to jab him in the neck with the needle.

"Join your sister, bastard."

What happened next made my heart stop.

Before I could even register what happened, Elderik appeared at Esilas' side and pulled him out of the way with enough force that he slid across the floor and slammed into the wall.

"Esilas!" I ran over with Avaline to help him up, but before I could even kneel at the dhampir's side, Avaline tugged on the skirt of my underdress. I turned to see her pointing back. When I followed her finger, I was in shock. The poison that had been meant for Esilas was jabbed into Elderik's neck.

"Elderik..." Esilas stared at the scene with wide eyes as his comrade held Eshrik by the throat, fighting his spasming muscles.

The poison was working through him fast, much faster than it had with the other victims.

"That poison wasn't meant for you, *little brother*, but no matter." Eshrik grinned maniacally. "That poison will eat through you like acid!"

However, despite the convulsions he was experiencing and his blood vessels bruising dark as the poison circulated through his system, Elderik was calm, and Eshrik's triumphant bravado diminished as the former's grip seemed to remain firm.

"I would have preferred..." Elderik strained as the poison took greater effect, "to have you pay for what you've done... the lives you've taken..." He tightened his trembling fingers around his adopted brother's throat. "But.. this will have to do..."

"E-Elderik...?" Esilas' voice was shaking, and Avaline trembled as she held onto my skirt.

"L-Lux..." Elderik turned his head back to look at me, the whites of his eyes bleeding red. "Take good care of them for me..." My eyes widened as he spoke, my heart breaking as tears built heavily in the corners of my eyes. "Tana... and Twiny... and Ephrem and Avaline... and take care of Esilas, too..."

"E-Elderik... don't—"

"What are you doing?!" Eshrik hissed as he fought Elderik's grip with greater fervor but without success.

"Remember your promise, Lux..." Elderik panted, his fangs protruding from his drying mouth and cracked lips; "the promise... y-you made... that first night... at the barracks..."

I swallowed my sobs, taking a deep, shaky breath.

"O-Of course..." my voice blubbered from my throat as I answered him.

"Dammit, let me go!" Eshrik continued to squirm and protest, clawing at his hand, but his grip was still strong.

It was his conviction.

Elderik turned to the man he had once called his brother.

He turned his head to the side, allowing him better access to his shoulder as he yanked his robes to the side.

"This ends... now!" Elderik declared with a hiss as he sank his fangs into Eshrik's shoulder, making him scream in horrific pain.

I covered Avaline's eyes and turned her head away, though I could not look away myself.

"Stop!" He pleaded. "Stop it, Elderik!"

Eshrik's eyes turned red with blood as the poison worked through his system, his own creation working to kill its creator.

"Brother, please!" He shrieked.

"You... said it yourself..." Esilas grunted as he stood from the wall, using his hand to keep himself standing. "You're not his brother."

Esilas' voice, though raw with emotion, was cold towards Eshrik. Elderik pulled away as he fell on top of his brother as they fell to the floor.

"Elderik!"

I ran over to him, pulling him off Eshrik and laying him on his back. He watched Eshrik pathetically turn onto his stomach and struggle to crawl toward his work table.

"I-I can survive this..." Eshrik strained as he reached out, only for him to fall limp. "I-I have to survive..."

Tears and blood pooled on the floor as he gasped for air. His eyes rolled into the back of his head as his life left his body. Esilas and Avaline came over to Elderik and me, the former dropping to his knees beside me as his eyes glossed over with tears.

"E-Elderik... you idiot...!" Esilas grasped his clothes as he fought not to cry as he screamed. "Why did you do that?!"

Elderik smiled despite his pain, coughing as blood filled his lungs.

"B-Because... Lux is here..." he strained; "I wouldn't want her to cry over your loss..."

"But what about your loss?" I whimpered as I held his hand in mine. "Elderik... please... take my blood... it can heal—"

"No..." he refused with a cough; "the poison has already become so ingrained in me... no amount of healing could stop this, Lux..."

Despite this cruel fate, Elderik seemed so carefree, as a soft smile worked its way onto his lips. I took a deep breath and looked at Avaline.

"Follow the corridor out... go find Captain Ailgraym... tell him what's happened..." the young girl nodded, even though tears were streaming down her face, and she ran out of the room, leaving the three of us alone.

"L-Lux..." Elderik spoke once more with a soft groan. "I-I have a request..."

"Don't talk like that, you idiot." Esilas said, his voice low as his shoulders shook. He gripped his comrade's tunic in desperation. "Just let her help you."

"Tell me, Lux..." he ignored his comrade, his brother, and continued to speak to me. "What... What was the name that my father gave you?" He looked at me as blood mixed with his tears. "C-Could you whisper it to me?"

My eyes widened at his words.

My true name.

It was his last wish to know what it was.

I took another shaky breath, and Esilas moved out of the way for me as I leaned down to whisper it in his ear. He let out a sigh of relief, and he then let out a soft chuckle.

"I-I should have known..." he whispered, his smile audible in his failing voice; "c-considering... you're..."

Elderik never finished his sentence; he fell silent, and when I pulled away to look at him, the cheerful light had faded from his eyes and he lay completely still. There was still a smile on his lips, that same smile that had been so warm and comforting.

"E-Elderik..." I whimpered. I gripped his clothes as I cried into his shoulder, wailing in frustration and anguish at his loss.

Esilas had been silent all this time, but he screamed, beating his fists against the stone floors to where they were bleeding. I looked at him.

"Esilas—"

"Elderik, you damn idiot!" He screamed. "How could you leave us behind like this?! Your mother and father...! Your little sisters?! How could you leave them like that?!"

I could only watch as he let his emotions burst through the floodgate of his heart.

And then... just behind Esilas, I saw a softly glowing mist in the shape of a person. It was soon joined by another apparition, and this one was much clearer.

"Luxia..." I breathed.

She smiled softly and then knelt beside her twin, gently touching his shoulder. The dhampir flinched, and when he raised his head to look beside him, I could see him freeze in place. Tears flowed silently down his cheeks and his mouth hung open as if to say something, but no words came out.

'He can see her... he can finally see her...'

I watched as Luxia put her hand on Esilas' cheek, and her mouth moved. I couldn't hear her words; they were meant for him. A moment later, Luxia stood from her mourning brother's side and looked at the hazy figure beside her. As she took the silhouette's hand, the haze cleared to reveal the figure of Elderik, his clothes white and gold, a sure sign that he was heading towards the light. The two of them looked at me and smiled.

Luxia nodded her head to me before she walked away, guiding Elderik behind her as they faded away. Esilas let out a shaky breath and then slowly turned his head towards me.

"S-She told me... that she was proud of me... that she was sorry..." he breathed as his emotions caught up with his voice. "A-And that she wants me to continue living..."

His tears streamed heavier down his cheeks, and I put my hand on his cheek, his eyes fluttering closed at my touch. He held my hand close to his cheek, almost as if he were afraid that I would disappear, too.

"Shhh, shhh..." I soothed; "no talking... just... cry..."

At those words, he let himself shake with every sob and I wrapped my arms around him. I cried as well, my chest tightening as our collective tears continued to fall. We didn't respond when the sounds of armored footsteps echoed from the corridor, nor did we respond when Captain Ailgraym called out to us before commanding his men to take action in securing the scene of our final battle. We were numb to it all, our nerves to raw to react to anything else.

Luxia and her baby had been avenged... but no one would celebrate this victory.

Not with the price that had to be paid.

23

The Return of Spring

I'M NOT SURE WHAT had happened after that; I vaguely remember the sounds of rapidly approaching armored footsteps and shouting as the adrenaline rush I had experienced ebbed away, taking my strength with it and reminding me of my injured leg. When I opened my eyes, white sunlight framed by dark walls blinded me. I definitely wasn't in the infirmary of the Royal Estate. As feeling slowly returned to my sore limbs when I moved, I could feel two hands holding mine as if in prayer. I took a sharp inhale of breath, alerting whoever was at my bedside.

"E-Esilas..." I called out hopefully.

"Easy, easy." I recognized the voice, and I found myself disappointed.

It wasn't Esilas.

"Cassius...?" I turned my head a bit, my vision clearing enough for me to find the demon prince sitting there.

"You've been asleep for a while." Cassius soothed as he gently squeezed my hand. "Nearly four days."

"F-Four days?!" I spoke louder, which made me cough because of how dry my throat was, and I tried to sit up and get out of bed. "W-Where is Esilas?"

"Take it easy, Luxahliah." He stopped me from getting out of bed, but helped me sit up against the headboard. "You can't overexert yourself."

I looked at him and then sighed.

He would not let me out of bed, so I resigned to relax a bit. I looked around, and I realized I was in my room at the clinic. I looked back at the Morgenstern prince.

"How did I get here...? I-I thought that this place had been caught on fire!" I asked. "The last thing I remember—"

"The so-called fire had been a ruse concocted by Eshrik to get you alone, from what the captain told me." He answered. "Esilas carried you here himself, Ephrem and Avaline following him." He stood from my bedside and went over to a small table to pour me a glass of water. "When I woke up, all of my memories of Luxia returned... and I was told about what happened to Elderik... Luxahliah, I'm so sorry..."

I recalled everything about those horrid events, and I felt my chest tighten once more.

"I came here to discuss things with the Passor family, but Esilas refused to see me. I, instead, talked to Elderik's parents. Esilas had already told them what happened, but they appreciated my condolences." He brought me the glass of water he had poured, and I took a sip to soothe my throat.

I remembered Luxia's last wish for Cassius and I looked at him.

"Luxia... I had a vision of her before I woke up in that place." I spoke carefully, and Cassius' eyes widened by a fraction. "She... wanted me to tell you something..." he sat down and leaned in close, listening intently and with an eager heart. "She said that she wanted you to keep living... and that she and your baby would be waiting for you when it was your time to join them."

Cassius' eyes fluttered closed as tears trickled down his cheeks. He bowed his head a little as he took a deep breath, trying to regain his composure.

"I miss her so much..." he whimpered; "but... I will live by her wishes. She was my life... and I'll continue living it for her..." He was still so devoted to her, and that made me smile a little. He then looked up at me. "Luxahliah, I-I think—"

The door suddenly opened, revealing Dahliah and a sense of dread engulfed me, making me remember Elderik's gruesome death and the promise he had me make.

"D-Dahliah..." I breathed.

"Cassius, I'll take care of her." Dahliah never took her eyes off of me. "Could you inform the others?"

The Morgenstern prince stood and gave her the glass of water.

"Y-Yes, ma'am." He nodded, looking at me for a moment before leaving the room. She walked over to me and sat on my bed, setting the glass on my bedside table.

"D-Dahliah... I-I..." I felt tears build once more.

"Shh, child." She whispered, gently petting my head as her voice cracked. She was close to crying as well.

"Dahliah, I-I'm so sorry... E-Elderik..." My shoulders jumped as sobs escaped my throat. "H-He's gone..."

"Sweetheart, you do not need to apologize." She pulled me into a hug, combing her fingers through my hair as I cried. "I should apologize to you... because of Eshrik... I never could have imagined what he was doing..."

"I-I couldn't save him—"

"Child, look at me." She pulled away and gently wiped my eyes. "He wouldn't want you to despair over his death, but rather remember the times you and Esilas spent with him."

I took deep breaths to calm myself, though with little success, and I looked at her.

"W-Where is Esilas...?" I asked, pleading for an answer to my question. "Please, Dahliah..."

Dahliah took a deep breath.

"Lux... he's gone..." She admitted. "He left this morning... to go back to the barracks..."

"H-He... went back...?" I felt my heart drop to my stomach.

"He said his goodbyes this morning." She informed me.

The shock of this new information caused my thoughts to race. Ignoring the soreness and physical pain I was feeling, I threw off the covers and stood from the bed.

"W-Wait, Lux! Your wounds still haven't fully healed—"

"I'm not about to let him go back to that place to be alone!" I shouted as I threw the door to my room open. "He's exiling himself because of Elderik's death!"

I ran past Tana and Twiny, Dargrin, Ephrem, Avaline, Cassius, and Captain Ailgraym.

"Luxahliah, where are you going?!" The Morgenstern prince asked with panic.

"Sorry, Captain!" I shouted, ignoring the prince as I opened the front door to the clinic. "I'm taking your horse!"

"Wait, what?!"

I ran down the steps to the street and mounted the captain's hellsteed. The necromantic horse reared back with a whinny and then galloped towards the Outskirts of the city.

Adrenaline coursed through my veins as the captain's hellsteed through the streets. The muted-colored buildings passed by me in a blur, and as I approached the Mid-Gate, the guards tried to stop me.

"H-Halt!" The guards tried to get the horse to stop.

"Faster!" I pat the hellsteed's neck. "Please, I have to reach Esilas!"

The demonic horse brayed loudly and galloped faster, jumping majestically over the Ebony Guardsmen at the Mid-Gate.

"H-Hey! Get back here!"

"That's the captain's horse!"

"Someone stop her!"

The guards shouted as they chased after me as the hellsteed's hooves trodden against the muddied streets of the Outskirts. We dodged and weaved through crowds of citizens towards the Outer-Gate.

'He's doing this to punish himself! I won't let him be alone!'

Soon, the outer gate came into view, and I caught a glimpse of the back of Esilas' head, his bag over his shoulder, as he talked with a patrol guard, giving his papers to him, and my heart leapt in my chest.

"Wait, Esilas!" I screamed, and the dhampir stopped and turned on his heel in my direction, his eyes wide in his skull.

I yanked on the reins of the hellsteed, halting him in the mud. I practically jumped from the saddle and ran to him, throwing my arms around his neck. He was forced to drop his bag as he returned the gesture, letting us fall to the ground.

"L-Lux... y-you're awake..." he whispered in shock, gently curling his fingers in my hair. "W-What are you doing—?"

"What do you think you're doing?!" I looked at him, gripping his tunic in my hands as I shouted and ignoring the amassing crowd. "Don't shut everyone out again! Don't shut *me* out!"

Tears spilled down my cheeks as I touched my forehead to his chest.

"Lux, I-I can't stay here..." he muttered. "Elderik is dead... and it's because—"

"Because he loved you! Esilas, he would have done anything for you!" I looked at him, screaming as I cried. "He watched you grow up, and he cared so much for you! He didn't want you to die by Eshrik's hand!"

I squeezed my eyes shut as I cried into his chest.

"Don't think for a second that he would blame you for his death." I whispered. "Please, Esilas... come back home... don't leave me behind..."

Esilas was silent, but I could hear his racing heart and his trembling hands told me he was holding back tears.

"Lux..." He gently put his hand on my cheek, pulling my head from his chest to wipe my eyes. "How could I say no... especially to you?" He whispered as he touched his forehead to mine. "But... what about Cassius?"

"I broke off my engagement with her since there's no need for it anymore." My eyes widened, and I turned to see the aforementioned demon prince. "Well, that's what I was going to tell her that before she heard you were returning to the barracks."

He was followed by the Passor family, Ephrem and Avaline, Captain Ailgraym and the guards from the Mid-Gate, and, surprisingly, King Claustus. The guardsmen and townsfolk that had amassed dropped to their knees in a kneel and bowed their heads.

"Cassius?" I looked at him.

"I had a lot that I wanted to talk to you about." He chuckled. "I have no right to break a Bond, especially *animae nexum*." He said as he stepped forward.

Esilas helped me stand, and Cassius smiled at us.

"After all... Luxia wouldn't have wanted that for her brother, right?"

I blinked and then nodded with a small smile.

'He's taking Luxia's last wish for him to heart.'

"And I think it's time that Luxia's wish was granted, don't you think?" Cassius asked with a knowing smile.

He looked at his father and nodded. King Claustus stood tall.

"I agree." The king declared. "The rank system of our society has yoked this city long enough. Starting with my son, there will no longer be a king and queen, no royal line."

The people murmured in wonder at this impromptu declaration. Most of them couldn't believe what they were hearing.

"No royal line?" I asked, looking at Cassius.

"I've discussed much with my father over the past few days." He explained. "The people of the Outskirts should and will be given equal opportunities and rights as those in the Mid-City and the Courts, and the city will be governed by a council and not a monarch." He looked at me as Esilas put his hand on my shoulder. "All people equal, never divided."

"So, from today on and every day after," King Claustus declared; "the gates of Obsiditourma are open to all."

The people of the poverty-stricken Outskirts cheered for the Morgenstern family's declaration, and some were so overcome with relief that they embraced their loved ones with tears in their eyes. Luxia's dream had been realized; her mother's people were lifted from poverty, the walls that separated the social classes of the city torn down.

"All people made equal." I repeated as I felt a great weight lifted from my shoulders.

I looked at Esilas, and I noticed his eyes were glossy. He was still so close to tears.

"Esilas?"

He looked at me and wiped his eyes with a chuckle.

"You truly are pure." He said as he caressed my cheek, this thumb gently stroking my cheekbone. He had been about to lean in close when—

"Captain Ailgraym!" A guardsman cried out as other Ebony Guardsmen clamored outside the Outer-Gate. "Prince Cassius—ah, a-and Your Grace! T-There's—"

He was heavily out of breath.

"Calm down, man!" Captain Ailgraym commanded. "Whatever is the matter?"

"I-It's... look outside the gates!" He pointed frantically. "T-The Pale Woods! They're budding!"

My eyes widened, and my head snapped towards the guard.

"Wait, what?!" I nearly shrieked.

"Come and see!" The guardsman gestured for everyone to follow.

What we found outside the gates of the city was awe-inspiring.

The pale trees that were once bare of leaves had flowered with golden blossoms and bud with rose-colored leaf buds, and the muddy ground had sprouted with bright green grass.

"What could have caused this?" Cassius asked as he looked around in wonder.

"I don't know," the guard answered; "but this isn't even the extent of it. It reaches past the Watch-Keepers' barracks. A rider was sent with the news."

"Could you take us there?" I asked as I looked at him.

He looked from me to Cassius and King Claustus. The two of them nodded, silently confirming that my request was valid. The guardsman then led us down the road, the population of the city migrating to a rather familiar spot, and my breath caught in my throat. We had been led to that same field where I had woken up. Where it had once been a field of dull-colored flowers and tall grass, it was now alive with vivid colors, surrounded by pale trees with scarlet and fuchsia leaves.

"This..." I breathed, gently squeezing Esilas' hand; "this is where I woke up..."

I put my other hand over my Heart-Mark.

"Legend says that life will return to the land when the Gods' Tree returns." Dargrin spoke up as he looked at me. "I think it's time that you introduced yourself, dear child." He whispered.

I felt heat rise to my cheeks, and I looked at Esilas. He offered a soft smile and then kissed my flushed cheek.

"Well, I've been curious about your true name for a while now." He said, gently running his finger across my forehead to brush my hair out of my eyes. He gently pushed forward. "Go on."

I took a deep breath, retracing my steps in the field as the tall grass brushed against the skirt of my dress, and I smiled at the memory of how my journey started. I turned to face the crowd as they watched me intensely, murmuring about my Heart-Mark being visible. Before this time, I would have been gripped by anxiety, but once again, I felt the warmth of Luxia and the other *Aster-Bloods* standing with me.

'We are with you.'

I felt another presence with them, too; it was a presence I recognized, one of such kindness and care, the one who had asked me to look after Esilas and the rest of his family. So, with a soft smile on my lips, I spoke my true name.

"I am the *Aster-Blood* of the Gods' Tree," I introduced myself. "My name is Arboriah Lux."

24
~Epilogue~

Two Months Later-

I sat at the vanity as I helped Avaline do Tana's and Twiny's hair. The young twin girls were dressed in light blue gowns with small butterflies embroidered into the skirts and tied in the back with a darker blue bow in the back.

"Alright," I declared with a soft smile as I finished Tana's hair, her silvery-white locks loosely braided with a matching blue ribbon at the tail; "looks like the two of you are done and ready."

The girls wore bright smiles on their faces as they squealed with delight.

"Thank you, Lux!" The two of them said simultaneously as they hugged me.

"Hey, you better thank your aunt Avaline, too." I laughed.

The girls giggled and happily thanked the mousy-brown-haired girl, who simply smiled at them. Dahliah and Dargrin had happily taken her and Ephrem in, seeing as their parents were both passed on. Avaline tapped me on the shoulder and pointed to my hair as if to ask if she could do mine as well when someone knocked at the door.

"Come in." I granted as I turned to face the visitor, pretty confident in knowing who it was.

Sure enough, Dahliah walked through the door. She was dressed in a gorgeous blue and white gown, and her long white hair was tied in a bun with a silver hair comb.

"Lux, you look like you've spent more time helping the girls get ready instead of actually getting dressed yourself." She playfully scolded in her usual motherly tone.

She wasn't exactly wrong; I was only dressed in a white underdress, my Gods' Tree Heart-Mark proudly displayed under my collarbone as its branches reached my shoulders.

"Sorry, Dahliah." I apologized with a smile. "I guess... I'm trying to distract myself..."

Dahliah smiled a knowing smile and turned to the girls.

"Could you three check on the guests... and make sure that the other half of the happy couple isn't pacing nervously? He is prone to do such."

The twins giggled and nodded as Avaline ushered them out of the room, a smile on her lips. Dahliah gently closed the door and then walked over to me.

"Come on, dear. We need to get you ready."

I stood up with a deep breath as she helped me into my dress.

The dress I was wearing was similar to the one I had worn for the Summer Soiree. The only thing that differed from the summer dress was that the sleeves were longer because of the cold weather and, along with the embroidered red leaves, there were golden apple blossoms. Dahliah helped me dress and then sat me down at the vanity once more so that she could do my makeup and my hair.

"You seem like you have a lot on your mind, Lux." She smiled softly as she ran the comb through my hair. "Penny for your thoughts?"

I fought to not pick at my nails and settled for nervously chewing on the inside of my cheek, to not mess up the rouge on my lips.

"I-I guess..." I finally mumbled; "I just have jitters..."

I chuckled nervously, and Dahliah gently put her hands on my shoulders.

"Sweetheart, you have nothing to be nervous about," Dahliah reassured me. "But, I can't blame you. It was the same way for me and Dargrin when our day came."

I looked at her reflection in the mirror as she gently started twisting my hair into a braid.

"Was it as big as this?" I asked.

"Oh, no, not at all," she laughed. "It was a small ceremony with a priest from the Outskirts. My family had absolutely no idea... or if they did, they certainly didn't approve or send their congratulations."

She finished my hair, pinning it in place with a hair ornament. It was similar to the one I had worn before, but it was gold in color, with sterling white jewels encrusted around the edge.

"There we go." She smiled as she brushed some long locks to frame either side of my face. "You didn't even need that light rouge. You've always been so beautiful." Her compliment made my face flush, even as I smiled softly. "Are you ready, dear? It's almost time for you to meet with him."

So much had happened in those two months after I had declared my full name as an *Aster-Blood*; King Claustus and Cassius had established the governing council, and Esilas and I had both been given seats. The Royal Estate had been renovated and opened up for the new council chamber, and since the estate itself was as complex as it was vast, it was also opened as an academy for equal education. In the weeks after King Claustus' declaration, the Nobles begrudgingly gave up their status and contributed whatever wealth they had to rebuilding the Outskirts into a better residential area.

Though it was still an uneasy beginning, the city was progressing forward, and it was only natural that Esilas and I did, too; he proposed to me again—not in bed this time—and entrusted the plans to Dahliah and Cassius, seeing as we were busy with council duties.

And all of that careful and loving planning led up to this moment.

The moment that Esilas seemed to have been waiting for with just as much anxious excitement as I had.

Our wedding day.

I took a deep breath and stood from the vanity, turning to Dahliah with a smile as I saw the happy apparitions of Elderik and Luxia in my periphery.

"I'm ready." I nodded with a smile. "I'm ready for my wedding day."

Character Reference Sheet

- Lux/Luxahliah: our beloved protagonist that was born from the will and the last apple of the Gods' Tree as a human. Her appearance mirrors that of the Gods' Tree, and being born of the Tree's will, she is also connected with the other *Aster-Bloods,* though she holds a most solid connection with Luxia, who was the only *Aster-Blood* born in the past century. This connection is part of the reason why she is so caring towards Esilas. She has long, red-gold hair, pale skin, and deep blue-green eyes.

- Esilas Solani: the dhampir boy and the twin brother of Luxia. Dhampir are exceedingly rare due to the nature of the vampiric mutative strain, and this mixed blood manifests as the features Esilas has: black hair that fades to an ashen gray at the tips, and amber-red eyes that glow in the dark. He doesn't trust anyone aside from Elderik and his family, and Ephrem. He is apprehensive about Lux when they first met, but upon discovering that she is an *Aster-Blood*, he becomes proctetive, considering how his sister was an *Aster-Blood*.

- Elderik Passor: the kind vampire who looked after Esilas when he was first brought to the Watch-Keeper's barracks. Like most vampires of older generations, his hair is silvery white and his eyes are a rosy pink as opposed to the normal red hues vampires normally have. He was trusted with Esilas' care when Ailgraym brought him to the Watch-Keeper's barracks. He

- Ephrem: the first-generation vampire of Esilas' group. Ephrem's behavior ranges from boyish to brattish because of the vampire virus in his system. Because of how young he was when he was turned, the mutation stimulates the hormones that he would have experienced when he was going through adolescence. So, in a way, he is still a growing child. As a first-generation, the mutative strain changed his hair-color to a light tone, and his eyes became red. These physical features of first-generations often match the features of the one who turns them, passing on the strain.

- Dahliah Passor: the head physician at the Passor Family Clinic. She is very kind-hearted and compassionate, a loving mother and a doctor. She is a seventh-generation vampire but gave up her status as an Aristocrat when she met Dargrin Passor in her youth and pursued her desire to learn about medicine. Like most Aristocrats, her hair is a brilliant snow white, but in her family, the eyes are either a rose-petal pink or a ruby red. She is where Elderik gets his rose-petal colored eyes from.

- Dargrin Passor: the skilled herbalist at his family's clinic. As a fourth, Dargrin is the first of his family to have silvery gray hair instead of white. His eyes are a dull red color. Dargrin was a student of his father when he first met Dahliah, who was interested in medicine. When she was abandoned by her family for wanting to deviate from tradition, Dargrin and his family took in Dahliah. The two of them were married a number of years later.

- Eshrik Passor: the "scholarly" bastard son who works in the Royal Estate Archives. Despite his heritage, Eshrik was born with stark white hair and reddish-pink eyes. He is very eccentric when it comes to his goals, and he is also misleading towards others. His plan has been a long time in its planning.

- Captain Ailgraym Solani: the captain of the Ebony Guard and the father of Esilas and Luxia. He knew that Lux was a woman the first time they met, but he didn't say anything because of how much he owes Elderk. His silvery-gray hair is always slicked back, and his eyes are a dull red. He met his first love, a human named Mariam, in the early years of his career in the Ebony Guard. And after an apology of their intial encounter and many visits, the two grew incredibly close, even having to sneak off to hide their relatinship. However, when they were found out, he was forced to break things off with her. Years later, he recieved word that she was dying, and he left his post to go to her bedside. He discovered his children, the twins Esilas and Luxia, there with her, and he begged Mariam for her forgiveness. She did forgive, and she asked him to take their children with him back through the Mid-Gate to give them a better life.

- Mariam: the human mother of Esilas and Luxia, and

the younger sister of Elaine. She and Elaine were barmaids at their father's tavern, and while she was the younger of the two children, she was incredibly outspoken and free-willed. She had raven black hair and beautiful hazel eyes. This is the amber hue that is part of Esilas' eye color. Mariam absolutely loved her children dearly, and she wanted nothing more than for them to live a better life than she could give them. That was what she wished Ailgraym to give them on her deathbed.

- Cassius Morgenstern: the half-demon/half-vampire prince of Obsiditourma. Very common traits of the Morgenstern Family are their black hair and honey-gold eyes. Since these traits are considered more dominant because of the Morgenstern bloodline, Cassius was born with these traits instead of traits as a hybrid. His relationship with Luxia was rocky at first, because she wanted nothing more than to go home and see her brother. It didn't matter; Cassius was patient and loving towards her. The two of them did end up falling in love, and it was perhaps the truest love in the history of the Royal Estate.

- Avaline: the younger sister of Ephrem. Avaline has mousy brown hair and deep green eyes. She is a first-generation vampire, but the traits of her human heritage are still present. No one really knows why Avaline is different from other first-generations. She is very fond of Queen Elaine, the woman having taken her in after she had been abused by a Noble in the Courts. She is the only one privy to the plan Eshrik put into play.

- Duchess Mareene: the mother of Dahliah and Ailgraym. This woman cares for nothing but symbols of status, and she clearly would do anything to stay in her position in the Courts. She is always dressed in lavish blue and gold gowns with her long white hair tied in a tight and intricate bun with beautiful silver combs and pins. She is very callous when it comes to traditon, and finds anything that deviates from the societal norm to be an abomination of nature.

- Queen Elaine: the Queen-Wife of Claustus Morgenstern and Mariam's elder sister. Much like her younger sister, Elaine was born with black hair and hazel eyes. However, when she was turned, all of her hair but a streak turned white. She tends to maintain her blood hunger in subtle ways as to not give away her heritage as a first-generation. She was very close with her younger sister, Mariam, before Elaine disappeared, being kidnapped by a Noble who had very obscure tastes. She was the object of cruel entertainment and turned by the Noble before being thrown out when he was bored with her. She was taken in by a half-demon named Goshryke, and the two eventually became close in their relationship. She ran when she discovered that Goshryke was very cruel, being a serial killer. It did not help that she was pregnant with his child, and with that knowledge in mind, she ran away from him, finding herself in the path of Dahliah and Dargrin Passor.

- King Claustus: the King of Obsiditourma and a pureblood of the Morgenstern Family. This kind and rather playful king is the picture of every descendant of Lucien Morgenstern. He has pitch black hair and gold-colored eyes. While he is often kind and understanding, it is best not to try your luck for too long. His strict side compels any vampire to kneel and avert their eyes. This side of him is very different given that he was quite the ladies man in his youth, fathering many bastards in Mid-City and the Outskirts.

Acknowledgments

A big thank you to my amazing parents, Daren and Lisa, for being so patient with me in my writing process and allowing me to live my dream as a writer.

To my awesome and loving boyfriend, Michael, who has had to put up with a lot since we got together.

To my dungeons and dragons group, where I was able to let loose and be myself whenever I needed a break from my work. Angie and Drake have been amazing friends since we met, and I wouldn't trade them for the world. Joe and Ryan have always been good comic relief whenever I needed a laugh, and they're the best friends ever.

To Kourtney, my best friend from high school, who has been encouraging more and more updates.

To my long time friend, Joe Newell, in Kingfield, Maine, who has been encouraging and just as excited as I have been about this book.

To my writer friend, Ellie, who was patient when I was asking questions and had many laughs with me in our chats. Thanks for all your help during the formatting and publishing phase.

And the biggest thanks to everyone who's been patient in waiting for the book to get finished and published so that they can read one of the many stories that has swirled around in my undiagnosed ADHD brain.

About Author

Born and raised in Alabama, Kathleen Lyons has always been a creative person. From an early age, she was drawing and making up stories to go along with the characters and creatures she made up. When she was a high school student, she wrote her first manuscript, but she never edited or planned on publishing that first novel.

Years later, Kathleen started another novel while working at an extrusion plant, and she started writing several other stories along with her first published novel. This novel, in fact.

It has always been her dream that her stories reach the people and help them to escape the pressures of the real world even if it was only for a little while.

Made in the USA
Columbia, SC
08 June 2025

59004918R00178